POOR REX THE DRUMMER BOY

EDWIN J. BRETT, "BOYS OF ENGLAND" OFFICE, 173, FLEET STREET, E.C.

POOR RAY.

"PLEASE, SIR, OH, SIR!" GROANED POOR RAY.

POOR RAY, THE DRUMMER BOY.

A STORY FOUNDED ON FACTS; BY A CONTRIBUTOR TO THE "ARMY AND NAVY GAZETTE."

CHAPTER I.

A SAD NIGHT'S WORK.

IT was a miserable, cold, wet, nasty evening, with rain falling in torrents, and dashed right and left by a cutting north wind, so keen, that it was enough, as the saying goes, to cut one in two.

It was dirty and slippery under foot; the gutters were choked up and overflowing; ponds of water, ankle deep and of a milky colour, covered the roads.

The lamps, too, as soon as they were lighted, blinked with a sad, watery look, quite in keeping with the weather; some struggled ineffectually to give their usual radiance, and fluttered out of existence.

Harder and harder the rain poured down, till half the tradesmen in the small, quiet, dingy unimportant town of Hockerton, had closed their shops, thinking, rightly enough, that no sensible persons who had any place at all to put their heads in would venture out.

Stronger and stronger the wind blew, till it was positively dangerous to walk in the streets; for slates and bricks, with now and then a chimney pot, were hurled from their lofty positions, to be smashed into a thousand fragments on the pavement below.

But stay, never mind the weather.

What is that crouched up in that narrow, filthy court?

God help us! that black-looking heap can never be a human being asleep, when not so much as a dirty beggar in rags, or a homeless, wandering street dog, can anywhere be seen; if it be, the very stones in the court-way ought to have compassion.

But hold, it moves slowly, as if in pain, for the wind has changed, and now the rain, like the furious tide that will not be kept back, dashes up the court unmercifully.

A sob can be heard of a wailing kind, followed, in quick succession, by a bitter burst of tears, as if the heart was breaking.

Perhaps the policeman, who is passing now, may see the miserable being; but he is thinking of a good supper, no doubt, and hurries on down the street.

A hollow, churchyard cough from a female.

God help us! it sends an unaccountable thrill through one.

A peculiar painful cry from an infant!

Yes, it must be from that carefully, well covered up lump, resembling a small bundle of rags, that lies on the female bosom.

At the sound, the miserable creature hugs the infant closer to her breast; but it's no use, the babe won't be quiet, and all the poor mother's coaxing is in vain.

If we could see her face as she sits up in that narrow court, doubtless there would be a wild, expressive light in her eyes.

It must be so, for in a twinkling she is on her feet, and with limbs shaking and teeth gnashing together, hesitates but for a moment, then hurries out into the street.

It is within a shade of pitchy darkness.

Evidently, from her slim figure, she is young; but she heeds not the pelting rain, but on and on she runs and walks alternately, till the town of Hockerton is more than a mile behind her.

Weak, and in a fainting state, she staggers against a large gateway.

It is too late to read the printed notices on the parish board, but she places her wet hand upon it, half with fear and fright, and to banish any misgivings as to the locality, takes a look round.

There could be no mistaking the dark outline of the massive building, though, as we have before mentioned, the night was so dark that nothing short of Egyptian darkness could have hid it from her sight; but still hesitating, she staggers into the middle of the road.

She knew it now; her palpitating heart confirmed it, as she nervously took off her shawl and wrapped it carefully round her child, for no one

but a mother would have done this, exposed her already drenched person to the fury of the elements.

Washing its face with her scalding tears, that the torrents of rain intermingled with, she laid it down at the gateway, and pulled a bell, which rang out a dull, dead-like sound.

Again the cold, wet hand jerked the wire; a suppressed scream, indicating symptoms of idiotcy, followed, and the wretched creature, stumbling at every step, hurried away, but to turn round at every dozen yards, fancying that some one was close at her heels, to drag her back for her inhuman act, in exposing her child at the gate, right under the very noses of the board of guardians.

Here was a daring act; not but that the thing had been done before, but the last occasion dated some few years back, and then the unfortunate mother had not strength to go many yards ere she fell down, only to be picked up next morning, stiff and cold, with famished features that bespoke unutterable misery.

It was not likely that the fat, pampered gateman, who was old in sin and wickedness, and who ate as much as six paupers, was going to answer the bell, leave his snug, warm, comfortable room, and get wet; perhaps that might bring on cold!

Oh, dear, no.

What business had tramps out such weather?—a pack of low-life scoundrels, who lived upon good-natured people; who came there to be fed, and went away next morning, giving insolence.

The gateman thought this, and, crossing his legs before a large fire, began to doze.

It was a much-coveted position, however.

The rain abated not, the wind howled and whined louder than ever.

Undoubtedly, the gateman would have gone to bed, only the workhouse doctor was out, and would not return till somewhere near ten; and so cun ning was the old sinner who nodded before the fire, that he actually knew the doctor's and the master's ring, as we know the time of day by looking at the clock.

At the first sound of the bell, he listened, thinking, perhaps, that the doctor could find no place to suit him like the house: the second sound was enough.

If ever he did make a mistake, and that was rare, he fell back upon the good old adage, " that there are none so deaf as those that won't hear."

It was a little past ten as the doctor came up to the gate.

He was apt to be impatient; the state of the weather jarred upon his nervous temperament.

" The devil take you," said he, as he heard the old man tramping through the rain, " for a slow coach," and kicking impatiently about, his foot came in contact with the bundle.·

Through his impatience the child was saved, for, in all probability had he remained quiet, as a medical gentleman ought to have done, the child would have escaped his notice, and consequently must have perished.

There was a terrible hubbub in the house.

The master and matron were called up.

Nurses had to leave their warm beds, and the doctor's assistant, an intelligent workhouse boy, made up a draught.

The child was carefully attended to, and, before morning, was consigned to the tender care of one of the pauper nurses; and, as it was a boy, it was in time duly christened by the master of the house as Ray Muggleton.

It would be simply tedious to record, even if we felt inclined, the events of a few years, except to say that the child grew, and was sent to school with other pauper children, where they got their lessons well kicked and caned into them, and invariably a couple of days or so after knew nothing about them.

CHAPTER II.

FATHERBY AND HIS IMP.

GOOD boys who never do anything wrong till they are found out, are plentiful in story books.

They are pretty, cheerful, generous and truthful.

Indeed, from the graphic descriptions given of their lineaments, they are so handsome that it is a pity models of them are not taken in wax.

We feel bound to say this, ere we pen another line, for poor Ray Muggleton wasn't good-looking, and at times his veracity was apt to be shaky.

Novelists devote page after page to describing the features of their imaginary personages; as a rule it takes another page to hit off the style of dress.

Fancy a writer, compelled to give a description of a workhouse suit—cord trousers and jacket—and the feminine beauty that peeped out of the large grey eyes of poor Ray Muggleton.

People would laugh, as well they might; but as our story is a true one, we shall be content to say that Ray Muggleton was not exactly an ugly boy; he was, as some lads say, betwixt and between; rather wild, but very obliging, and easily frightened; in fact, too sensitive for a workhouse boy.

The schoolmaster—who was a sly rogue, and little better than a villain—took a positive hatred to the lad, and as the man of letters was noted for his brutality, poor Ray soon received a full share of caning.

All the boys in the town of Hockerton knew Mr. Fatherby—a look from him would send them flying—and as the brute stood nearly six feet, it may be easily surmised that no pauper ever dared dispute his authority.

Besides, who ever heard of a schoolmaster being taken up for knocking pauper boys about?

Not but that some of the larger boys in the house conspired, at times, to upset his authority.

But the look of the man invariably brought their secret and hot-headed plans to the ground.

Above all things, be it known, that Fatherby had a son, the biggest coward and dunce in the school, who certainly inherited a good share of his father's propensities.

It was Monday morning, then, and Fatherby was in one of his revengeful and savage tempers.

The boys used to whisper that Sunday made him worse instead of doing him good, and, as may be guessed, Monday was a dreaded day.

It was said that Fatherby could see out of the back of his head.

You never caught any of the boys talking if he was feigning to read or looking up at the ceiling.

Oh, no, they were up to those dodges, and could tell by the twitching of his disagreeable features that he was only waiting to pounce upon his prey.

His head and face were larger than the school globe, which was a pretty good size, and his hands, that wielded the cane so unmercifully, were in proportion.

The first sight that met Ray Muggleton as he entered the school was the schoolmaster and his imp of a son punishing one of the paupers.

The slight noise he made on opening the door made Fatherby desist, for he was more cunning than a fox.

The master of the house or the parson might drop in; but then his lying tongue would soon colour up a plausible story.

Ray Muggleton stood with his cap in his hand, hesitating where to go, and, as no one seemed to take notice of him, he stood trembling from head to foot.

"Come here," shouted Fatherby, and the very rafters in the roof of the school-room shook again. "Quick, you lump of ignorance! So I have to mould and shape you into a little like order, have I? Speak, will you?"

"Yes, sir, please," faltered poor Ray.

But the savage feigned not to hear him, and struck him down.

Fatherby then walked away unconcerned, to administer condign punishment on other unoffending heads.

It is almost unnecessary to say that little Ray Muggleton's learning in the shape of letters was not much that day, for a kind of singing in his right ear hindered him from hearing and understanding.

Most boys soon take to one another, but Ray was one of your shy fellows, who, whenever they take to a companion, do it in real earnest—not for what they can get, but some one to love; for poor Ray lay many a night thinking, as boys will think, whether his mother was alive or dead, rich or poor, and what her face could be like; perhaps he might some day be fetched away in a carriage, and what would Fatherby say then?

But the master soon dispelled those ideas.

For months Jack was on the look-out for a companion whom he might trust with some of his warm-hearted thoughts.

He had tried a good many, but found them ready to betray him for a spoonful of skilley, and as Fatherby was so much against him, that was a sufficient reason for most of the boys to shun him.

One, evening, as the bell called the inmates to their food, the ravenous boys ranged themselves in the dining-room, as Fatherby ostentatiously called it, a miserable white-washed room, without a sign of a picture of any kind.

"Sit down," said Fatherby.

Each boy willingly obeyed; but the master frowned at the boys whose eyes glistened with hunger at the skilley, and then came this farce—

"For what we are about to receive, the Lord make us truly thankful."

In an instant spoons went to work! Such a licking and blowing!

It was a queer sight; but suddenly there was a pause, and one boy cried out with amazement—

"Oh, if you please, sir, there's Ray Muggleton ain't touched his."

"O-o-oh!" said all the boys, and each eye was turned upon poor Ray. It was such a rare sight to see a boy sit down and not eat.

Fatherby stared; a dead silence ensued as the brute caught Ray by his ears, and pulled him out by main force from his seat.

"Please, sir; oh, sir!" groaned poor Ray, not daring to touch the arm of the schoolmaster.

"You sneaking scoundrel," he cried. "I can see through you, as I can see through that window yonder. You don't feel well, I suppose, eh? Do you hear me?"

"Yes, sir."

"Go to the school-room at once, and you'll eat your skilley to-morrow evening, never fear." The brute's laugh was taken up by the chief part of the boys, who, apparently, were trying to win favour.

Ray Muggleton, with tears in his eyes, sat down on a form.

There was no one that loved him, no one ever spoke kindly to him, and when he thought of this the tears oozed down his cheeks; he thought of the other boys who had friends, but no one ever came to see him.

He loved one person in the house, and that was Bill Jones, who was so clever at figures, and could write such a beautiful hand; but Bill Jones cared nothing at all about him, would turn against him in the playground, and take the part of the others.

Ray, though a quiet lad, had a little spirit.

When aroused he felt that he would do some mischief if Fatherby didn't mind; and, as for staying in the house, he was sure he never would.

Numerous traditions were handed down from pauper to pauper how Tom So-and-So ran away, and was brought back and put in the dead-house to sleep with a corpse, and how Dick Somebody was skinned alive, and other dreadful cases, all of which the boys fully believed.

Hour after hour went by, and still no Fatherby came, for a friend of his had dropped in to see him, and poor Ray was forgotten.

He, however, went to bed, feeling sick and tired of life; he said his prayers, and wondered in his simple way why God allowed Fatherby to be so wicked and brutal.

Next morning at school most of the boys thought that the master had forgotten the freak of Muggleton, in not partaking of his allowance, and though the boy made a great show of eating his breakfast, literally he partook of none, for he felt ill.

Fatherby took his seat, and called the school to silence.

"Come here, that boy who showed his temper yesterday evening, and wouldn't eat his supper."

Poor Ray, with his head bent down, approached him.

"What have you say, that I shouldn't punish you? Somebody else, you know, will say to you some day, what have you to say why sentence of death should not be passed upon you?"

"Nothing, sir," faltered the boy.

"I should think not."

"I don't feel, sir," he said, making a great effort, "feel——"

"Ah! ah! he, he! ah! you scamp, don't feel well, isn't that it?"

"I don't, sir, indeed I don't; don't punish me this time, please."

"Silence," roared the monster, "whining won't save you."

In an instant he was hoisted upon

the back of one of the strongest boys in the school.

"Boys," said Fatherby, solemnly, "I am about to punish this ungrateful wretch in a manner that I hope will do him good, and be a lesson to you. Refuse to eat the good food that gentlemen and invalids send here for! Refuse his supper! Ah, the wretch, thousands of boys outside would thank God for it; but that skinny rushlight is not fit to live. He's a sneak; I can see it in him, and he will be hanged yet, as sure as I am standing here. He has a good bed to lie on, and a kind master to look after, and educate him, but over-feeding has made him saucy!

"I am too old to be caught by chaff.

"Shamming illness won't do for me."

After this style he delivered a discourse, which lasted for some time.

He wound up by asking the boys whether Muggleton didn't deserve what he was going to get.

"Yes, sir," was the cry.

Fast and heavy fell the birch upon the naked skin of Poor Ray, till the blood trickled down, yet the monster would not desist, though the boy screamed and turned in all manner of conceivable ways.

After Fatherby had gratified his revengeful spirit, the poor boy was sent into a corner of the school, where he continued to sob, and his sobbing caught the ear of the schoolmaster's son, who was not present at the castigation.

He went up to Muggleton, and struck him with his fist at the back of the neck.

The boy looked round, with fire glaring in his eyes; he forgot everything, and with a furious spring bounded upon the young imp, who began to bawl lustily; but right and left poor Ray drove his fists into his face.

He was about to throttle him, when a blow from Fatherby dashed him to the ground.

"Oh, you murderer!" he roared. "What! kill my poor boy?"

"Yes," replied poor Ray, not at all frightened; "and so I will, too."

"You forget," said Fatherby, out of breath with passion, "that I'll cut you to pieces."

"I don't care. You may kill me. I wish I was dead. I'm starved here, and kicked for nought."

"Starved, you scoundrel? I'll starve you yet; see what you have done to my poor innocent boy; blackened one of his eyes. You shall go to the dead-house for it, where the rats will have a feed off your skinny carcase."

"He shouldn't touch me then," returned poor Ray. "Do you think I'm going to let a fellow like that knock me about, and run needles into me?"

"Ah, you forget the dead-house, and the rats."

"I hope I may never come out; that's my wish."

This reply to Fatherby was unparralleled in the annals of the house.

The boys opened their eyes and drew in their breath as the schoolmaster ordered him back again to the corner.

The wretch knew that he dare not inflict any further punishment on the lad, as there was no telling what the consequences might be, but he made up his mind that Ray Muggleton should have a few hours in that dreaded habitation, the dead-house.

And no doubt he would have carried his threat into execution, only the lad was taken so ill that the doctor was sent for, and for once Fatherby shook in his shoes.

Severely the doctor called him to account, and it was only after begging and whining that the medical man gave his word to hush the matter up.

In the meantime the terrible excitement, and the beating, with the horrid thought of the dead-house, brought on a fever, and in a few days poor Ray was given up by the doctor.

He, however, got the better hand of death—and then returned the determination to run away from the workhouse.

It was his constant thought how he might get away.

He planned in bed, shunned most of the boys, and inwardly resolved that the first favourable opportunity should see him clear of the hated walls of the workhouse of Hockerton.

CHAPTER III.

POOR RAY TAKES FRENCH LEAVE

HOW tedious the days passed to poor Ray, and how long they seemed, as evening after evening, he was kept in school to learn his lessons.

He soon picked up the mysteries of arithmetic and letters, and felt half inclined to relinquish his bold scheme, and stay some time longer in the house.

His mother or some relation might turn up, and then his last chance would be gone for ever.

Fatherby spared him not, though he was as submissive as a lamb, and did all in his willing nature to please, but to no purpose.

It was after a severe flogging that he found himself in the schoolroom one evening alone.

Impatiently he looked out of one of the schoolroom windows, with deep thought strongly marked upon his brow.

The bell called the willing paupers to supper, and the scene among the boys was laughable in the extreme, as they pushed and scrambled to be first in the dining-room.

As poor Ray was to stay no longer in the school than supper time, he left it slowly, as if he were taking a picture of the place in his mind, which would at least take some years to efface.

He made a show of eating his supper, but a lump seemed to bar the way, and adroitly he gave his allowance to another boy.

Supper over, the boys marched to their dormitories; each dormitory con-tained three beds, the doors, as a rule, being generally locked.

Wednesday night generally found the man in charge intoxicated, as he went every week to give orders at Hockerton.

Ray thought of this, and to his great joy the lights were turned off, and the dormitory left unlocked.

The other two lads in the room were inclined for talking, but Ray, feigning to be poorly, trembled in his bed at the harrowing idea that he might be caught in attempting to make his escape.

A shudder ran through him as the traditions of the house flashed across his mind, yet the two other lads kept on talking; restlessly he turned in his bed, and the perspiration rolled from him, as he heard the sharp, snappish sound of the workhouse clock striking ten.

Yes, the boys had dropped off to sleep.

He was dressed in an instant, but had the good sense not to put on his shoes.

He scarcely dared to breathe as he glided along the corridor with a face as white as the walls, and his heart beating terribly against his ribs.

Suddenly he heard footsteps, and almost sank down with fright.

It was impossible for him to retrace his steps; nearer and nearer came the firm heavy tread.

His heart rose up to his mouth, as

he caught sight of the dark outline of Fatherby.

Panting for breath, he crept close up to the side of the wall, as Fatherby passed up the middle of the passage, talking to himself.

" I'll cut the heart out of him," he muttered, and at the very sound, Ray Muggleton covered his mouth with his hand, for fear Fatherby might hear him breathe.

The schoolmaster passed on.

But not daring to move, Ray Muggleton began to crawl along the corridor, after some time had elapsed.

Gaining the front door of the workhouse, he found it doubly barred and locked; climbing up to one of the windows, he undid the fastening, slowly pushed up the sash, and by dropping down, he crept along near the gateway.

The walls were exceedingly high; but scarcely knowing what he did, he hurried to the gate, and peeped in at the lodge window.

There was a dim light burning, and he heard the old gentleman snoring.

If he could get the key! but he was too frightened to try it.

He went to the gate, thinking it would be easy to get over; however, he tried the latch, and to his amazement the door opened.

The gateman had evidently forgotten to lock it.

CHAPTER IV.

ON THE TRAMP.

IN an instant he was out, and running for his life.

On he went along the high road, not meeting a soul.

He began to lag, but the thought that Fatherby and his gang might be behind, made him redouble his efforts, till he was sure he must be a good many miles from Hockerton.

He sat down upon a heap of stones by the roadside, feeling a something within that almost made him wish that he was back at Hockerton again.

Every object that met his eye seemed dim and mysterious, and he thought of ghosts and goblins.

He felt so tired that he must lie down somewhere.

A few yards from the road stood a large straw rick; creeping though a hedge he made a hole in the side of it, crept in, and tried to sleep.

But fear reigned predominant in his bosom; he found it utterly impossible to sleep.

As soon as the grey dawn appeared in the horizon, he was up and on the road again.

As it got lighter, several men stared very hard at him, and when the sun had risen, he overtook a farmer's lad driving some sheep.

If he could get work, and save up money, that would be capital.

So he asked the boy, who looked at him with wondering eyes, whether he could tell him of a place.

It didn't matter what the work might be.

" I think our master will give thee a job at ox keeping. Would thee like that ?"

" Oh, shouldn't I ?" said Ray, and he rubbed his hands with glee.

" Dost see," said the lad, who was sharp for a country boy, and who took a secret fancy to his cord jacket, "thy clothes ain't what farmers like. I'll give thee a fine smock for thy jacket, then Farmer Snoxall won't know thee from an old hand."

After a pause, he remarked, abruptly—

"What be they letters in thy cap for?"

Ray never thought of this—H. W. were the initials of the workhouse of Hockerton—and made some silly excuse.

A bargain was struck, and as the farmer's boy lived hard by, he brought out an old slop and a billy cock, for which he received many thanks.

"I'll tell thee what thee must say to old Snoxall. Say, 'Zer, can thee give I a job at ship kiping, or mindin' oxen?' That's the house, with the poplar in front. Dost see it?"

"Yes," said Ray, who, without further ceremony, bade the boy good bye.

He was fortunate enough to meet the farmer a few yards before he got there.

There was absolutely not a vestige of good nature in the features of the farmer.

His face was the counterpart of Fatherby's, and he carried a ground-ash stick in his hand.

"If you please, sir," said poor Ray, timidly, "can you give me a job at minding sheep or cows?"

"Humph," growled the farmer, "where dost come from?" And he looked so fierce, that Ray thought in a moment, if he told a lie, the farmer would be sure to find out, and, perhaps, get him sent back to the house again.

"From Hockerton, please, sir."

"Oh," he grunted. "Well, what can you do?"

"Anything, sir."

"I suppose that means nothing at all."

"I hope not, sir."

"Are you honest? If I can trust you, I'll give you a job to look after my oxen. What you'll have to do will be to keep them off a field of turnips. You can do that, I suppose."

"Oh, yes, sir."

"Why, you look famished. Have you had anything to eat?"

"Yes, sir, a little," replied Ray.

The farmer then gave him to understand that as soon as his day's work was done, he should have a large basin of hot milk, which made the anxious listener's mouth water.

Not many minutes after, he was on the downs, and the farmer having pointed out what he must do, left him.

The morning passed.

The oxen were very quiet, and did not even attempt to go on forbidden ground.

He was very lonely, and began to conjecture what the time could be, for the basin of hot milk and bread was uppermost in his mind, and the thin smock that he wore was a rag, compared to his warm cord jacket.

The oxen kept chewing away, scarcely deigning to notice him.

At length, he wandered some distance from the turnips, when, to his horror, one of the oxen gave a bellow, and immediately the whole herd rushed into the field of turnips, snorting and tearing them up in a most furious manner.

Ray hallooed and bawled till he could hardly speak, and the appearance of the enraged farmer who came running up to him, out of breath, frightened him so much that he could not say a word for himself.

"You young vagabond. You take care of oxen! Fifty pounds' worth of turnips destroyed."

And with that he commenced to beat poor Ray, who in vain roared and implored for mercy.

CHAPTER V.

A BOLD DECISION.

"GET out of my field," cried the farmer, as poor Ray fell down, and with that he commenced to kick him.

Ray managed to get up, and soon found himself once more on the high road, every bone in his body in pain, and his frame so weak with hunger that he could hardly stand.

Boy-like, the tears flowed faster and faster, as he saw a long road before him, but hunger compelled him to resume his painful walk.

As he went along, he plucked a few leaves from the hedges.

Then it occurred to him that he might have had a turnip or two.

He was getting near some town.

He could tell that by the milestones, though the inscriptions were nearly obliterated; not being a good reader, that made it still harder for him to decipher them.

The sun was going down as he crawled into the town of Littleford.

Boys were scampering about, others shouting and playing leap-frog.

How happy they all looked.

He was sure he could not walk much further, and his only hope was that he might die.

He sat down near a baker's shop, eyeing the loaves in the window wistfully, and the smell of hot bread that came from the shop was delicious.

The hardest crust, that had been lying by for weeks, would have been a treat, but no one gave unto him.

While thinking of hunger and where he should lie for the night, a large waggon-load of wood stopped at the baker's shop.

In a very short time, two biggish boys asked the baker if they might help to carry it in.

Poor Ray heard them, and he looked longingly at the baker, who caught his famished look.

"Yes, and you can come, too," he said.

Without further bidding, he moved with alacrity, and was soon staggering under the wood.

But what did he care now? Perhaps he might get sixpence for the job.

A couple of rolls, and then there would be fourpence left.

Two hours and a half, and the waggon was empty.

"Come this way," said the baker, to the two fellows before mentioned, "and you as well."

This was to poor Ray.

They entered the bakehouse, and it was as much as poor Muggleton could do to resist the great temptation of picking up some crumbs.

The baker gave them some beer.

"Now, I think," he said, "if I give you half a crown between you, that will be paying you pretty well."

"Of course it will," was the response.

"Well, here, take this half crown and divide it between you."

The biggest lad of the party eagerly seized it.

"Come on," he said to poor Ray, who followed at their heels.

But as soon as they got a few yards from the baker's, they walked very fast.

Then the idea flashed through poor Ray's mind that they meant dividing it between them.

If they took to running, he was sure he would never be able to keep up.

"What do you want?" said one, turning round.

"If you please, will you give me

"I WANT TO 'LIST, SIR."

my share. I'm so tired and hungry; oh, please do give it to me."

"Your share, eh; that's a good un, too."

And with that they went into a public-house.

"Stay, we'll bring it out to you," replied the younger of the two, who was one of the scamps of the town.

And stay poor Ray did for a long time, till he got tired.

He then went and quietly asked the landlord to tell them that he was still waiting.

One of them came out and began to bully him.

The other slipped on tiptoe to the pump, filled a bucket of water, and threw it over him.

With that the two young vagabonds took to their heels, laughing.

Poor Ray was drenched.

He told his pitiable tale to no one, but walked slowly up the street, with large tears oozing down his cheeks.

It was dark, and the gas lamps burned dimly.

There was a bridge to pass over, and all at once the thought shot through his mind to drown himself.

He couldn't be worse; no money, no food, nowhere to lie his head; and he looked up into the dark sky, thinking whether it could be so wicked after all to take one's own life.

Perhaps God would forgive him, for he was only a poor lad, who never received kindness from anyone.

Those at Hockerton wouldn't so much as know his name; but his mother—she must have known the place, and for that reason above all others he loved the town, it was so familiar to his ear.

If she was alive, and should some day go to the house and find him gone!

But suddenly he remembered Fatherby's words that he had often told him—"that he came from a bad stock."

Yes, he could hate her.

Perhaps she was driven to it—who could tell?

He was positive Fatherby knew nothing about her.

He drove these thoughts from him.

He was hungry.

Why not steal?

But the fear of being taken and sent to prison overcame all other evil promptings that were busily at work within him.

He looked down at the water that rushed along so rapidly, still hesitating whether to leap off the parapet or not, when the rough hand of a policeman came in contact with his right ear, and ordered him away.

That settled the affair.

But he did not go very far.

He sat down in a courtway and soon fell asleep.

He slept as he slept many a night after, cold, wet, and in rags, that clung to him like grave clothes.

Getting a day's work at this place, and a job at breaking stones at another, more than a month passed away, and, after many more days of wandering he reached Bristol, when he fully made up his mind to go as a sailor.

But he was soon kicked off the deck of nearly every ship he boarded.

Who wanted the services of a boy in tatters?

He could see that sailoring was out of his reach, and in a corner of the ship gave way to his grief.

But he found that crying only made him weaker, instead of filling his belly.

He strolled from Bristol about three miles when he saw two soldiers, the worse for liquor, drinking at an inn by the roadside.

He looked at them very hard, and, though he had not the slightest idea of soldiers or what they were like, yet when one of them addressed him, and asked if he would like to be a drummer, he instantly jumped at the proposal.

He had seen military bandsmen, and had noticed how smart and clean they all appeared though he himself was so ragged and dirty.

In fact, it was at these times that he took stock of his own wretched attire.

"Would you like to go?" said the soldier, jesting.

"Oh, shouldn't I!"

"Then you shall. What would you like to be—a fifer, drummer, or bugler? But the drum; listen—

"For the rat-tat-too
I love to hear,
With the drums and fifes
So sweet and clear."

"I don't care which, sir."

"That's right!" cried the tallest of the two, handing him a glass of ale. "Now I'll tell you what to do; go to the barracks. You know where they are, of course?"

Ray said that he didn't.

After pointing out the locality, the soldier resumed with a grin—

"Ask to see the drum-major. You don't know who he is; that's the gentleman who will teach you playing. Ask to see him, and you'll get on well. Plenty to eat and drink, a good bed, and finish up with a medal on your breast."

CHAPTER VI.

THE GREEN RECRUIT.

POOR RAY, without waiting for further instructions, set off to Horsefield Barracks, a distance of a mile.

Arriving at the barrack gate, he saw the sentinel on duty, pacing to and fro.

"What do you want here, you ragamuffin?" asked the sentry.

"I want the drum-major, please; I'm going to enlist for a drummer."

"I'll 'list you, you ragged scamp," said the sentry.

At that moment the orderly bugler, who was reading a book to pass the time away, hearing the word 'drummer' mentioned, walked up to poor Ray, and inquired his business.

"Oh," said the bugler, winking slyly at the sentry, "it's all right; you're just the chap we want."

And away went poor Ray, following the bugler to the bandroom.

The bugler was a harum-scarum sort of a fellow; was up to all manner of pranks, and commenced by introducing the homeless wanderer to a dozen other drummers in the room.

"Brother comrades and sheep-skin smashers, this most intelligent youth is dying to join the service. He has a beautiful lip for the bugle and big drum. His face and clothes match each other, and for that reason, I propose that he be enlisted without further fuss or ceremony."

"Agreed on," was the ringing cry.

As there were no non-commissioned officers in the room, they soon commenced their tricks upon him, though not until they had given him something to eat.

One of the drummer boys put his hand up the chimney, and commenced rubbing his face, saying at the same time—

"I do like you; we'll be chums."

And poor Ray innocently enough replied—

"Thank you; I hope you won't have cause to repent it."

A roar of laughter followed, for his face was like a sweep's.

"What are you laughing at?" he asked, smiling himself.

"Laughing," was the response, "because we have got such a fine recruit. But you know," they said, "you must have a bath, or the doctor will never pass you."

And forthwith he was taken to the bath-house, and half drowned.

After playing all the tricks upon him they could, one of them hinted that as he had not seen the colonel, he had better make sure at once and do so.

"But why am I to see him this evening?"

"Oh, if you don't, you may lose pounds by it, and the colonel may be in the backwoods of North America to-morrow by this time."

"And while you are about it," remarked one, "tell him, if he pleases, to send our *Weekly Grumbler*."

"As well as two bottles of wine that he borrowed," added another.

"Yes," said a third; "and the money that's due for playing no end of dark nights at the regatta that terrible siege which can be seen at all the fairs for the low price of one penny."

"But what will he say?" asked poor Ray.

"Say!" they all repeated, with great emphasis. "Go! You know it is in our power to decide whether you shall be a drummer or not."

This was enough for poor Ray.

If he doubted ever so much about the matter, the terrible threat of not being a drummer was amply sufficient to counteract any wavering on his part.

Away he went, simple fellow as he was, to the officers' mess, the drummers in the meantime getting out of the room, as they knew that there would be a noise over the matter if the adjutant heard of it, not that they ever imagined for a moment that he would see the colonel.

The waiters would take great care of that, and kick him about his business.

From some unknown cause, not a waiter was to be seen as poor Ray opened the mess door, after repeatedly knocking; for Fatherby, to give him his due, kicked manners into him.

He walked into that magnificent scene.

To him it appeared as a fairy land.

The dazzling brightness all but took his breath away, as he stood for a moment gazing at the glitter of sparkling gold and silver, bright scarlet uniforms, and the perfume.

"Oh, oh!" cried one of the officers, "who have we here?"

"If you please, sir," said Ray, going up to the officer, "may I see the colonel?"

"Won't the adjutant do?" said another, a cavalry officer, who was visiting the mess for a bit of fun.

"No, sir."

"Colonel, you are wanted."

"Come this way, boy," said the colonel, frowning. "Speak out."

"I want to 'list, sir," said Ray.

"But who sent you?" said the colonel.

"The band boys. They want a paper of theirs sent—the *Weekly Grumbler*, I think they called it—and you are to send the wine that was lent."

"And what else?" said the colonel, looking round at the officers, who were all on the broad grin.

"The regatta money."

"Is that all?"

"Yes, sir."

"Why, you dirty little rascal, what do you mean by coming here? I've a good mind to order you a sound thrashing."

"Would it not be advisable," said one of the officers, winking, "to put him in the water-butt below or throw him out into the back yard, that the dogs may tear him to pieces?'"

"He is not so green as he looks," said another.

"Keep an eye on the plate," added a third.

"Yes," said the colonel; "and send the sergeant of the guard to me, for allowing the confounded vagabond here at all."

"I shouldn't wonder," remarked another, as he beheld the terrified countenance of poor Ray, "if he has pocketed something in the spoon line already."

"Mercy, sir!" cried poor Ray, putting his hands up.

"Where do you come from, boy?" said the colonel.

"Hockerton," he sobbed.

The officers stared at each other.

"My boy," said the major, "Hockerton is a long way from here. Did you tramp it?"

"Yes, sir."

"Have you a father or mother?"

"No one at all."

"Not even a brother or a relation?"

"I have no one, sir; no, I haven't," and poor Ray lifted up his voice and wept.

The company got interested, and by dint of coaxing, the outcast told his tale.

The drum-major was sent for.

"This boy wishes to join the drummers. See that he has a good bath, and take those rags off him and put them in the dust-hole."

"But, sir," said the drum-major, "consider the brat ought——"

"That's my order; there's the boy," and away went poor Ray.

"You cursed lump of humanity!" exclaimed the drum-major, breaking out at him, "what brought you into barracks at all? There will be no end of things stolen now."

"I'll be good, sir."

"Be good! By the living jingo, if you are not to a hair's point what I expect you to be, you had better be dead; do you understand that?"

Without waiting for a reply, he entered the drummers' room.

"I should like to know," he said, appealingly, to the men and boys in the room, "who induced this lump of vagabondism to go to the mess? Now, tell me, boy, what's your name?"

"Ray Muggleton."

"Ray what?" repeated the drum-major.

"Muggleton."

"Oh, great Heaven! we shall all have our throats cut some fine night. Who sent you to the mess?"

"I think it was that one," pointing to one of the boys.

"Me!" cried the boy, "why, I haven't been in all the evening. Oh! my, can't he tell lies?"

"Never mind, now," said the drum major, frowning.

So saying he left the room, upon which all the drummer boys turned upon poor Ray, and pushed him round the room spitefully.

At bedtime they tied a piece of string to his bedclothes and pulled them off repeatedly when he got into bed; others threw bread at him; some more daring got basins of water and drenched him with it.

This game was carried on for some time after the usual hour for retiring.

The corporal, who was on leave, was to return that night, and the drummers frightened poor Ray by saying, "Wait till Corporal Slasher comes in; won't he wallop you?" and with that pleasing information ringing in his ears, the wretched boy dropped off to sleep.

Corporal Slasher was as sharp as a razor, and thought there was no one like him.

He was abhorred by the band, and he knew it, for they told him of it often; but what cared he for their hatred, as long as he was their master?

In height he stood five feet four, and was so ill-looking that he was considered one of the ugliest men in the regiment; to the boys, as we have before intimated, he was a savage.

Most of them waited upon him, and licked his hands, so to speak; but he only ill-used them the more.

His feet, like his hands, were abominably ugly, and whenever any of boys saw him walking across the parade, the cry was, "There goes old Leftlegs," for his legs knocked together in an unsoldier-like manner.

He arrived in barracks somewhat late; but he went to bed in pretty good spirits.

But joyful evenings generally bring sorrowful mornings, and as soon as the bugle sounded for the men to turn out, and make up their beds, he called out—

"If every bed ain't made up as it ought to be, I'll wait on you."

With that he curled himself up for a comfortable snooze.

"Please, corporal," said one of the boys, whispering in his ear, "the new boy ain't got up yet."

Corporal Slasher turned heavily on his side, and the boy repeated in his ear the second time that the new boy was still in bed.

"The what?" he growled.

"The new boy, corporal."

He started and shook his head.

"I'll 'new boy' him."

Putting on his trousers, he took down a stick from the regulation shelf and cut away viciously at poor Ray.

"Oh!" he roared, smarting with pain.

"Get up, then, you lazy fellow; wait till I see what you are like. Merciful power!" he groaned, pretending to be horror-struck; "the service is going to old Scratch. Who enlisted you?"

"The drum-major."

"Ah! he's going mad. Your name?"

"Muggleton, sir."

"Worse still. If you don't tell me what part you come from and what you have been doing, you shall have the cat-o'-nine tails and be cut to ribbons. Go on!"

"From Hockerton."

"Who dragged you up there?"

"I was at the house."

"What house?" exclaimed others, chiming in.

"The workhouse!" he faltered.

"I knew it," returned the corporal, turning up the whites of his eyes. "A workhouse brat!"

But the corporal stopped and changed his tone, for there was the bounty to come, and as he had not a copper in his pocket, he made the best of it under the circumstances by saying—

"Well, after all, it's nothing to be ashamed of. Better boys than you have been there. Mind you boys don't play your tricks upon him. I'll have him under my superintendence for a week. I'll see what I can make of him."

As the drummers' room was occupied only by boys, the corporal had his own way in most things.

The grown-up drummers generally held a consultation in the room of an evening, but Corporal Slasher found ways and means of getting rid of them.

But the bounty, that was the main point to be looked after.

"Oh, my gracious," said one of the F flute players, "you haven't passed the doctor. You'll see some awful sights."

"What will he do, then?" inquired Ray.

"Do!" replied several. "Why, he'll half roast you before a fire, to see if you can stand it. He'll run a ramrod down your throat, and give you dozen cartridges. Let us hope he won't keep you there, as we shall never see you again."

In this foolish way they terrified Ray Muggleton.

However, he passed the doctor's examination, and experienced none of those horrible things that his comrades were so kind in acquainting him with.

He was sworn in, received his bounty, and in his "small book" he read the following description of himself—

"Ray Muggleton, enlisted for the — regiment of foot, on the 4th of April, 1866, at Horsefield Barracks, in the county of Gloucester, at the age of 12 years. Born in the parish of Hockerton, in the county of Wiltshire. Trade or calling, nil. Size, 4 feet 8 inches; complexion, fresh; eyes, grey; hair, brown; marks, none."

On the front part of the book his regimental number was 280, and he repeated it over to himself.

Further on in the book he read "that obedience is the first duty of the soldier;" then came copious extracts from the Articles of War, which were terrible to read.

A court-martial may award "death, penal servitude, for mutiny, desertion, cowardice, sleeping on or quitting his post, in action, or previous to action, using words tending to create alarm."

Ray Muggleton wondered whether he should ever go into action, and what it must be like.

He might turn a coward, or just the opposite, and get a Victoria Cross for his bravery.

Whilst he was deeply studying the Articles of War, the drum-major was thinking of his bounty, and as this unworthy individual was not unlike his inferior, Corporal Slasher, it is easy to conjecture that at times they were not the best of friends.

Let it not, however, be imagined that the drum-majors in the service are all like the individual introduced here; there certainly may be a few like him, but only a few.

"Come to my room," he whispered, about an hour after the lad had been sworn in, "I want you to go on an errand for me."

With that he closed the door.

"Yes, sir," replied Muggleton, going, but Corporal Slasher stopped him.

"Do you know," he said, in a half whisper, "that it is the custom to give the corporal of the drums a present out of your bounty? It's what they all do."

And he appealed to the boys, who of course could say nothing but yes.

Poor Ray generously put his hand into his pocket and pulled out half-a-crown, which the corporal indignantly refused; he required ten shillings, and would not take a farthing less.

"And if you'll be judged by me," he whispered, "I'll take care of the rest."

Without the slightest hesitation Ray Muggleton handed him over the remainder of his bounty, and ran off to the drum-major, who commenced operations at once upon him.

"As you are a boy that don't know what money is, you had better let me mind it for you; you can have a shilling whenever you require it. What do you say?"

"Corporal Slasher's got it, sir."

"The villain! Come with me."

"Oh, dear," thought poor Ray, as he had to keep step with the drum-major, "I shall be killed."

"Corporal Slasher," said the drum-major, in a tone of authority; "return that boy's bounty money to him."

Slasher commenced to grumble, but all to no effect; he had, as the boys said afterwards, to fork out.

"But this can't be all," exclaimed the drum-major, counting the money, "one pound two out of two pounds, where's the remainder, Muggleton?"

Corporal Slasher stared at the boy as if he could kill him, but Ray had to tell, and the money was handed over to the drum-major.

A few days after, through dishonesty in charging the officers for worthless instruments that were little better than rubbish (for they were afterwards sold to a marine store dealer), the drum-major was tried by court-martial and "reduced to the rank and pay of a private soldier."

CHAPTER VII.

HARD TIMES FOR POOR RAY.

CORPORAL SLASHER had no one to keep him in check, but as he did not wish to get a worse name than he had, which Heaven knows was bad enough, he behaved kinder than usual to the boys, told them whenever the colonel was good enough to make him drum-major, that they should, generally speaking, do what they pleased.

But as he daily expected without obtaining the coveted rank, he got tired at last of curbing his brutal propensities, and became more cruel than ever he had been to the boys.

It was no good to whimper or whine, and that poor Ray soon found out.

Evening parade was over. The drummers' room was like a church or graveyard for quietness.

Corporal Slasher was in one of his savage moods.

"There," he said, pitching a slip of music paper to poor Ray, who was seated round the barrack table with half-a-dozen more lads.

The music-paper was blotched so that it was rather difficult to decipher the notes; the tune was simple, but if it had been hard, it would not have made the slightest difference to Slasher.

His fingers were itching to beat poor Ray.

He had not forgotten the bounty, and as he was of a very vindictive spirit, ne never spared his inferiors.

Corporal Slasher coughed like a wild beast that roars in readiness for its prey.

"You can read writing, I suppose?" he said, in a tone that was enough to put one's teeth on edge.

"Yes, sir. 'Lily of the Vale,' isn't it, sir?"

"Play it; see the time it is written in—two-four. How many crochets are there in a bar of two-four time?"

"Two, sir."

"How many quavers?"

"Four."

"Right, now go on."

Poor Jack shivered as he put the flute up to his mouth.

He knew what was coming, and so did his companions, who still treated him coldly.

He had proceeded as far as the fourth bar of "Lily of the Vale" when a blow from the corporal sent him swinging off the form.

"Playing!" he roared. "Is that playing? Go it, I say."

And he put his foot on the bosom of the boy, who was stretched on the floor.

"Is that playing, I say again?"

"Yes, sir, please, I did my best," he sobbed.

"Stand up! By Heaven, I ll alter this."

Ray tried again, but failed to play the piece, as the fiend was determined he shouldn't.

Down came the thick heavy stick upon his fingers.

Ray forgot who his terrible antagonist was, jumped off the form, and kicked Corporal Slasher in a manner that made him drop on one knee.

For a moment the other boys cried shame and hissed, and one, more plucky than the rest, shied a drum stick at his head, which, had it hit him, would undoubtedly have made a vacancy in the corps, but in the twinkling of an eye, Slasher laid the fellow low.

Foaming at the mouth, he rushed at poor Ray, and with one blow felled him.

"You shall be tried by court-martial," he gasped. "Kicking a non-commissioned officer! You know what it says in your 'small-book?'"

"Oh, dear," groaned poor Ray, "I'm hurt."

Corporal Slasher turned deadly pale.

If such a thing got to the officers' ears it would be all up with him.

He wisely refrained from saying more, and dismissed the boys from practice.

He made his bed and got into it, and for once Corporal Slasher gave him leave from tattoo.

As they were alone, he went to him, pulled down the bedclothes unceremoniously, and asked him if he had any bruises about his body.

There were two at the side of his bosom, which covered as much space as the crown of a man's hat, very much discoloured and of a jelly-like appearance.

He coaxed round the boy, and begged him not to show the marks to any one, and if the following evening was fine, he would take him for a walk.

This little bit of humbug, which poor Ray looked upon as the forerunner of better days to come, pleased him very much, and he wondered, as he fell off to sleep, where Corporal Slasher would take him to on the morrow.

Corporal Slasher, after making sure that he was in a sound sleep, partly turned down the light, as it was dark outside, and very near the hour of tattoo.

He then went to a large chest, on which was painted in large letters, "Music-box."

After selecting a piece of rope, or, more strictly speaking, some cords that are used in bracing up the drums, and satisfying himself as to their strength, he opened a hole in the bosom of his tunic, where there was a considerable quantity of wadding.

Placing the cords with a careful hand into it, he sewed up the lining that he had unripped, and sat down to think.

The bugle sounding the drummers' call for tattoo, and the drummer boys tripping in from their merry games to get their instruments, roused him; however, he said not a word to any one.

As he got into bed some time after, he threw a terrible glance at poor Ray the Drummer Boy.

CHAPTER VIII.

TERRIBLE MOMENTS IN THE LEA WOOD.

MAY was drawing to a close. Scarcely a breath of air was stirring, which made it rather unpleasant for pedestrians.

But, as the evening drew on, a breeze sprang up, which was a very agreeable change.

Poor Ray went to the ablution room—such is the fine name given to wash-houses by the Horse Guards—had a thorough good wash, oiled his hair, and even went so far as to try and part it behind.

The piping on his tunic was as white as the pipe-clay that cleaned it, and his buttons had received a brilliant colour from his brass brush. Corporal Slasher, too, was getting ready at the same time. Acting with caution, he sent poor Ray on some way before him.

His heart was full as he saw Corporal Slasher walking towards him with his white gloves on.

"Shall we go into Bristol for an hour or so?" were the first words he uttered.

The slightest wish or hint on his part, had it been to go to California, would have met with a hearty response from the boy.

"If you like, corporal."

They walked on in silence for some distance.

A thousand little things passed through the lad's mind, the uppermost one being that his superior had no coin with him, and, as he had a shilling, he would ask him to take whatever he liked at the first public-house.

Acting upon this impulse, he asked the question.

"Well, yes; I don't mind having a glass of brandy and water and a cigar. Give me the shilling; I'll pay for it."

And in they went.

Poor Ray had a glass of ale, which cost a penny; his superior, brandy, that cost sixpence, and a threepenny cigar, leaving Ray twopence.

They sat for some time talking.

At last the conversation took a turn.

"I have been thinking," said Corporal Slasher, "as the evening is so fine, that we'll go the Lea Woods bird's-nesting. It will be fine, you know, to bring home some eggs and young song thrushes. You can look after them."

"Oh, won't it!" exclaimed poor Ray, ready to dance with joy; and off they started.

They slipped into the wood, and were soon in the thickest part of it.

"I think," gasped Corporal Slasher, "that there's a nest in that dark fir— a pigeon's, I shouldn't wonder. You get up; I'll lift you."

As the tree was rather high, it took poor Ray some time to get to the top.

But there was no nest, except a fragment of an old one.

As he was climbing the tree Slasher unbuttoned his tunic, tore open the lining, and took out the drum cords.

"I see no one about," he muttered. "Why not here? He'll be frightened, and perhaps make a noise; but I'll quiet him first."

By this time it was dusk.

Corporal Slasher trembled slightly.

He sat down, and called poor Ray to make haste out of the tree, taking care to conceal the cords.

"Sit down," he whispered, as if he feared some one might overhear him, "and rest awhile."

Poor Ray obeyed.

But there was a kind of gloom hanging over the spot, that struck terror into the boy's heart.

"Shan't we be late, corporal?"

"No; at any rate you won't, for where you are going I am not aware that they have any roll call, or that they play tattoo."

Like an electric shock the thought flashed through the agitated bosom of the poor boy that Slasher had brought him to this terrible spot for some horrible purpose; and, as he was hesitating whether to jump up and run, Slasher produced the cords.

"Do you know what these are for?" he whispered, seizing him by the right hand. "Do you know what they are for?

"No, corporal."

And he commenced to cry.

"By Heaven! I'm going to hang you."

"Oh, Corporal Slasher!" cried the boy, falling on his knees, and clinging to the monster.

"Your time has come. I haven't forgotten the bounty, and you shall swing."

The tears streamed from poor Ray's eyes, as Slasher endeavoured to free himself from the convulsive grasp of the boy.

"Save me!" he sobbed.

But a blow from the fiend partly stunned him.

The rope was put round his neck, and Slasher threw the other part over a stiff branch, and caught it as it came down.

"Oh!" groaned poor Ray, with his eyes protruding from his head.

"Hi!"

There was a shout of a man's voice at the moment ringing in the wood.

"Hi!" cried the voice again.

It seemed evident that the man was lost.

"Hi!" again was the cry, much nearer.

Slasher in an instant stopped from his diabolical purpose, loosed the cord, and hissed between his teeth—

"Don't make a noise; sit down."

He listened.

"The next "Hi!" was further off.

It seemed a long time to the poor boy sitting at the trunk of that dark fir tree, waiting to know what his tormentor would do next.

"I won't hang you, as I intended," said Slasher, when the lost man was no longer heard, "but I'll do something else. Strip; take off your clothes. I'll give you twenty on the back with these cords."

Poor Ray, crying, took off his tunic.

"Off with your shirt! Now place your arms round that tree."

Poor Ray was too frightened to resist, and Slasher fastened his hands round the trunk with a small cord, then he began to flog with the double rope.

The terror-stricken countenance of poor Ray was hid partly by the surrounding darkness, but as the cords fell upon his skin not a cry escaped him, though a kind of spasmodic action threw them off again.

Ten were given, and he heaved up his shoulders.

The corporal had heard a sound which filled his mind with uneasiness.

A carriage was coming towards them, along one of the paths or drives that had been cut through the wood.

Then a voice was heard exclaiming—

"Stop, coachman! stop!"

The sound of wheels ceased, and a husky voice was heard inquiring—

"Wot's the matter, sir?"

"Did you not hear something in the wood?"

"No, sir."

"A groaning sound like someone in great pain or distress."

"I didn't 'ear nothink, sir."

"I wish you would just look about, I cannot go away thinking that perhaps I may be abandoning some distressed fellow creature."

The next minute the heavy feet of the coachman could be heard crashing through the underwood.

Corporal Slasher looked desperate.

This was the second time he had been interrupted in his evil practices against poor Ray.

He drew a sharp-pointed, broad-bladed knife from his pocket, and muttered a fearful vow that any intruder should perish.

"And hark, you young whelp," he whispered in Ray's ear, "if you whimper or moan, or make the slightest sound, I'll cut the flesh from your bones."

"For Heaven's sake, don't!" replied Ray, in the same tones.

Both remained motionless.

They heard the coachman plunging about among the bushes, and Ray, in his heart of hearts, began to hope that he would come that way.

But he was doomed to disappointment, for the footsteps gradually died away, and soon afterwards the carriage drove on.

Then Slasher turned once more to his victim, who was still bound up to the tree.

"You young rascal, you shall have it all the hotter for this," he said.

And once more the cords fell upon the bare back of the poor drummer boy.

At the twentieth stroke Corporal Slasher desisted.

He helped him to put on his shirt, buttoned up his tunic, and struck out in a direction that he must have been familiar with.

THE CORDS FELL UPON HIS SKIN—NOT A CRY ESCAPED HIM.

They once more gained the high road.

It was not till then that poor Ray began to feel himself again.

Slasher was kind enough to give him a glass of stout, reminding him with a horrible oath that if ever he breathed a word to mortal about what had occurred, so sure as his name was Corporal Slasher, he would hang him.

Much more did he say of a threatening nature, and the listener began to shiver again as he did in the Lea Woods.

As they drew near the barracks Corporal Slasher, with a menace, left him to come into barracks by himself, taking care to be only a few yards behind, as on the night previous.

He gave him leave from tattoo for that evening.

The boys, for a wonder, were not at their games.

They all seemed inclined to be chatty, but poor Ray was silent, for his back pained him very much, and he felt the large wheals like whip-cord.

Then he got into bed, in a feverish state, to doze and wake up, to be one moment falling down frightful precipices, another in the Lea Woods with Corporal Slasher bending over him, with the cord round his neck, and the lash torturing his back.

And that wild, piercing cry of " Hi, hi!" he never forgot; that saved him for a time, but he little knew what trials were yet in store for him.

CHAPTER IX.

POOR RAY GETS INTO A SCRAPE—A FRIGHTFUL LEAP.

A STRANGER could easily find the band or drummers' room in any barracks.

Invariably, from morning till late at night, some one or the other is practising away.

Beginners are either thumping away on the bassoon, or with a cracked cornet coming in to fill up the intervals.

In a drummers' room new boys are going up the scale like a waggon heavily laden going up the hill, and coming down again in the same slow, monotonous manner.

The drummers' room could boast of showing what no other room in the barracks could display, and that was a large photograph of the corps, standing to attention, with their drums and fifes ready—to use a civilian term—to strike up.

Save this, it was no more than another room: bare walls, that had been whitewashed no one exactly knew

when, beds arranged round the room, blankets and sheets neatly folded, and a printed card on each cot setting forth the name, company, &c., of the owner.

The photograph was hung rather high over the fire-place—there is no such an ornament known as a mantle-piece in a barrack room—so that if any of the boys wished to have a good look at it, they had to stand on one of the barrack forms.

The taps had sounded for tea a few days after the adventure in Lea Wood.

Poor Ray began to get a little stout.

He received fourpence per day to spend, and to him, as it ought to be to every boy, it was a large sum.

After tea, Tom Sparks called, a young fellow gifted with the gab, and the very identical one who first fell in with poor Ray at the barrack gate.

" Now, you know," he said, " Mug-leton, that you have not seen all the corps. One is sick; this is him, looking rather thin and pale; not a bad fellow."

"He does look delicate," answered poor Ray.

"Ah! but, Muggleton," returned Sparks, "this is the fellow, Tom Welsh."

And he pointed with his finger to a youth about sixteen, dark, and as upright as a piece of board, good-looking, feminine.

Poor Ray took the picture in his hand, and gazed very closely into it.

"He's Irish," went on Tom Sparks, "a Dublin boy; nearly lost the dialect now, but still has a slight Irish accent in his speech. That's the fellow for learning; he came out of the Hibernian School; he can confab in Latin, knock off the ancients, and, as for geography and arithmetic, he is not equalled in the regiment."

"I have not seen him, then!" exclaimed poor Ray, greatly interested.

"No," the boys answered; "he's on detachment. Ain't he kind; do anything for you, yet we never treat him properly."

"It's a fact," broke in Tom Sparks, who was of the Duke of York's School fraternity, "there ain't a better chap than he. Stay till you see him. If you wanted the price of a glass or a crust of bread he'd give it to you; but never mind, we'll put the picture up; he'll be here next week, and now for a game. Follow me."

Tom Sparks generally led the drummers into scrapes, but somehow managed to keep clear himself.

Poor Ray was no longer called the new boy; he knew most of the drummers by name; the boy who slept next to him, he didn't like.

Though young he had men's ways about him, which are detestable in a boy, and, what was worse still, selfish.

George Hancock did not suit him, and up to the present time there was no one in particular that he cared much about.

Tom Sparks was certainly the best.

That being so, he never hesitated much about following him.

They had put out all the lights in the barracks the evening before between them by blowing down the gas pipes; they had torn up a lot of the defaulters' books, and now they were bent on drowning the sergeant-major's cat, because puss some evenings before came to their door and made a noise.

Tom Sparks, full of devilment, caught the cat having her evening nap on the little door mat.

He gently began by stroking it, then whipped it up into his arms, and the remainder of the boys trooped after him into the washhouse, where they held a conference, and agreed unanimously among themselves to half drown the cat, then hang it.

Tom Sparks tied a piece of drum cord round the cat's neck, and doused the animal into a cold bath.

The drummers set up a shout; some got stones, others old bricks, and threw at it.

"Now, then," shouted Sparks, his eyes dancing, "we'll hang her; what say, boys?"

"Hang her!" was the response.

"I think," remarked poor Ray, "that she's had enough."

At this Tom Sparks swung the cat round and nearly knocked him down with it.

Poor Ray could not help but think of himself when he saw the animal hanging over a beam kicking and her eyes shining like burning coals.

In the midst of their cruelties some one had overheard them in the washhouse and informed the serjeant-major, who went on tip-toe; but the boys were too cunning, they jumped through the window, all but Ray, who undid the rope.

So great was the rage of the sergeant-major, that for a moment he was at a loss for words.

"You ragamuffin, hang my cat!" and with that he caught poor Ray a tremendous box on the ear.

"Tell me the names of those who crawled through that window," he continued.

In cases like this the boy was plucky, and he did what none of them would have done for him—said he did not know their names.

"Why, you lying scamp, they are the drummers; tell me, or you will go to the guard room."

"If you please, sir, I was loosing the cat, when you came up," he replied, all of a tremble, and evading the question.

The end of it was, he was marched to the guard room, and after a few hours released.

Master Tom Sparks laughed and giggled when he heard it, but most of them felt very uncomfortable, for the birch was often used in the drummers' room, and no one could wield it better than Corporal Slasher, who enjoyed such work.

The sergeant-major informed the corporal of the circumstance without delay, and he rushed for the defaulters' book, and wrote the following report—

"Supernumerary drummer, Ray Muggleton, for inhuman conduct in trying to hang the sergeant-major's cat, and inflicting other unheard-of barbarities upon it, by endeavouring to gouge out its eyes.
"CORPORAL SLASHER."

"You are in the report, Muggleton," said one.

"My eye, won't you get it," added another.

"Only, whatever you do, don't split," said a third.

"No, not for your life. Stick to it like a brick," chimed in Tom Sparks, "and don't betray your friends. What's a dozen or so with the birch? Pshaw, I have taken fifty before breakfast; be plucky, and we'll lush you in the canteen to-morrow night."

"We will, we will," was the cry from the faint-hearted lot.

"I won't tell, then," faintly answered poor Ray, who was sitting on his cot, nibbling a piece of straw that he had pulled out of his bed.

"I don't like going before the colonel."

"Pooh," returned Tom Sparks, "you are not used to it; the first time I was in the report, my eye, didn't I shiver, and my teeth went through the Dead March in Saul, and from that to the Rogue's March,

'Once, twice for selling my kit,
Three times for desertion;
If ever I list for a soldier again,
The devil shall be my sergeant.

"That was a nice ditty to march into the orderly room with; I thought I should have dropped."

The boys laughed very loud at this; but poor Ray could only smile, he dreaded the coming morrow; the orderly room, as it is called, or, in words more intelligible to civilian boys, *the Military Court of Justice*, where Tom Sparks said justice was kept down with a stern frown under the table, and punishment reigns in full sway in the narrow little inkstand at the colonel's elbow.

After tattoo, when all the boys were in bed, Slasher turned on the light, and gave this pleasant bit of comforting information for poor Ray to sleep upon—

"Perhaps, my lad, by this time to-morrow you'll be walking the streets again, starving, and setting in defiance what is laid down in the eighth commandment; it must prick you, I know, whenever you say it."

No more was said.

Try how poor Ray would, he found it impossible to sleep; he turned restlessly from one side of the bed to the other, thinking of the morrow that he so much dreaded to see.

Perhaps he would have to leave the regiment, to be kicked through the world again, ragged and without money.

If he had to go!

The perspiration trickled down his cheeks as he turned the matter over in his mind.

He drew a long breath—he would starve for no one any more.

It was some hours before sleep overcame him, and when he woke, nearly all the drummers were making up their beds, and whispering to each other.

He guessed the topic of their conversation.

If the colonel sentenced him to a whipping, he would—he began to breathe hard and fast—do something that none of the drummers ever thought of, but it might not be a whipping.

He drank a little coffee for his breakfast; he was too much alarmed to eat.

He went to parade, but his thoughts were not taken up with music.

How long the morning parade seemed!

Would it never be over?

At length he heard the bugle sound for orders.

"Come to orders," it rings out.

Wildly his heart beats.

The orderly room—there it stood, frowning upon him—its portals he must soon pass and know the worst.

Corporal Slasher was there, book in hand; and several of the drummers kept peeping out to see how matters went.

The colonel came out of his quarters like a monarch, with the step and air of a general.

The sergeant-major called the non-commissioned officers, privates, and prisoners to attention.

Ray looked with dread into the colonel's face, as a boy might into a cage of tigers, to see if he could read any hope in his lineaments.

There was none; and the unhappy boy drew a very long breath, for the colonel's features betokened an unpleasant mood, particularly when he glanced out of the corners of his eyes at poor Ray, who shivered and turned deadly pale.

Then came sharp, decisive words from men in authority, which pricked the soft, penetrable heart of the boy.

It was not very long before the time came for him to be marched into that dreaded room.

"Quick march!" said Corporal Slasher, sticking out his chest, that had ever so many handkerchiefs on it for padding, and holding up his head so high that he nearly fell over an orderly-book that some careless sergeant had left in his way.

Of course he was never so smart as when the colonel had his eye upon him.

The orderly-room, like every other of its kind, was an unassuming chamber of justice; a couple of plain deal tables, a few books, court-martial records, and the Articles of War posted up, were the principal regimental ornaments.

If you went to India, Australia, or to the uttermost parts of the earth, and took a glance at any barrack occupied by English troops, the orderly-room would be nothing more than what we have just described.

Captain Jenner knew everything, as most adjutants do; could hit off a man's character verbally, as a Cheap Jack does his worthless goods.

Who could colour up a case like the adjutant?

Yet he was very meek and lamb-like in the orderly-room, scarcely ever said a word one way or the other, and left it all, so the generality of the men thought, to the colonel, whereas he was continually pouring *ex parte* statements into his ear; a crime ungentlemanly and unworthy for any man, and, above all others, a soldier, to so debase himself.

We have digressed thus far because Captain Jenner, who was as thin as a rake, had, to use an every-day term, pitched a horrible tale against poor Ray.

Corporal Slasher had been to the adjutant's room and begged, as a favour, that poor Ray might be sent about his business, on the world again —rag gathering.

The adjutant and colonel were whispering together as the sergeant-major said, "Halt, front," to poor Ray, and then he stood in front of the dreaded tribunal.

The report was read.

The colonel stared, and sat up in his chair like a statue.

Corporal Slasher, in a rambling, hesitating manner, went on in broken sentences—

"A very bad boy; a worse couldn't be found in any prison. Contaminate all the others. I can do nothing with him, sir. At practice, he laughs at me when I speak to him; he's thick-headed; he plays second. But Lor', sir, he spoils the corps, and as for his swearing, it's dreadful. He's so very sly, sir; he'd not only murder a poor cat, but I fear, sir, he'd murder——"

Here Corporal Slasher stopped, and left the colonel to finish the sentence according to his fancy.

"Shocking—a most shocking boy," said the colonel, and though poor Ray was standing at attention, he felt his knees shake together.

"You see, sir," said the adjutant, "that from his general appearance he's a most slovenly fellow. I'm continually finding fault with him. There, sir, do you see those buttons? And look at that tunic, sir. In short, he's a disgrace to the regiment, and I beg to suggest that he be discharged. We may take it for granted that murdering cats and dogs is nothing to him."

Corporal Slasher's eyes twinkled with infinite satisfaction, and he glanced at the adjutant with adoration, as if he could worship him.

"You hear that, boy?" said the colonel. "If I am not much mistaken, this is the lad who came into the mess that night in such a deplorable condition."

"Yes, sir; yes, sir," chimed in Corporal Slasher.

The adjutant said nothing, but he turned his face round to the colonel that he might see the sneer upon it; but the colonel broke out in a different strain—

"But it seems somewhat extraordinary to me that this boy is the only one brought before me to be punished; there were several others."

"Yes, sir," exclaimed the sergeant-major, "there was a great lot of them, only he wouldn't tell."

"Why won't you tell their names?" asked the colonel.

Poor Ray never answered, but the adjutant did in a whisper—

"A most obstinate and surly fellow, sir."

"So I perceive, Captain Jenner," but still the colonel secretly admired the boy's nature in not betraying the others.

"You hear what has been said, boy?" said the colonel quietly. "Have you anything to say against it?"

"No, sir," was the answer.

"You are a very ungrateful boy," remarked the colonel, solemnly; "you came here in rags and filth, you are now clean and respectable, made so by sheer compulsion. What would you do if I discharged you, eh?"

"I don't know, sir," and poor Ray's eyes filled with tears.

"Corporal Slasher, he must receive a severe whipping; let the number of strokes be twenty, and you yourself inflict the punishment."

"Oh, yes, sir."

"Next time, boy, mind," said the colonel. "March," and he thumped the table.

"To the right, face," said the sergeant-major; "quick march," and out went poor Ray, his heart thumping in his bosom, with Corporal Slasher at his heels all smiles.

A whipping!

Oh, and shouldn't he have it too, that very afternoon?

When poor Ray reached his room, the boys crowded round to hear what punishment the colonel had sentenced him to.

"A whipping!" they all cried. "Old Slasher will cut pieces out of you; what a fool you were not to split."

"Would any of you do so, then?"

They all laughed.

"Would you?" he repeated.

"I should think so," said one, "get off easier, you know."

"Tell all that the colonel said," demanded another.

But Ray was indignant.

Yes, he could see they would have split had he escaped; and with that he turned away from them, and sat down on his cot to think.

It was a long, miserable, painful morning to him.

The bugle call for dinner sounded, but the poor boy could not touch a morsel.

Slasher had been in to tell him that he should receive his punishment at two o'clock; a little before that time he got very uneasy, went to the window, and looked out.

Now the drummers' room stood on the second landing, a high brick wall encircled the barracks, somewhere about twenty feet high, and the drummers' room window looked down upon it, at a distance of ten feet.

Poor Ray measured it with his eye, and he began to wonder, if he did jump out, whether he could drop on the wall.

The time was at hand.

Slasher appeared with a very large birch, a fiendish light playing in his eyes.

All the drummers were assembled to add solemnity to the scene.

One of the forms was raised in a slanting position, and the end laid on the barrack table.

It was on this form, poor Ray knew well, that he had to stretch himself with his shirt off, and a few of the big drummers to hold him down.

Slasher hemmed.

"I am very sorry," he said, "that I am called upon to perform this painful duty, but a sneak like Muggleton is a nuisance in any corps. The colonel, only for me, would have kicked him out of the barrack gate; but the very next time he goes before him he'll be drummed out, the cruel wretch. But I'll cruel him; I'll make him think that he's been skinned alive, the little sneak; and if some of you boys don't mind what you are doing, you'll be the next; some of you must associate with him, the ragamuffin. Come, undress, you snivelling coward."

How poor Ray's heart beat, and his face was as white as a sheet.

He turned his eyes to the window.

It was half way up.

A couple of the drummers went to take hold of him.

In an instant he was upon the window.

The drummers stood petrified, with their eyes staring at him.

Slasher turned a deadly, sickly colour, as the unfortunate boy threw himself out.

CHAPTER X.

IN WHICH RAY IS TAKEN TO THE MILITARY HOSPITAL—STORY OF THE PARSON'S SON—A QUEER SIGHT.

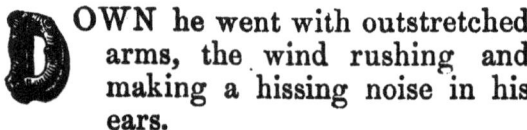DOWN he went with outstretched arms, the wind rushing and making a hissing noise in his ears.

He clutched at the wall, missed it, but his legs and hands came in contact with it.

He fell upon the ground, and there lay, without moving, as if dead.

In a moment the whole troop of drummers rushed downstairs, and picked him up.

The news spread through the barrack-rooms, and deep and angry threats at Slasher for being a villain trembled violently on the lips of the men, as poor Ray was borne across the parade to the hospital.

The adjutant, who was playing a cracked flute at his window, suddenly stopped, and inquired what was the matter.

The flute dropped from his hand when he heard the news, and he immediately communicated with the colonel, who at once wrote the following note—

"Horsefield Barracks.

"DEAR DOCTOR MAPP—It is with great regret that I hear Drummer Ray Muggleton has thrown himself from one of the barrack-room windows.

"You will please let me know at once, without delay, whether it will terminate fatally or not. I hope you will use all the skill at your command, as it is a most ugly affair, and would create a great noise if it got to the papers or Horse Guards.

"Yours, etc.,
"COLONEL DUNN."

The orderly who took the colonel's note to the doctor received a verbal answer from the sergeant of the hospital that the doctor was out, but that he had been sent for.

An hour later the colonel received the following—

"Hospital.

"DEAR COLONEL DUNN,—I have great pleasure in acquainting you that Drummer Muggleton has only received a very severe scratching; no bones are broken, and he will be all right in a week or so, but the nervous system has received a great shock.

"I am, dear Colonel,
"Yours sincerely,
"J. MAPP."

Like everything else, this was a three days' wonder, and in less than a week poor Ray was allowed to get up.

It was the first time he had been a patient in a military hospital, and as he got stronger and stronger every day, he took cognisance of what was going on around him.

The patient who slept next to him was a pale young fellow, with very large, dark, impressive eyes, an intelligent countenance, and who spoke but very little.

In some of the wards the men were hearty and strong, playing draughts, dominoes, and other amusements; but in the ward that poor Ray was in there was nothing but coughing, and, like the pathetic words in the immortal *Song of the Shirt*, it was cough, cough, cough, till the eyes were bright yet dim.

And, to harrow up the feelings of the patients, the orderly man who waited upon them and got sixpence a day extra for his trouble, was a low, mean, dirty, sly, drunken scamp, who never bothered his head about the eighth or any other commandment.

Robbing patients, or even dead men, was thought no more of than sitting down to a good dinner.

Those in the last stage of consumption he kept a very watchful eye upon.

'Twas evening—as Ray lay upon his bed reading the Bible—that this drunken soldier walked up to him, and then sat down by the side of him.

Ray could scarcely conceal his disgust when he took his hand and held it within his own; he put his mouth close to his ear, and that pestilential breath was sickening.

He chuckled as he muttered—

"That man won't live long. Have to cut him up; can come and see me if you like."

"Ss-s-h," was the only answer Ray made, shuddering; but, after a pause, he whispered, "he'll hear what you are saying."

"Pooh, what do you think I care? I say, neighbour," he cried, touching the patient, with a grin, and showing his foul, black teeth, "I shall soon require you down below," and with that he brought his thick, heavy hand upon the shoulder of the sick man with the dark eyes, whose name, by his card, was Joseph Winter.

The sick man shrank as in pain, and turned his head away; as he did so, Ray observed the orderly ransacking the little box that stood by the side of Joseph Winter.

Ray closed the Bible, turned on his

side, and pretended to be asleep; but the orderly got up and left the room.

"Drummer, drummer!" gasped Winter, "I'm going to die."

Ray's blood rushed violently through every vein in his body.

"I have a lot of things here, but the orderly will take them from me. You may have them, they are not regimental."

"Oh, but you won't die," whispered Ray, trying to smile.

"But I shall," and the poor fellow coughed and spat up a small portion of lung. "I should like to talk to you, drummer, do you know. Look at me; only a skeleton; once there wasn't a straighter fellow than I, but it's my own fault. I have noticed you reading your Bible—for a long time I never believed in it."

"You didn't!" exclaimed poor Ray, with emphasis.

"No, listen. I'll give you advice, and when I am dead, as I shall be before many days, think of Joseph Homesdale, that's my real name. Drink made me a soldier, drink made me a robber, drink brought me to this.

"Yet when I think, oh, my God! of the happy days I spent a few years back, it nearly drives me distracted; but I got mixed up with such a lot, that there was no help for it.

"You wouldn't believe that my father was a clergyman; of course I never told any one here, why should I? His only son, too; but he's dead now, poor man.

"And my mother, oh, great Heaven! why do I think of her now? It was in the middle of winter, the horrid gang that claimed me as one of their fraternity were hard up. For weeks I had taken all I could clap my eyes upon.

"Four nights out of seven saw me rolling home; but there was one crime which I hesitated to commit—sacrilege, rob the church.

"The keys were kept in the rectory —our rectory. It seems all a dream now; but my companions, brethren in wickedness, were urgent, and I was led as easily as a lamb to the slaughter.

"We had been drinking a week and more. My father through me was ruined, his name blighted.

"I was in his hearing called a profligate; and my mother said I was killing her by inches.

"She loved me—Muggleton, I think your name is—loved me, ah, how much, the same, perhaps, as your own mother.

"Well, it was arranged that I was to get the key of the church, and with an iron bar break open the box that contained the communion service.

"That night, how can I forget it?

"It was late.

"My mother was expecting me; but the key of the church door I required.

"I scaled the wall, then went on tip-toe through a grove of fir trees, and avoiding the laurel path that led to the house by a circuitous route, crept near the door.

"Great Heaven! my mother was standing there!

"I darted back and concealed myself behind one of the dark firs, and I heard her say distinctly—

"'My poor boy, he's killing me.'

"Many's the time she went on her knees to me, and implored me to give up my evil companions, but I couldn't; but now to-night her words wrung my heart.

"'My poor boy, he's killing me.'

"I was on the point of falling down at my mother's knees and confessing all, when the angry voice of my father called her.

"The spell that had bound me only for a moment was broken.

"I got the key, broke into the church, smashed up the strong oak box, took out the plate, and was locking the door after me, when I heard a rustling noise.

"I turned with horror; within a yard or so of me stood my father and the parish clerk.

"Evidently they recognised me not, for I had one of my companions' suits on; but they called me to surrender. I heeded them not, but slung the bag, in which the plate was, across my shoulder, and made off at my greatest speed, with them after me.

"There was a frightful noise; the parish clerk bawled out, 'The church has been broken into and robbed.'

"The people came running out.

"I made for the high road; but to my horror, found that they had cut off my retreat, and my only chance was to run back and conceal myself in the garden; but they were close at my heels.

"I threw the bag down under the shrubs, broke off a large stick from one of the firs, resolving in my own mind to knock down the first who came up.

"What I am going to tell you now makes me shudder.

"My mother was a very courageous woman, and there was a foolish cry— 'The parson's killed, good Mr. Homesdale!'

"Out rushed my mother, but I knew her not; Heaven knows I did not.

"I must have been blind; the devil must have deprived me of sight.

"She ran close to where I lay; she heard me panting for breath, and, to my unutterable surprise, she clutched at me, as dark as it was, for the moon only showed herself at very long intervals.

"I eluded her.

"She had on one of the servants' shawls, or I must have known her; I think it was the housemaid's that I abhorred.

"I uttered not a word, but struck her one blow of my stick on the head; the hot blood spurted all over me, but the blow was deadened by the stick coming in contact with the branches under which I stood.

"'Take that,' said I.

"She fell reeling, but caught at one of the trees.

"'Oh, oh!' she groaned.

"My blood curdled within me, as conscience whispered—

"'It's your mother!'

"I cannot even now at this distance of time forget the piercing yells that rang in my ears.

"'Where is he?' I heard voices crying out.

"And, to my amazement, my mother rallied and darted at me.

"I felt her soft tapering fingers round my throat, as she screamed—

"'I have him!'

"My heart ceased to beat! the screams she gave!

"'Mother,' I cried in bitter anguish, 'it's your son, poor Joseph. Release me; let me go, I'm choking.'

"A mother's love! define it, ye philosophers.

"Great God, how quickly she composed herself, and with the blood all streaming down her face.

"'He's gone from me,' she cried, 'that way,' and she pointed with her finger to the front of the house.

"There was no time to lose.

"'Mother, forgive me,' I cried, falling on my knees, 'I didn't know it was you, upon my soul I did not.

"She embraced, and passionately kissed me, but she never spoke—never spoke, drummer.

"Are you listening?

"I am, eagerly," was the tender reply of poor Ray, as he gazed sorrowfully into the sick man's face.

"It killed her, that blow; she died a fortnight after, but she never spoke to any one, and there was I for weeks like Cain, my punishment greater than I could bear; but I dare not go back, for somehow I fancied I had been recognised.

It was more than a twelvemonth after that I went to the rectory, taking care to go in the evening.

"The blood rushed to my heart; there were fresh faces there, and those who loved me so well slept quietly in the churchyard beyond.

"They had no property to leave me, for they were very poor, ah! much poorer, Drummer Muggleton, than the sergeant-major of our regiment."

The sick man paused as if for breath, but seeing the eager eyes of the lad fastened upon him, he continued—

"Let me tell you briefly what first sent me out on the road to perdition.

"The party that I belonged to did not believe in the Bible, and having taught me their belief, made me careless of my soul, and thoughtful only how to gratify my own inclinations, which were evil."

The speaker fell back on his pillow, and remained for some time in an unconscious state.

Death was upon him.

Poor Ray was frightened as he looked upon him, and thought again and again of what he had told him.

He spoke, but received no answer; at intervals there was a rattling in his throat, and Ray perceived that the skeleton hand was tightly clasped round the Bible.

Blood oozed out of the ears and mouth.

A groan, and imperfect mutterings of Scripture fluttered on the blood-stained lips.

A convulsive throb, and the spirit of the parson's son fled, let us fervently hope, to happier realms beyond the sky.

Poor Ray turned his face away; the other patients got out of their beds and peered curiously into the dead man's face.

The orderly was, as some of the patients said, boozy; and when he heard that Joseph Winter was dead, he brought the usual shell and commenced to drag the corpse out of bed by the legs.

"Pray don't," cried Ray, with a look of entreaty.

"Don't what?" said the drunken orderly.

"Be so rough."

"Rough be hanged! ain't he stiff?" With these words on his lips, he dragged the corpse on to the floor,

amid the threats of the patients, who said that such inhuman conduct deserved a court-martial.

The brutal fellow paid no attention, and wheeled the shell away.

It was hours before poor Ray could sleep.

In the middle of the night he jumped up in bed very much frightened; he heard some one moving by the bed.

It was the orderly examining the dead man's clothes.

He gripped poor Ray by the throat, saying—

"If you speak I'll put a piece of steel through your heart. Come, get up and dress. The doctor wishes to see you."

"Me!" cried poor Ray, trembling in every limb.

"Do as I tell you. He's waiting in the surgery for you. Follow me," which the boy did.

As they went along the passages the orderly whispered—

"I have that corpse to get ready for the doctor by the morning. Come, you can make yourself handy by holding the light and using the knife. You shall have a glass for it."

Poor Ray besought this monster in human shape to let him go back to his bed; but the scoundrel made use of such terrible language that the lad in a fainting state accompanied him to the dead-house.

There—stiff, white, and cold—lay the corpse, and by the light of the candle the dead-house had that ghastly glare, that, in the words of Madame Tussaud, might be termed the Chamber of Horrors; at least, so it was to the boy, who was so horror-stricken that he fainted away.

The vagabond orderly tried restoratives, but, finding them fail, he carried the lad back to bed, and gave him, when he came round, a sleeping-draught.

It was late when Ray awoke, and what occurred in the night was as he had seen a vision.

THE INTERVIEW BETWEEN RAY AND CORPORAL WELSH.

No ill effects ensued, and, some days after, Ray was sent out from the hospital.

He was greeted in barracks with smiles, and familiar faces laughed to see him return; some spoke kindly to him, and shook him by the hand, but Slasher, who had the heart of Pharaoh, frowned and bullied the poor boy even before he got to the drummers' room.

CHAPTER XI.

TOM WELSH.

UP in one corner of the room sat Corporal Thomas Welsh—a clever, humorous, witty youth of sixteen, a native of Dublin, who spoke with rather a deep Irish accent; he had returned from a very long furlough, and was the young man that Sparks and others had said was such a stunner for spinning tales.

Corporal Slasher required another corporal to assist him, but when some of the sergeants in the mess proposed Welsh, he shook his head, thinking he might jump into the drum-majorship, for Welsh was a good flute player, an expert drummer, and, as for blowing a bugle, Slasher was not to be mentioned in the same breath with him.

However, Captain Jenner liked Tom Welsh, because he was good-looking, smart, and a remarkably clean soldier; and, as some one had to take the stripes, the adjutant, in looking over the roll of drummers, ran his finger down the column till he stopped full at Thomas Welsh.

Slasher was spoken to.

He offered some very frivolous objections, but the adjutant was firm, and in a week Welsh was called out in order to be lance-corporal.

Tom Welsh had a pair of eyes of jetty blackness, with fringy eyelids that kept guard over them, when half-closed, like drooping willows.

Everybody in the regiment praised his eyes.

Even envious Slasher said, "Yes, they were passable," and, he might have added, "strong and powerful."

Whenever he took a walk in the streets, if half a dozen young fellows were with him, as if by magic every female riveted her eyes upon him but, wonderful to say, he was not much taken up with the female community.

A high, noble forehead that a physiognomist loves to see—as smooth as a child's—yet he had seen poverty in all its dark, grim awfulness; a small nose—Slasher called it a pug; teeth as even as a company of soldiers on parade, and so white, that they appeared to those who admired them to be transparent.

Slasher sneered whenever his teeth were mentioned, and said that he cleaned them with milk, and it was a pity Providence had not given him a pair of wings.

This being the case, Welsh knew that he stood but a poor chance of ever being made a corporal; he was well aware that he had no one to thank but Captain Jenner; and Corporal Slasher soon afterwards got permission to have a room to himself, thereby giving the colonel and officers a very hard hint that it was time he was made drum-major.

The drummers leaped for joy when he took up his traps.

With Welsh they could almost do what they liked, as soon that soft-hearted individual found out.

If Slasher required a drummer to

run a mile he had only to speak, but if Corporal Welsh asked one to go ten yards he grumbled.

We repeat again that Corporal Welsh sat in the corner of the room thinking; he must have been in a deep study, or he might have perceived poor Ray staring with all his might at him.

Love at first sight is unaccountable to some people, but during Ray's wanderings he never saw a face that he loved so much.

He felt a strong inward desire to go and make himself known; perhaps Welsh might take notice of him, and, as there were no other boys present, he might talk to him.

He did not know his name, and even forgot that this could be the young chap that was so taken up with boys.

Ray's countenance fell—he was not good-looking; but he actually smoothed and wiped the corners of his eyes, as if to rub away the recent traces of tears.

If Welsh required his boots cleaned every morning, he would do it; if he smoked tobacco, or wanted a sixpence, he should have it from him; his endeavours would be to try and be a servant to him.

But some other boy might have forestalled him; if he could only take a fancy to a poor fellow like him, would he not be happy?

And he began to thank his stars that he was not killed when he jumped out of the window.

In moving the rag that he had covered up his face with, he made a slight noise which at once attracted Tom Welsh, as he was generally called by the boys, though if they addressed Slasher it was, "Yes, corporal," "No, corporal."

Welsh had heard of the new boy's freak in jumping out of the window, though he was not present.

Welsh got up, and Ray's heart fluttered between hope and dread, as he held out his white, ladylike hand that Ray took, but was afraid to squeeze it, as he imagined it would be taking too great a liberty.

"You are Drummer Muggleton, I believe?" he said, in a winning tone.

"Yes," answered Ray, timidly.

"I was sorry, indeed, to hear that you jumped out of window; you are well again, I suppose?"

"Yes," was all Ray could say.

"If you are at all attentive to your music, I'll do my utmost to get you on. Now tell me, or, I should say, give me the brief outlines of your history; I heard such a lot from Corporal Slasher about prisons and workhouses, that I don't know what to make of it."

With much coaxing, Ray was prevailed upon to tell his little history; which he did in a simple manner that won the heart of the listener.

"We must be friends, then," said Welsh, taking Ray by the hand. "If you require to be shown how a piece of music should be played, or if you don't rightly understand the flats and sharps, come to me, will you?"

"Yes."

"Why, what's the matter?"

The tears streamed down Ray's anxious face.

It was the first time that he had ever been spoken so kindly to.

"I—I should like to clean your sword and belt, or run errands for you, or do whatever you require of me."

"Nonsense, Muggleton, you have not known me more than ten minutes. Pooh!"

But Ray was right, and Welsh knew it after.

He threw aside melancholy, hopped about, made Tom Welsh's bed for him, cleaned the boots that were lying under the cot, went to the sergeant of his company and drew six shillings pay, and, as his heart was so full, he gave four to Welsh; but Tom, being quite a different character to Slasher, returned it.

But he sent to the canteen for stout, and they were making merry, when Tom Sparks came bounding in, with the rest of the tribe at his heels

"Lushing, Welsh, I see!" he cried, smacking his lip as he and the others came round them.

"What's the matter?" asked Welsh, smiling at the boys.

Some commenced to groan, looking all the time at the stout.

"I suppose," said Welsh, "you had better send for some more, Muggleton."

A gallon came in, and as there were more than twelve to drink it, they were by no means light-headed.

Above all things the boys could never get any one to tell them tales like Welsh.

If you said better tales could be found in books they only groaned.

To hint that another soldier was as good a hand at it as he, produced derisive shouts of laughter.

Tom Sparks was averse to tale-telling.

He preferred that Welsh, with Muggleton, and six more, should form sides, and hammer one another with pillows.

Welsh consented, and the game commenced; upsetting cans of water, tables, knapsacks, and a shelf full of basins marked with the war office stamp W. D.

If Slasher had only popped in!

But fortune favours the silly and the brave.

He did not.

At a sign from Welsh the ball was brought to a close, and the barrack-room, in military language, "put square."

More stout was sent for, and, will it be credited, since the hour that Ray was born he was never so happy.

He had some one to love.

"I propose," said Tom Sparks, "that we go to the schoolmaster's quarters and set fire to those books of his."

"Agreed on! agreed on!" was the cry.

"Come on, Muggleton," said Sparks.

Welsh shook his head.

"How I hate school," said Smith.

"Not more than I do," remarked a second who, through over-feeding, had a tremendous big head, and a very appropriate name, Joll, who set grammar at defiance, and whose mournful lamentation was—

"What does I do at school? I tries to learn, but a master like that I'se could wollop him; and he pretends to teach Woolling, King, and Cole grammar, he does."

"Oh, mercy!" interposed Welsh, groaning.

"Why, bain't it the English grammar?"

Muggleton thought it curious for Joll to speak like that in front of Welsh, a corporal, but he soon found out that Welsh in the barrack-room was no more than themselves, only when duty required him to be alert then he was capable of acting energetically.

"Geography and history!" continued Sparks, who only wanted to draw Welsh out on the point, as he put such a masterly piece of workmanship on every subject he handled.

"What does he bother us with collects and King Alfred the Great?

"Why, he's trying always to get us extra schoolings; he and Slasher ought to be tied together and thrown into that sweet-smelling river of yours that runs through Dublin bounded on the west by the river Liffey. How is it bounded, Joll, on the north side? by the Royal Barracks, eh?"

"I don't know. Why does he learn us such stuff? Bounded! I can't make out."

"It means," said Muggleton, "that ——"

"Stop!" cried Sparks, Smith, and King, all in one breath, "you don't know what it is."

"I'll bet twenty pounds," cried Sparks, "that he don't give us a full explanation. Mind, bounded by the hemispheres; the horizontal poles in the equator acts on the needles."

"Silence!" cried the drummers, as

Sparks got upon the table, and began to address the audience.

"Ladies and gentlemen," he said, flourishing his hands, "the observed toryism of the wrangular season of diabolically severe. The atmospheric causes — ahem — supernaturalism of meteorological—ahem—ladies."

This nonsensical stuff continued for some time when a pillow, thrown with unerring aim, fetched Master Thomas off his perch.

"But bounded," remarked Woolling, who, because he knew a little Latin, wished to carry on the debate, particularly as the Latin class styled themselves the educational staff.

"Do you know?" inquired Welsh, turning to poor Ray.

"Yes; I can give the definition."

"Oh, mercy, my jaw!" groaned Sparks.

"I'se," said the fat-headed drummer, "wants no more jaw-breakers."

"For Heaven's sake," returned Welsh, who had a delicate ear for the English language, "stop those 'I'se' and 'does's.' I'll recommend the schoolmaster to give you lessons in grammar."

"Go on," cried this elegant youth, in a surly manner, but Welsh took no notice. The lad continued—

"What's Muggleton perched by the side of you for? He's thinking of cutting me out. O-o-o-h!" and there was a groan.

"Give the definition," said Welsh; "never mind about betting."

"To be limited on such a side," said poor Ray, who turned very red.

"That's in the dictionary," shouted Woolling.

A dictionary was scanned by Welsh, who read the meaning given by Webster. "To limit—to restrain."

"You have answered very well, Muggleton, indeed. If you give your mind to school-work, you'll cut some of these boys out."

"What good is Latin," observed Sparks, "that the schoolmaster makes such a fuss about?"

"You'll see shortly," replied Welsh.

"Listen, boys," he said. "As I don't stand quite in the same light as I did some weeks ago, I must request you, one and all, when on parade or in the presence of Corporal Slasher, to give me my title. When here by ourselves it is not necessary."

Sparks turned up the whites of his eyes.

"Neither should you be criticising the conduct of any schoolmaster as regards merit. However, as I and the present Norman gentlemen are on very good terms, I'll say this, you might get a worse."

"What do you think of that assistant in the school-room, Corporal Smith, who takes notes and keeps a diary?" observed Woolling, a lad with a good education, and who paid the greatest attention to Welsh, as he sometimes assisted him in Latin.

"Ah," replied Welsh, laughing, "the affectation of the fellow is sickening. Not long ago, at an examination, he came into the school with as many books under his arm as would stock a small library.

"Behold you, after awhile, a certain uneasiness crept over the fop, Corporal Smith; he put his hand to his forehead, looked round the school, then at me; he was licked, the dolt, at algebra! He shook his head at it, and directed my attention to the papers; he was puzzled.

"At the close he ought to have left the school and hid himself for ever, for his work was abominable."

"Yet he still sticks in the school," interposed Woolling, "knocking the privates' children about. They say he came from the Guards."

"So he did. Ah, the Guards! fine body of men, but awfully strict; a lance-corporal there is more than a colour-sergeant here. I was attached to them in Canada for a week."

Welsh was not in the humour of talking any longer, so he took his flute and asked a couple of boys to play over the second and F flute parts to some waltzes that he had composed—an introduction, sweet, gliding through delicious groves of fairyland; then tempo, grand, striking, that made Ray Muggleton rise up in his seat.

Waltz number one.

The boys listened with rapt attention, as Welsh played with such a mellow tone, and poor Ray began to wonder if he ever should be able to play in like manner.

"They are a finer set than those rubbishing things we practised all last week," said Sparks, in a withering tone.

"Wouldn't they publish them, and put a picture on the outside?" asked poor Ray.

Welsh shook his head.

"Who do you think would go to the expense of printing and publishling the composition of a soldier?

"If one of the great musical composers of the day, say Meyerbeer, Verdi, D'Albert, Karl Buller, Strauss, Finney, or the Godfreys, lent me his name, in the fashionable world these waltzes might be received with acclamation; the name is, and ever will be, everything.

"I remember reading of a poor musician, whose father and mother were dying with hunger.

"The poor fellow, even in the midst of poverty and wretchedness, had a few sheets of music paper by him, so he sat down and wrote some of the finest waltzes that you ever heard.

"He took them to a great composer who was living in the neighbourhood for a time, and besought him to put his name to them. He told his story of woe.

"The great man promised—mind, only promised—to look over them, and finding them to be better than a good many of his own, put his name to them, and thousands of copies sold.

"But the poor musician omitted to leave his address, and, after repeated inquiries, it was found that he, with his father and mother, were buried by the workhouse authorities a week before in a pauper's grave.

"The great man himself told the tale and vouched for its authenticity."

"What a pity," was the feeling response from all.

Welsh made no reply.

The bugle sounded the drummers' call; the flutes were taken out of the little leathern cases; and some commenced playing in the room, others in the passage down to tattoo.

Slasher bawled out—"Fall in!"

The buglers, eight in number, stood in a line.

"Slow march!" said Slasher, and the buglers commenced to blow, "Dark hole, dark hole."

The sounds appeared to reach the very heavens, besides causing every window in the barracks to vibrate with the martial sounds.

Tattoo commenced.

Slasher was in the habit of walking round the circle, and putting his ear to the boys' flutes to hear if they were playing their parts in tune.

Poor Ray dreaded him.

Up he came, and in a moment bawled out—

"What are you playing?"

Smash came down the stick which he held in his hand on Ray's fingers.

'Leave off! Take down your flute, you dirty, thick-headed scoundrel!"

These bitter words sank deep into the heart of poor Ray, and gave him more pain than the blow on the fingers did.

"The Queen," growled Slasher.

The kettle drummer gave a flam, and "God save the Queen" brought tattoo to a close.

The drummers hurried back to the room, making remarks and comments on Slasher not by any means complimentary.

"Never mind, Muggleton," whispered Welsh in his ear. "I'm your friend. Do whatever I tell you, and all will be well yet; good night, don't be afraid;" and the bugle sounded a long, solemn G, that meant "Lights out."

CHAPTER XII.

ALONE IN A BARRACK ROOM—A FIEND IN HUMAN SHAPE.

ALONE! It is very seldom that a soldier is alone in a barrack-room; to be so produces a feeling of uneasiness and wonder, with moralising thoughts breaking upon the soul—wonder that the room should be so solemn—thoughts of what has become of all the fellows who sat down to meals at the same table and slept under the same roof.

Ray was alone—alone as much as the Arab in the vast trackless desert of burning sand—and for a time he was monarch of all he surveyed.

The drummers—every one — had gone to an engagement in the country, some twenty miles distant.

That morning two fine horses, in a break, champing and gnawing their foaming bits, drew up to the drummers' passage, and took them away in high glee.

They were to get six shillings each for playing, plenty of refreshment, and a delightful drive through a charming picturesque country.

Ray was left at home to practise "Napoleon's March," or the last new set of waltzes that Slasher wrote, which were wretched to hear.

It would take columns to describe what passed through the boy's mind during the day.

Towards evening he sat down on his cot, and as he was up very early that morning, he fell asleep.

It was dark when he awoke; it must have been after tattoo.

He undressed himself and tried to sleep, but to no purpose, he only turned about in bed.

Feeling frightened in such a large room by himself, he prayed that the drummers might come in.

The barrack clock struck one.

It was nearly three-quarters of an hour afterwards when he heard Tom Sparks laughing.

With that, he arranged the clothes and feigned to be asleep.

In they came, laughing and talking as if they were all intoxicated.

Corporal Slasher ordered candles from the sergeants' mess, as the gas was turned off at the main.

Several bottles of excellent wine were placed on the table, and some choice viands, the fumes of which greeted the nose of the boy lying in bed.

Down they all sat, cutting and slashing away, drinking and wishing one another good health.

After each had partaken of more than was good for him, one of them said—

"There's Muggleton; let us wake him up."

Ray partly opened his eyes.

Welsh had gone out somewhere.

"He ought to be burnt," sneered Slasher; "let's see that hang-dog face of his. Up to tricks, you know, since we have been away. Shouldn't have been surprised to have found the barracks in ashes. I must examine the music-books, and see that he has not torn any leaves out. Hi! wake up."

He shook him roughly.

Ray had heard every word; they cut into his heart like a lance; but he was cunning enough to rub his eyes and make believe that he had been in a sound sleep.

"Did you practise my waltzes?" inquired Slasher, nearly tumbling upon him.

"Yes."

"Yes what, you brute?" said the

ruffian, as he struck him with the hand across the face.

After a pause Ray sobbed—

"What did I do that you should strike me like that?"

"By Heaven! if you presume to talk and question, you shall be put in the guard room, you mutinous cur."

Poor Ray sat up in bed, all eyes upon him.

"Put me in; you are for ever threatening me with it."

"Silence, you young scamp! There's enough mutiny in that infernal blood of yours to set the whole British army in rebellion."

"I'm knocked about like a dog for nothing."

"I'll make you jump out of the window again. Only let me have a chance to get a cut at you, I'll tame you."

"I wish I was dead."

"Ah; and so you shall be."

Poor Ray got bold.

"You are like no other corporal in the service. I'll report you to the colonel for striking me."

"Report me!" hissed the monster.

He screeched as he struck at the boy, who eluded the blow by jumping out of bed; but, like a bloodhound, Slasher followed and kicked him.

Down fell poor Ray between the cots.

"Shame! it's a shame, Slasher! You have killed the boy!" was the cry.

The drummer boys clenched their fists, and out went the two lights, and whilst Slasher was demanding who it was that dared to blow out the candles without his permission, some good-natured drummer caught him behind the ear with a drum-stick.

"Murder!" he roared.

"Give it to him!" cried the boys. "Kill him!"

"Murder! Sergeant of the guard!"

In popped Welsh, who heard the shouting.

"What's all this?" he inquired.

"Oh; Corporal Welsh, I'm dying! My head's cut open by a lot of murderers. Light a candle; please do."

A candle was lit, and a ridiculous spectacle Slasher looked.

His face was covered with blood, one eye was completely bunged up, and, what made matters rather surprising was, that all the drummers were sitting quietly on their different cots.

In the background poor Ray lay unconscious.

"How is this?" inquired Welsh, again. "Are you all going mad? I left you amid jollifications; now you are like a lot of undertakers' mutes."

All eyes turned in the direction of the boy lying on the bed.

Welsh understood matters in a moment.

He went up to the lad and touched him.

"Muggleton, what ails you?"

There was no answer.

"This fellow, Slasher here, has kicked him. He woke him out of sleep, then gave him blows and kicks," said the big drummer.

"It's a lie!" returned Slasher, who by this time had got a handkerchief round his head.

"At any rate," exclaimed Welsh, "here's the boy with his cheek swollen by the brutal kick."

Slasher made an attempt to get to the boy, but Welsh ordered him away.

The cry was taken up by all—

"Away, away."

Hisses and groans followed him as he rushed out of the room.

Cold fomentations were applied to the part kicked, and the agitated boy took a glass of wine; his bed was brought next to Welsh's—for it is against the regulations for soldiers to sleep two in a bed—and, with one arm round the neck of the good-hearted Irishman, he fell asleep.

CHAPTER XIII.

FORGIVENESS.

SLASHER woke early next morning in a terrible fright; the proceedings of the last night rushed vividly through his cowardly mind.

He thought if he could get the upper hand of Welsh, by swearing to behave well to the lad, the affair might blow over.

Acting on this judicious idea, he sent for Welsh.

But Welsh refused to go.

The drummers eyed Slasher as he walked into the room, especially poor Ray, who was very pale, and he turned away.

"I am extremely sorry," he said to the boy, "but I was drunk. Here's sixpence."

But it was refused.

"Oh, Corporal Welsh, I regret exceedingly that I was so brutal as to kick the boy in the manner I did. Be merciful this time; and I give you my word that I will look favourably on the boy for the future, to make amends for my bad conduct towards him."

Welsh shook his head, as he replied—

"At any police court in the kingdom, Corporal Slasher, you would get six months for what you did last night. The newspapers would head the account—'A Monster in Human Shape.' Besides, the youth can hardly walk."

"I'll give him leave from parade till he gets round. Welsh, don't be hard upon me; and if ever you require a shilling or a glass, come to me."

"No. I won't be bought! If I hush this matter up, it won't be beer or money that will make me do it. I'll leave the case in the boy's hands. Muggleton, come here."

"You boys, please leave the room. We are alone.

"Corporal Slasher has desired me to say that he feels very sorry indeed for what occurred last night, he being then under the influence of liquor, and he begs me not to bring the subject before the colonel.

"Don't be frightened—fear not; Corporal Slasher cannot harm you. I beg you to be guided by the dictates of your own conscience."

Welsh ceased; and poor Ray peered into his face, as if to take his cue; but the flashing dark orbs gave no signs either way.

"I forgive you, Corporal Slasher."

And poor Ray extended his hand, which Slasher shook triumphantly; that little hand was now clasped within a greater that had knocked him down times enough.

Surely that hand would never do so again.

"I approve, Ray Muggleton, of the step you have taken; and you, Corporal Slasher, let us hope we may never have to meet like this again."

Thus they parted, and, in the words of Lord Byron, all went "merry as a marriage bell."

The boys went out bathing every day; played cricket, quoits, rounders, and enjoyed themselves very much, Slasher taking part in the games occasionally.

A swimming match was on the *tapis* among the boys, the distance being one hundred and fifty yards.

Every favourable moment was taken advantage of; and when it became known, it made quite a commotion among the officers and men.

To the surprise of every one, Ray carried off the prize, much to Slasher's regret and disappointment.

CHAPTER XIV.

PRACTISING FOR THE CONCERT.

NO boy that ever lived loved singing, sacred or secular, with a more passionate love than poor Ray.

The corps he had the honour to belong to was noted for the number of concerts they gave every year.

Ray thought he had a good voice, for he occasionally tried a ditty in an under tone in the barrack-room.

To do Slasher justice, he had a capital bass voice, and was very good at getting boys on.

He devoted hours to teaching the boys chanting and to sing by music, but to him Ray was an outcast.

Great preparations were made for the concert.

The general of the district, besides his brilliant staff, officers of other corps, were to be present.

The colonel spoke to Slasher, gave money for music, and begged that the concert might be the best that was ever given.

The adjutant encouraged him in like manner, went to practice, and sat down between Sergeant Cole and Private Woodstock to sing bass.

Two hours every evening all the corps but Ray were practising in the school-room.

A duet for two boys, "On a Bank," formed part of the programme.

The fat-headed drummer tried it and broke down; another tried, but likewise failed.

"Who are we to get?" asked the adjutant. "It will never do; the boys sing so ropy. The alto part was very well sung indeed, Woolling. Let me see, where's—what's his name—Muggleton? I miss him."

Slasher laughed.

"He can't sing, sir."

"Have you ever tried him?"

"Oh! yes, sir; such a squeaky, harsh voice I never heard."

"Where is he?"

"He may be in the drummers' room, sir."

"Just for fancy, Corporal Slasher, send for him, will you, and we'll then hear what he can do."

The corporal sent one of the boys.

Fortune once more favoured poor Ray, as it did at the swimming match.

He had previously tried over the treble part, and sang it to perfection.

Up came Ray, very red, for the drummers were laughing; but Slasher was furious, the more so because he considered himself the man at every concert.

"Oh, drummer Muggleton," said the adjutant, "can you sing?"

"A little, sir, I think."

The conductor shook his head with a pitying look, and the adjutant noticed it.

"This is a part," the adjutant continued, "that we wish you to sing. None of the other boys can manage it; now don't be frightened; sing out. Fancy that you are in a wood alone, and that we are trees."

Ray's eyes encountered Welsh, whose orbs spoke volumes of encouragement.

That was amply sufficient for the boy; he took his place by the alto singer, and sang so beautifully, that the adjutant stared at Slasher, and the drummers at each other.

"Bravo!" cried the adjutant at the end of the first verse. The drummers clapped their hands, and Slasher reluctantly admitted that it was very good.

The remaining verse was sung equally as well.

"Here, Muggleton," said the adjutant, giving him a shilling.

"Thank you, sir," and he glanced at Welsh.

"I very much fear, sir," remarked the conductor, "that when he gets in front of an audience he will be timid, and break down."

"No, no, he won't; let his name be put in the programme. They are not printed yet, I suppose?"

"No, sir, they will be done tomorrow."

As a matter of course, some of the boys were jealous of poor Ray for getting a shilling and such praise.

"I never heard a boy sing better," said Welsh to him. "I shall like you all the better."

And the eyes of poor Ray leaped in his head for joy.

The bills were printed, headed "Musical Entertainment to be given by Her Majesty's — Regiment, on Friday night, commencing punctually at seven o'clock."

The first on the programme was "On a Bank," Drummer G. Woolling, Drummer Ray Muggleton."

That was the first time that poor Ray saw his name in print.

He kept one of the programmes, having a slight idea that he might yet meet with his mother, and, boy-like, display it to her view.

The bills were posted up all over the barracks and the principal hoardings in Bristol.

It was to be a grand turn-out.

The colonel wrote a polite note to the editor of the *Bristol Mercury*, requesting as a favour a reporter to take note of the proceedings, a request that was immediately granted.

Friday was drawing near.

The schoolroom was decorated with the prettiest of flowers, evergreens, and devices.

At the farthest end stood a raised platform, made of barrack tables, covered with rugs.

Forms filled up the body of the school, but in front a good number of chairs had been borrowed from the officers' mess and library.

About an hour before the time stated in the programme, the colonel received a telegram from the general, who had been kind enough to give his word to honour the concert with his presence, to the effect that an unforeseen circumstance had occurred, which prevented his being present, and requesting that the concert should be postponed till the following evening.

A line was sent in return, complying with the general's request.

Most of the other visitors were made acquainted with the arrangement, but the reporter of the *Bristol Mercury* stuck to his post.

The concert was opened; but it was only to be a rehearsal. Most of the officers were present, besides noncommissioned officers, their wives, and children, and a large number of privates.

The drummers were as clean as soap and water could make them.

Time was up, and the performers arranged themselves in a semi-circle on the platform, the conductor taking especial care to talk loud, and be seen by the officers.

Poor Ray gazed round timidly to see so many persons present, and all those upturned faces filled him with awe.

He began to feel nervous, and feared that he should not be able to sing his part—exactly what Slasher had been saying all along.

In front were the colonel, adjutant, and a formidable array of officers, as they appeared to him, including the doctor.

The conductor tapped with the stick he held in his hand, and poor Ray all but tottered as he bowed to the audience.

And then came a tremendous clapping of hands.

The lights danced before him.

He was conscious of holding the music paper, but he could no more see the notes than a blind man.

RAY CLAMBERED OVER THE PARAPET, AND JUMPED INTO THE RIVER.

The conductor gave two sharp beats —one, two!

The alto singer struck manfully into his part.

Ray followed in a maze.

At the fifth bar he faltered and lost mself.

But the alto singer, Woolling, still ept on.

In vain did the terrified lad try to pick up.

Slasher's malignant eye was upon him.

The alto singer stopped and looked at him.

"Go on! go on!" shouted the audience.

Some laughed, some hissed ignominiously.

Ray was pushed from the stage, in the presence of the audience, by the conductor.

The other parts were gone through in an exceedingly creditable manner.

Poor Ray, sick at heart, hurried away to his room, and gave vent to tears.

The next morning he rose sorrowful enough.

Welsh spoke not.

After dinner Corporal Slasher said to him—

"As there will be no practice, you can go out of barracks, and don't show your face at the concert to-night, you coward. Go, and may you never come back."

"I'm not a coward," was the reply that Ray made as he sallied out of the room, through the gate at the guardroom, and into Bristol, with a heart as heavy as when he first tramped through it.

He walked he knew not where, to keep out of sight till the concert was over.

If he had only another chance to sing at the concert!

In the midst of these conflicting emotions he walked by the side of the river.

There was a shout, then a piercing shriek.

He looked up.

People were running, with white, terrified faces.

Ray ran too, and in the middle of the river was a wretched woman struggling in the water.

Without thinking, Ray clambered over the parapet of the bridge, and jumped pluckily into the river after her.

He struck out resolutely for the creature, whose features were undergoing convulsive emotions.

Now he was within a yard, and had the presence of mind to grasp her hair, which was floating.

"Bravo, boy!" cried the spectators with enthusiasm. "Mind she don't get hold of you! There will be a boat in a moment."

The woman suddenly turned, and grasped him tenaciously by the right wrist.

"Release me!" cried Ray, with horror, "or we shall both of us be drowned."

But the words fell unheeded.

The creature clung to him so closely, that both of them began to go under water, and then rise again.

Some of the spectators screamed, others held their breath.

"Oh, God!" said Ray fervently, as the water came running out of his eyes and mouth, "save us—save me!"

With the strength of despair he wrestled and tugged to liberate himself, but she still clung to him.

He was going down, but he held his breath—down, lower yet, till the water got colder and colder.

He was bursting; he must breathe.

Opening his mouth, the waters rushed in.

In this harrowing moment the thought struck him to dive down lower yet, and down they kept going, the woman still clinging to the body.

It was getting dark, and large stones and pebbles, covered with weeds and slime, were magnified to double their size, but consciousness was leaving him.

"Lord have mercy upon me!" and again they still went down! down! down!

Such awful moments as these are beyond the limits of imagination.

The unhappy creature had clung tenaciously so far, yet in her delirium —she must have been aware that she was going down among the springs and weeds—she relaxed her hold.

Ray had an indistinct feeling that he was rushing up through the waters, and that he was now being roughly bundled into a boat.

Such was the case; the boat came up in the nick of time, or all the doctors and boats in the world would never have saved him.

Brandy, a drop at a time, was poured down his throat, and a good rubbing with a pair of soft, kind hands brought him round.

After an hour he was himself again, only that he felt weak and giddy.

Some one put half-a-crown into his hand, and he had to ride to barrack, with a benevolent gentleman by his side.

As they approached Horsefield, Ray begged the gentleman to accompany him no further.

No one passed any remarks as he walked across the parade into his room, which was empty.

Visitors were pouring in at the barrack gate.

Then he bethought him of the con-cert, changed his dress, and brushed the weeds out of his hair.

The concert was just going to commence.

The general, his lady, and a numerous staff, besides the upper ten thousand of Bristol, were present.

The place was crammed.

As before, it opened with "On a Bank," Drummer Woolling as alto, and Rutter as treble.

Verily the ways of an audience, or crowd, or mob, are altogether unaccountable.

There was a cry for "Drummer Muggleton — Muggleton!" till the rafters rang again.

Muggleton was sent for, and when found he pleaded indisposition.

But that did not save him.

He was carried in on the shoulders of the drummers.

How different the lad looked this evening—pale, calm, and melancholy; no violent palpitation as he took one corner of the music, and sang with all his heart and soul.

A thousand hands beat violently together in admiration at the end of the first verse.

The general, officers, and ladies joined in heartily at the finish.

"Bravo, Muggleton; Encore! encore!" was shouted.

The conductor was forced to comply.

Again the hearty round of applause greeted the two lads.

Poor Ray slipped off to his room, and quietly got into bed.

CHAPTER XV.

SUNDAY MORNING.

SUNDAY morning in a barrack is, as elsewhere, different from other days.

There are the usual guards and pickets to be found, but no regular drill.

The monotony of polishing buttons, pipe-claying and brushing, may be said to form the whole existence of a private soldier.

Yet, in spite of all the shining and brushing, a profound silence ushers in the Sabbath morn, broken only by the sentinel's dull, heavy tread.

Of all sweet, heavenly sounds, "The Church Calls" played by every band in the service, cannot be excelled.

How Poor Ray loved the Church Call!

Slow and thrilling were the sounds this morning, as the men walked to and fro, clean, erect, and smart, carrying that fine, undaunted air that led many of them right up to the cannon's mouth.

The band played the inspiring psalm, then glided swiftly into the well-known "Hark! The Bonny Christ Church Bells."

A thousand red-coats stood still to listen.

Out of that vast number one was looking dull and melancholy, as if he dreaded the moment the bugle should sound "Fall in."

It was Poor Ray.

His clothes were of a very peculiar colour.

The river water of yesterday had shrunk and made them rusty-looking, and, as the adjutant was particular in this respect, Poor Ray knew that Slasher would notice them like a hawk, and direct the adjutant's attention to them.

The bugle sounded cheerily the "Fall in."

Slasher's features were thick and swollen.

He had carried on a debauchery till a late hour, got up cursing church parade, could eat nothing, and was savage as a bear.

"Will you stand steady there?" he cried. "Yes, you, Muggleton. Hold up your head, and press your knees back."

Slowly Slasher walked down the ranks.

The drummers who were as big as himself he passed by, either pretending to arrange a waistbelt or brush a speck of dirt off the trousers, but found fault with the younger ones.

He made a full stop at Drummer Muggleton.

"Ah, I thought so; beastly dirty from head to foot. If you had been sweeping chimneys, you couldn't be more black and filthy. Look at those trousers—new ones, too!"—and Slasher commenced tugging at them—"Stay till the adjutant comes."

"I brushed them this morning, corporal."

"Silence! How dare you talk on parade?"

Ray turned as red as fire as Slasher took him by the shoulder from the ranks, and placed him face to face with all the drummers.

"Look at those trousers."

The drummers laughed and tittered.

Welsh kept his eye on his superior with such a steady gaze that Slasher moved uneasily.

"Some of you might think," continued Corporal Slasher, "that I am hard with this brute. Ain't it enough to make me put him in the guard-room? Go back to your place. Ah, here comes the adjutant."

Slasher made a most natty, cringing salute, as he answered some observation made by the adjutant, who seemed in a great hurry, for he passed Muggleton.

But the corporal was not the man to let him off like that.

"This boy here, sir, is in a most shocking state. Belt greasy, sword not clean, and here's his best trousers."

"Dear, oh, dear!" said the adjutant. "What do you mean, Muggleton, by this? I thought you were going to be a better lad. You'll be discharged yet. What makes your trousers so bad? The others, you see, are clean and black, but yours are as brown as a berry, as if you had been washing them."

"I brushed them this morning, sir, please," and Ray's eyes filled with tears. "I can do nothing right for Corporal Slasher," he faltered; "he never lets me alone, not even in the room. I'm knocked and kicked about like nobody else. I wish——"

Here he broke down, and commenced to sob violently.

"Come, come," cried the adjutant, sharply. "This is childishness; I will not tolerate crying on parade! Remember, you are a soldier. I don't believe Corporal Slasher would touch or injure you."

"Ah, he's a sly 'un, sir; it's only put on."

"Humph!" returned the adjutant, "as he sang so well last night, I shall overlook it. He need not be reported for being in a dirty state."

"Very well, sir," replied Slasher, giving a most wheedling salute.

"Let him off because he sang well at the concert," muttered Slasher boiling with rage.

"Well, some people have got queer ears too. I'll let you know yet, you lying ragamuffin, whether I kick and knock you about! To tell the adjutant such a monstrous lie! I chastise you when you deserve it, and always will; mark my words!"

"Don't keep threatening me," answered Poor Ray, boldly, for Slasher was standing in front of the drummers.

"Will you keep silence?" he roared. "Don't you know the regulation, blockhead, that no private soldier, drummer, or bandsman is allowed to speak in the ranks? Stay, only stay till to-morrow's parade time!"

"I don't care much," was the faint rejoinder; which Corporal Slasher pretended not to hear.

The colonel called the regiment to attention.

"Fours!" was the word of command; "right!" the troops moved like machinery. "Quick march!" and the band struck up, leading the way to church.

As usual, Poor Ray sat with the privates: he was not even now good enough to join the choir; Slasher still kept to his opinion.

CHAPTER XVI.

A PEEP AT THE PAPERS.

ON Monday morning the newspaper boy left in the sergeants' mess, copies of the London *Standard* and *Bristol Mercury*. The papers were anxiously sought for, as an account of the concert would appear, at least, in the *Bristol Mercury*, if not in the *Standard*.

The *Bristol Mercury* alone contained an account of the musical entertainment.

It was headed—

"Grand concert given by the Colonel and Officers of the distinguished Corps now lying at Horsefield Barracks."

Slasher was present, and one of the sergeants read in a loud tone of voice—

"A most distinguished party of officers and the aristocracy of Bristol, including no less a personage than the general of the division, honoured this popular corps with their presence on Saturday evening."

After describing the concert in gushing language, the reporter wound up his account in the following manner—

"But we must not omit to mention a duet sung by Drummer Woolling and Drummer Raymond Muggleton

"The previous evening, at a rehearsal, the last named drummer broke down in a soft, bewitching duet, 'On a Bank;' on Saturday evening, he sang his part in a most exquisite manner that was highly applauded. The conductor deserves all praise."

Slasher grinned when he heard this.

"Ah," he said, "I told you we could do it. That must go to the *Gazette*."

"I was not aware," remarked the sergeant who had read the account, "that we had a reporter present."

"I was, though," replied Slasher; "that pale gentleman. You must have seen him—sitting up in the corner."

*   *   *   *

At that moment the postman entered.

He brought a carefully sealed registered letter for Corporal Slasher, who on looking at it, found that it bore the Hockerton post-mark.

It ran thus—

"Get rid of Drummer Muggleton, and you shall receive a thousand pounds: the writer will see you ere long."

It bore no signature, and Slasher carefully concealed it.

As soon as Slasher had concealed the letter, he once more turned his attention to the sergeant who was reading the paper.

"By jingo?" the latter exclaimed, as the following in the columns of the *Standard* caught his eye—

"'Gallant Conduct by a Drummer-boy.'"

Slasher pricked up his ears like a horse.

"Ah," observed the sergeant, "and in Bristol."

"Read it!" was the cry.

The sergeant gave a hem and commenced—

"'On Saturday afternoon a woman, respectably dressed, threw herself into the river, to the consternation of a large number of persons who were passing. No boat being near, the struggles of the woman were painful to witness.

"'In the midst of the excitement a

lad, wearing the uniform of a drummer in the line, climbed the parapet of the bridge, took what is called "a header," and at once struck out for the unfortunate creature. Amid prolonged shouts of applause he grasped her hair, and then ensued an exciting and most painful scene.

"'The woman, in her desperation, clutched the boy by the arm, who by this time was terribly frightened. The lad resolutely did his best to free himself, but in vain, and they both went down together struggling, amid the shrieks of the spectators, some of whom fainted away.

"'At that moment a boat dashed up with the grappling irons; the lad was taken out.

"'A seaman jumped in and dived down for the woman with success. The boy was immediately taken ashore and speedily recovered. When asked to give his name, the brave fellow with simplicity only said "Poor Ray." He deserves a medal for his brave conduct.

"'We regret to hear that the unfortunate woman, who, after repeated efforts, was restored to consciousness, has since died. An inquest will be held to-morrow.'"

"What do you think of that, Slasher?" asked the sergeant.

"That he is a brave fellow. I hope he will get a reward."

"I say," continued the sergeant, "what if it is one of our drummers, eh?"

Slasher grinned.

"If it was for eating and drinking they'd soon get medals enough."

This announcement in the paper, coupled with the concert, made quite a sensation in Bristol: it spread over barracks in a very short time.

Welsh and Ray had gone out together for a stroll, so that they heard nothing of it.

"You see," said Welsh, in reply to a simple remark made by Ray, "such a course would never do. Above all

things, Muggleton, never tell lies if you never do, I shall place the greatest confidence in you.

"Those trousers of yours, Slasher was right, they are spoilt: but I'll get some stuff and dye them."

"I got in the water, Tom, that's what spoilt them."

"Water—what water?'

"In Bristol."

"That's queer too. You were awkward enough, I suppose, to fall in?"

"No, I jumped in."

"For what? Not to drown yourself, I hope."

"Oh, no, Tom! A woman was in, and I tried to get her out. She nearly drowned me; it was fearful!"

"My good fellow, Muggleton, then you are plucky. Why did you not tell the adjutant, and Slasher, too?"

"I was thinking they might make me pay for them."

"Stuff! I am glad you have told me. Let no one else know."

"Why, Tom?"

"I have reasons. There may be an account in the newspapers."

"What—in the papers!" exclaimed Poor Ray, with astonishment.

"Yes, and your name, too."

"But I didn't tell them my name; I only said 'Poor Ray.'"

"Well, that's capital; you are in luck's way. Come along; we'll return to barracks."

The drummers' room was empty.

Sparks and his gang had gone out.

A long conversation was kept up between Poor Ray and Welsh till the latter got music-paper and sat down to compose.

Poor Ray knew he never liked to be disturbed, so he went to the library and looked at the pictures in the *Illustrated London News.*

Of this he soon grew tired and fell asleep, so that he heard not the bugle calling the drummers—

"Drummers all, fifers all, don't you hear the drummers' call?"

Two policemen were on the parade ground, evidently inquiring after some one.

Slasher was talking to the adjutant.

All the drummers were present, with the exception of Poor Ray.

"Fall in!" cried Corporal Slasher, and the drummers fell in with a rather nervous dread that one or the other would be walked off to the station-house.

"You have nothing to fear," said the adjutant.

"This is not a case of murder or sheep-stealing, but one of bravery. What drummer, on Saturday last, jumped into the river to save a woman's life? Step out at once; pace to the front."

But no one came forward.

Welsh said nothing, and kept in the background.

He evidently knew the turn matters would take.

"I don't think it's one of ours," observed Corporal Slasher.

"Policemen," inquired the adjutant, "do either of you know the lad?"

"I think," said the taller of the two, "that I should know him again. It must be here, sir."

"Are the drummers all present?" asked the adjutant.

"Yes, sir."

"There's Muggleton, sir," called out Welsh, "he's not here."

"There, you see," replied the adjutant, "you say all are present; I wish you would be more careful."

Corporal Slasher was very red, as he replied—

"It could not be him, sir."

The adjutant turned away.

"Let him be sent for, Corporal Welsh; in fact, you go for him."

These words were like a knife cutting the bosom and entering the heart of Corporal Slasher.

"Come on," cried Welsh, joyfully, when he had found Ray; "you are required on parade."

Ray turned very white.

"Don't tremble. It's about the jump into the water."

"That's him," said the policeman who had spoken before, when he saw Ray; "I know it is."

"Muggleton," said the adjutant, "did you jump into the river to save a person's life on Saturday?"

"Yes, sir."

"And why did you not mention it?"

"I was afraid, sir—afraid of Corporal Slasher."

This was a slip of the tongue.

However, the words were uttered, and they could not be recalled.

"He means," said Corporal Slasher, speaking up, "that—that——"

"That's what spoilt your trousers," remarked the adjutant, who looked daggers at the corporal by his side.

"Yes, sir."

"You are a brave boy. I should have been sorry, indeed, had I punished you. The police will require you to-morrow morning at the inquest.

"Here are five shillings for you."

"Thank you, sir."

And the adjutant patted him on the shoulder.

The drummers were dismissed, and all that evening men were shaking hands with Poor Ray.

"May I send for beer?" he asked.

"Oh, yes," said Sparks, "we will."

"May I?" he appealingly asked Welsh.

"As you please."

A good drop of ale was brought from the sergeants' mess.

Welsh filled out a glass, and said—

"Here's fortune to Poor Ray!"

"Hurrah! May he find his mother!"

The individual alluded to felt tears rising in his eyes.

His mother!

CHAPTER XVII.

CORPORAL SLASHER STROPS HIS RAZOR.

SLASHER was alone in his little room.

A fire, a very small one, was burning.

The corporal sat over it thinking till it grew quite dusk.

"Let me see," he muttered. "Have I locked the door?"

He stood up.

The key was turned in the lock.

In one corner of the room stood a box, with "Corporal Slasher" written thereon.

He unlocked it, and from a drawer produced two phials.

One contained a deadly poison, the other vitriol.

Slasher sometimes found vitriol useful for cleaning bugles—and removing others that stood in his way.

He clenched his fist, and brought it down violently on the table, nearly upsetting the two phials.

"I knew it," he murmured, biting his lips; "it is in his eye. Shall I, after all these years, give in—allow another to cut me out? No!"

And he took up the bottle that contained the vitriol.

"Ha, ha, ha! They think in the regiment that I am such a good man.

"Perhaps I am; but other people mustn't knock me down to jump into my shoes. I read it in the adjutant's eye only yesterday that the drum-majorship will be given to that cursed Welsh.

"I'll suffer death on the gibbet—be hung up by the nails—crucified—boiled in molten lead—buried alive before he shall have it!

"How easily it might be done to—to—cut—cut—his—his—or if I fail, this beautiful liquor will help me. But stay."

And he pulled out a razor from the box, felt its keen edge, as if doubting its practicability, turned it several times over, and then commenced to strop it.

Again he took the old seat by the fire.

"Roberts is no good," he soliloquised. "What information does he bring me? Yet I read in his face the living representative of myself, but let me now——No.

"Here then, on my knees I fall and pray that the Almighty may give me the drum-majorship, and if he don't, then, imps below, I suppose you'll claim me."

A slight knock roused him.

In the twinkling of an eye the phials were replaced in the box, and the razor and strop concealed from view.

Gently he turned the key.

"It's you, is it, Roberts?"

"Yes, sir."

By nature Roberts was bad.

He was a light-haired fellow, addicted to taking what did not belong to him.

This it was that got him turned out of the drummers' room.

Corporal Slasher swore that he should go back, and back he went.

"How goes matters, Roberts?"

"Not very well."

"What do they think about the promotion?"

"They say the officers are determined upon making Welsh drum-major."

Involuntarily Slasher's eyes turned to his box.

"And the drummers — their opinions?"

"Run in the same channel, corporal."

"Roberts, come nearer. Lock the door. Are you sure it is locked?"

"Yes."

"You are short of money, eh?"

"Rather."

"Suppose I employed you to do a job for me, and I paid you well, you would not be the idiot to say no?"

"That all depends upon what it is?"

"Do you like Welsh?"

"No."

"Welsh hates you as much as he does me. Suppose you were full corporal, and I drum-major, eh?"

"That would be fine."

"Of course it would, Roberts."

"What am I to do?"

"You shall know after tattoo. As you come into my passage, take off your boots; I'll leave the door ajar. See that no one watches you. I'll have a beautiful drop of spirits ready for you. Mind, I rely implicitly on you. Doubtless you may guess then what will follow."

Roberts went out on tip-toe, though there was no occasion for that.

But a guilty conscience makes people very cautious.

Roberts, as we have before stated, was, in the words that the men in the regiment called him, "a downright bad un."

Slasher made him a great deal worse.

The many promises he made, and money he gave, and what he intended to make him, bought him over, for Roberts could scarcely either read or write.

All the evening Roberts felt very uneasy.

He did not join in any of the sports, but lay down on his cot, wondering what it could be that Corporal Slasher wanted him for.

After tattoo, when every other soldier was in bed!

That was a puzzle.

He tried again and again to conjecture the remotest probability that induced his superior to require him at such an hour.

But the perplexing thought only harassed his mind.

Welsh noticed him, and asked—

"Don't you feel well, Roberts?"

"No, corporal, a little poorly."

"What ails you?"

"I hardly know."

"If you require an article, and have no money to get it, I will send you some."

"Thank you, I have."

At tattoo Roberts kept his eye upon Corporal Slasher.

A kind of fascination drew his eyes towards him, and he encountered a glance that made his heart beat.

He then began to wonder in his own mind, whether he had better not keep away, and say he forgot to come.

After tattoo the drummers rushed away to their beds, but Roberts hung about till the bugler sounded "lights out."

Walking on tip-toe, he went to the passage where Slasher's room was.

Every light in the barrack was out, and the non-commissioned officers, who lingered a moment to chat to each other, went to their respective rooms.

Roberts took off his boots, according to instructions.

The door was ajar.

In he walked.

Slasher immediately locked it after him.

Roberts heard his heart thumping.

Some hot water in a jug, and brandy, stood on the table.

"Did anybody see you come in?" whispered Slasher.

"No," returned Roberts.

"That's good. Sit down while I pour out a glass of hot brandy and water."

After these preliminaries of drinking had been gone through, for it was nothing more, Slasher coughed very gently.

"Guess now what I require you for."

"I can't," said Roberts.

"To the point then; do you think you could use a razor?" asked Slasher.

"How?"

"Never mind; say to cut my throat, or any one else's."

Roberts was made for petty crimes, but this made him shudder.

"Hark!" whispered Roberts, "I hear some one."

"Pshaw, you coward."

"Let me go out."

"Suppose I wouldn't?—who would be the wiser?"

"No one, corporal."

"That's true. Can you and I come to terms?"

"I don't feel well."

"Drink some more brandy, it will give you pluck. Do it; won't you?"

"Tell me what it is. But can't you do it yourself?"

"At present, no."

They were both sitting, and Roberts felt most uncomfortable.

He inwardly resolved never to visit his superior after tattoo again.

Slasher could read the human face.

He saw in a moment that Roberts was no good.

Cautioning him not to say a word to any one, he unlocked the door, and wished him good night.

CHAPTER XVIII.

MIDNIGHT—SLASHER'S VISIT TO THE DRUMMERS' ROOM.

IT was midnight. All was still. No light was to be seen anywhere, except a wavy glare from the windows of the guard-room.

Not a soul was stirring; even the sentinel leaned against the box.

Occasionally the flicker of a light from a fire might have been seen had any soldier had the audacity, at such an hour, to walk into Slasher's room.

He was bent over the fire the same as we saw him in the evening.

The devil was at work within him.

The brandy and water he had taken had given him false courage, but now the moment for action arrived, he felt a peculiar sensation at the heart, which said—

"Don't you; some of them may be awake."

He got up very slowly, walked across the room on tiptoe to the box in the corner, took out the phial that he knew by that uncertain light to be vitriol.

He took out the cork, and gently let fall one single drop into the fire.

It sent forth such a flame that he cursed himself for being so stupid.

The razor was the article.

Which should he use?

That was rather a distracting question.

It was no use worrying his brain; the moment the time arrived to do the deed, it should be done promptly and in a business-like manner.

A rushing train of thoughts made his heart beat most violently, and a whisper in his ear said—

"With the one you produce disfiguration for life; the other requires

"DO YOU THINK YOU COULD KILL HIM?" ASKED SLASHER.

speedy burial, without any fuss or ceremony being said over the grave."

The former, if detected, was the safest.

The latter would be seen, and give a good job to Jack Ketch, whose trade was then rather dull.

There need be no doubt that the hand, swift and unmerciful to take the life of an innocent boy in the Lea Woods, only Providence stepped in to the rescue, would not now, at the dead of night, hesitate to pour a drop of spirit upon a sleeping form, or draw the razor in defiance of that commandment which says with trumpet tongue, "Thou shalt not kill."

All being prepared, he stepped forth, without his boots.

It was darker than he expected.

He stood a chance of stumbling over some of the sleeping forms of the boys.

Should either of them awake, they would never recognise him—back like lightning to his own room—he must be safe.

A terrible cry there would be in the morning.

Searching inquiries, the papers would say, are being hourly carried on by the police, who have obtained a clue.

What need he fear?

A calm countenance—no trace of guilt to proclaim him the man.

Then the drum-majorship must be his.

To him that rank was as a diadem.

No prince ever aspired to and worshipped that of a king more than he did that of drum-major.

He crawled, cat like, along the passages, and, in spite of the brandy and water, his heart thumped so loud, that he put his hand to his breast to stop it.

He paused for a minute or more at the door of the drummers' room.

It was safe.

With a nervous dread that some eye might be watching him, as well as the all-seeing eye above, he opened the door.

The heavy breathing he heard was a sure sign that they slept sound.

He crept on his hands and knees between the cots, towards Welsh's bed, who was sound asleep, and lying on his back.

He caught the dark outline of his form, and with a wildish eye, looked round the room.

"The night favours me," he muttered, "and the light of those bright orbs, that has bewitched so many people, shall be out for ever.

"But what if he wakes with pain, and gives an alarm? Shall I silence him for ever?

"Hark! that's the clock striking a quarter to one. He shall never hear another."

Involuntarily his fingers clutched the phial, but the cork resisted all his efforts.

"Curse it!" he hissed, between his teeth, "fate has pre-ordained that he should die by the razor."

Creeping up close to him, he peered into his face.

The bedclothes were wrapped tightly round his neck, which was a great obstacle to the would-be assassin; as, in trying to remove them, he might wake, and then there would be a hand-to-hand struggle.

Holding his breath, he opened the razor, and endeavoured to remove the bedclothes.

Welsh breathed heavily and turned on his side, offering a most tempting part of the neck, which was exposed, so to speak, to accommodate the assassin.

But Providence guards over us all.

Roberts' mind was disturbed; and, if his superior had never sent for him that evening, Providence alone knows how matters would have turned out.

Corporal Slasher's features terrified the boy in his sleep; that horrid leer he saw playing on his cheeks when he eft him set him dreaming, and Roberts shrieked out—

"Corporal Slasher—mercy!"

The razor fell out of the villain's hand, and his heart rose to his mouth as he crouched down, having a vague idea that Roberts would yet wake all the room; he crept towards him; another shriek, which was terrific, and reached the ears of some of the guard who sat over the fire.

"Slasher, spare me! I'm choking! Father—mother—I'm choking! Oh —oh—oh!"

Several of the drummers started out of their sleep very much frightened, but Welsh still slept soundly.

"Who's that?" cried Poor Ray, as much frightened as he was when he was going down with the drowning woman clinging to him.

"Who is it screamed like that? Wake him, somebody," said Woolling; "he's been dreaming."

"Mercy! mercy!" cried Roberts again.

Poor Ray got out of bed, and, as he went towards Roberts, his legs came in contact with Slasher's rough head.

The youth jumped and gave a shout that woke Roberts and Welsh.

"What's the matter?" cried the last named person. "Who is it?"

Poor Ray, half dead with fright, and trembling from head to foot, said, in an undertone—

"There's somebody in the room. Roberts was dreaming; I went to wake him."

"I was dreaming, Corporal Welsh," replied Roberts, who was in a perspiration; "I thought Corporal Slasher was hanging me."

At that moment—"hanging me"— the door was gently opened, and Slasher hurried for his life downstairs.

"There," exclaimed Poor Ray, recovering a little, "didn't you hear the door open? I wonder who it could be."

"Some drunken fellow came to the wrong room," said Welsh. "He's made a mistake, you see, and he's off. Go to sleep, all of you."

It was hours before Poor Ray slept, —he began to try and think if it would be possible to know a man in the dark by the touch.

He was beat for a considerable time; but in an instant Slasher came up before him in imagination.

That dreadful evening in the Lea Woods made him feel confident that it could be no other person; he deemed it prudent to go and tell Welsh, who was dozing off again.

Welsh started.

"It's only me," whispered Poor Ray. "I have come to tell you who it was that crept out just now. It was Corporal Slasher."

Welsh felt as if a shot had hit him; it made him very uneasy.

"Do you think they are all asleep?" whispered Poor Ray.

"Yes, I think so. Why?"

"Because I have a terrible disclosure to make—that I vowed should ever be locked in my breast—relating to Slasher."

Welsh sat up in bed.

Poor Ray whispered in his ear—

"He took me to the Lea Woods after I first enlisted, and nearly hung me with a drum-cord on one of the branches of a tree, only some one cried out and stopped him."

"My God, he may murder *me* in my sleep some night. What a fool you must have been to hush the matter."

"I was so frightened; don't mention it."

"I dare not, Poor Ray; it's gone by so long."

"I feel afraid to go to sleep, Welsh."

"You are not sure that it was him, but the hangings. Don't let us talk any longer. Go back to your bed."

"I will."

"Good-night, Poor Ray."

"Good-night, Tom."

Corporal Slasher in his flight had

dropped the phial; he missed it when he reached the room, but to go back and search would be a suicidal step.

A bottle was nothing.

There was no harm done, and the would-be man of guilt got into bed.

Early in the morning one of the boys picked up the phial and handed it to Welsh, who asked who owned it, but no one spoke.

But Roberts, after looking at it, said it was Corporal Slasher's.

"What did I tell you?" whispered Poor Ray. "I knew I was not mistaken."

"I'll keep it," said Welsh.

On parade, Corporal Slasher gave several hints about the room, evidently wishing to know whether they were disturbed in the night by any of the drunken privates.

Welsh said there was a slight noise, but nothing to speak of, and then the affair passed over.

CHAPTER XIX.

CORPORAL SLASHER IS MADE DRUM-MAJOR.

TIME, like the tide, which waits for no one, was hurrying by.

Poor Ray, what with bugle practice, and weeks at the drum, found that he had been at Horsefield better than eighteen months.

He could hardly realise the astounding fact.

Eighteen months; yet it only seemed as yesterday that the drummers sent him to the officers' mess.

Corporal Slasher would never leave him alone, and as the colonel and adjutant were away for a short time, he got many frivolous reports against him.

There was a whisper that the colonel was thinking of making Slasher drum-major at once now that he had returned.

Slasher could not sleep for thinking of it; and he thought, too, of that night which found him crawling along the passage to the drummers' room.

The band was hard at practice when the colonel's orderly walked in and said—

"The colonel is waiting to see you in the orderly-room."

"Drum-majorship," said the big drummer. "I hope you may get it."

But the boys turned up their noses, and pulled very long faces at it.

"I hope I may get it," said Slasher; "they have been keeping me a long time. I'm hanged if I wouldn't have given up the corporalship if it had been much longer in coming."

This was making sure with a vengeance.

Out he rushed.

"May he break his neck downstairs!" said one.

"May he be choked!" replied a second.

"There will be no speaking to him at all," remarked a third.

In this way they spoke of their superior.

Slasher was out of breath as he marched into the orderly-room.

The colonel and adjutant were sitting before the table, the former smoking a cigar, the latter balancing a pen between his fingers.

"I have sent for you, Corporal Slasher," said the colonel, "as I have been thinking of making you drum-major.

"The adjutant has spoken privately to me in very strong terms, recommending you for the appointment. How has the corps been going on since we have been away?"

"Very well indeed, sir."

"Very happy to hear it. I promote you, then, to the vacant drum-majorship."

Slasher's heart beat audibly.

"Remember," said the colonel, "that I shall keep a good watch over you. Be strict with the boys, but be just, and allow them to play after practice hours, and you will be all right; I shall be your friend."

The adjutant said very little, and Slasher thought the little he did say sounded rather ominous of bad luck.

Drum-major Slasher left the orderly-room as light as a feather.

He could jump and sing, and felt that he shouldn't require food for a week.

"No more practice!" he cried in ecstasy, as he entered the room. "I am appointed drum-major."

But no one said—

"Glad to hear it; hope you will live to keep that rank, and retire honourably from the service."

But when he volunteered to send for beer, it opened a few of their hearts, as beer will, and they told him a pack of stuff that they did not believe themselves.

Next day Drum-major Slasher appeared on parade to the best advantage.

An arithmetician might have been puzzled to tell how many pieces of cloth he had stuffed in his bosom.

No king ever walked with more stately step than he, as the eyes of the whole regiment were upon him.

He treated the sergeants handsomely in the mess, but his own former comrades got very little.

For a time he was very easy, but he soon broke out into his old ways, and it won't surprise any one to hear that he showed more authority than ever.

It was hard times for Welsh, as Slasher would sometimes say in the presence of the corps—

"I might as well have no corporal at all as him."

The route, or marching order, came for the regiment to proceed to Manchester.

Such a scene ensued in packing, and, literally speaking, taking the barracks to pieces, that it would take a column to describe it.

After several months' stay, we find it recorded that the ages of the three following personages varied thus—

Drum-major Slasher, twenty-two; Corporal Welsh, eighteen; Poor Ray, sixteen, and, nothing marvellous to relate, better-looking than when he first joined the regiment.

Welsh and Poor Ray were not so fond of each other as formerly.

Friends, good, warm-hearted fellows thus far, a coolness sprang up between them, all through a young lady.

And very shortly Poor Ray, for Welsh's sake, wished that he had never seen her.

CHAPTER XX.

RACHEL WILLIAMS.

THE hour of evening parade was fast approaching. The drum boys, with Tom Sparks as their general, dashed on to the drill ground, right into the midst of a little party, who had travelled many a long weary mile by rail, nearly upsetting the few boxes that were lying on the parade.

There was nothing extraordinary in seeing an old sergeant with his wife and family about him; yet the men were peeping from the barrack-room window, in admiration, at a young lady apparently seventeen, who wore a blue dress.

" Lor'!" exclaimed Sparks, opening his eyes, "what a fine un!" meaning thereby a pretty girl.

" Isn't she ?" said Drummer Woolling, and with that they gathered round the party, volunteering to carry their luggage.

As yet neither Drum-major Slasher, Corporal Welsh, nor Poor Ray, had seen this slight, delicate creature, whose father—we won't say gambled —but lost his property, died in action, leaving the tender Rachel Williams (how familiar this name became in a few days !) a very small annuity.

There were no relations, except very distant ones, and, as she was so very poor, they left her to take care of herself.

She became *The Child of the Regiment.*

Colour-sergeant Jones, of the eighth company, became her guardian, sent her to school with other sergeants' boys and girls, where she was taught by an assistant, a drunken corporal.

It was with deep regret she left he 69th Regiment; but Colour-sergeant Jones being transferred to another regiment, she could but follow, leaving many a sorrowful heart behind.

Evening parade was at hand ; Sparks and his mischievous gang hurried away to prepare for it.

Corporal Welsh sallied from his room and came in close contact with the young lady, with hair and eyes the same hue as his own.

Welsh felt an extraordinary sensation at his heart, as if, were it requisite, he could die for her !

He walked on.

Drum-major Slasher came next, went up to Colour-sergeant Jones, and introduced himself.

" Your humble servant, sergeant. Have you travelled far ?"

The young lady turned round.

" A great way, drum-major."

And the dark, soft, melting feminine eyes gazed upon Slasher.

" By jingo !" he thought, " just the girl for me."

And already he fancied himself in love, and commenced to open a siege.

" We are going to play, Miss—Miss —what shall I say ?"

" Rachel."

" What a sweet name. Have you a fancy for a waltz, polka, or a gallop?"

Rachel laughed, and Slasher fell in love with that fine even row of teeth.

" I should like to hear a waltz. Do you know the ' Madolina,' by Karl Buller ? I love it so much."

" I regret exceedingly that I am obliged to answer in the negative."

Drum-major Slasher bowed gracefully as he gave her a meaning glance.

The bugle sounded the " fall in."

" I'm all right; by Jove, I am," muttered Slasher. " What shall I send her—trinkets or a watch ? I'll write a line to her—perfumed note-paper, of course. I'm first in the field; if another should pop in, I'll get rid of him."

Slasher thought of the razor and vitriol.

Corporal Welsh, as a true Irishman, experienced a pang of jealousy when he saw his superior addressing her.

Evidently he intended making her his wife.

Drum-major Slasher tapped his sword with a stick.

"Number 1 Waltz," said he.

And the sweet tones of the flute, with a rich accompaniment, were delightful to hear.

From Slasher, down to the littlest boy with the drums, all were taking sly peeps at the young lady.

A flutter went through the heart of Welsh as she came up, and turned her eye to the music-book to see what they were playing.

Drum-major Slasher stepped up politely to her, and called out the name of the waltzes.

"What do you think of her, Poor Ray?" inquired Sparks.

But Ray made no answer.

"Did you ever see such eyes? Does she paint, as her face is so white?" remarked Woolling, addressing those near him.

"I'se should like to marry she," whispered Joll.

"Would you, Poor Ray?" asked Welsh, eagerly, with a smile on his countenance.

"Not I."

"What, not an officer's daughter?"

"It would make no difference to me if she were a general's daughter."

Evening parade was over.

The men hung about that they might look at the young lady.

Welsh followed her with his eye.

Poor Ray never gave a second thought about her.

To the surprise of Slasher and the drummers, Rachel Williams called out to Poor Ray—

"Drummer."

Poor Ray stared, and looked round to see if she really meant him.

"Is it me, miss, you wish to speak to?"

"Have you any relation in the 69th Regiment?"

"No, miss."

"What instrument do you play?"

"The second flute."

"You would like to play first?"

"Yes, I shouldn't mind."

"Suppose the drum - major—— What is your name?"

"They call me Poor Ray."

"Indeed! A sweet pretty name, and very suggestive. Shall I ask the drum-major to put you to play the first flute?"

Poor Ray laughed, and said—

"It would be no use; he and I are not very good friends. I must be going, miss."

"Good evening, then," said Rachel, but the second flute player made no reply.

Drum-major Slasher saw this, and he would have given five shillings to know what it was that she was saying to Ray.

However, he would ask.

"Muggleton, here. What was that lady saying to you?"

"She only asked me whether I had any relations in the 69th Regiment, and a lot more silly stuff."

"A lot more silly stuff," repeated Slasher, laughing.

He liked the sound of that sentence very much.

However, in a few days Ray was advanced.

One afternoon, after practice, Welsh whispered to Poor Ray—

"What say you for a walk under the verandah?"

"With pleasure," was the reply.

Welsh had a motive in this; Rachel might see them, and join their company.

He was cunning enough to see, that at present, Poor Ray cared little or nothing at all about her.

His eyes flashed again with unbounded expression as Rachel came up—

"Oh! you two conspirators, I should not like to know what is passing in your bosoms."

"I wish you did, then," said Welsh, who felt more cheerful that moment than he had been all day; "our conversation is generally edifying and amusing."

"That I am pleased to hear," and she turned her eyes upon Poor Ray, who looked in another direction.

"What do you think?" she asked; "the drum-major has asked me to go in the country next Sunday. Would you go, Welsh?"

"I hardly know."

"Would you, Ray? Why, you don't speak."

"Yes, go, of course."

"He's very kind, but somehow—"

Here Poor Ray broke in by saying—

"Welsh, I must be going."

Welsh perceived that after he left, Rachel's tongue did not go so fast.

The conversation grew dull and insipid, as if the essence had departed with Poor Ray.

CHAPTER XXI.

POOR RAY IN TROUBLE AGAIN.

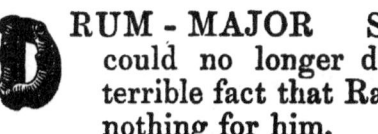RUM - MAJOR SLASHER could no longer disguise the terrible fact that Rachel cared nothing for him.

He had reached the highest pinnacle of happiness, only to be dashed down unmercifully by the hand he loved so well.

He saw, and not only that, but heard she had a decided preference for Welsh or Ray.

Had she not begged him to put Ray a step higher?

Was she not always speaking about him, and his generosity, and that he bore evident lineaments of aristocratic birth in his countenance?

It was maddening.

But she who had thrust the iron into his soul should suffer a similar pang.

From this time forward Muggleton should be his cat's paw.

If it made her heart bleed to see him with a shaved head, or on parade with a knapsack on his back, then he should rejoice.

If Welsh was the fortunate individual, he, too, should suffer.

A chance soon came.

Poor Ray was never much given to drink, but one evening, as Slasher paced about his room like a wild beast in a cage, with his eyes continually fixed on the box in the corner, Ray went to the canteen, drank more than he ought to have done, and never left till the bugles called the drummers to tattoo.

He staggered slightly, though Slasher observed it not, but as the bugle sounded the last note, Roberts whispered in the drum-major's ear—

"Muggleton has been to the canteen all night. He's drunk; didn't you notice him."

"Yes," replied the drum-major, "when he's in bed I'll go up and have him confined."

" I'se like my bed, I do," said Joll; " it be fine a cold night."

" Ah," replied Welsh, " there's no place like it."

" Shouldn't like a night in the guard-room," said Sparks, as he turned into bed.

" Nor should I," said Poor Ray, throwing a glance at Corporal Welsh.

In walked the drum-major.

" Muggleton," said he.

At the sound Poor Ray's heart rose to his mouth.

The icy manner in which his name was pronounced by his superior, sobered him.

" Did you think I was asleep at tattoo? You were drunk, and are now."

" I think you make a mistake," said Welsh, in a very low voice.

" By Heaven! Corporal Welsh, I'll not suffer this! The drummers are all going mutinous through you! I'll put you under arrest if you speak another word! Come, get up, Muggleton, and go immediately to the guard-room."

" But what for?"

" Answer me not!" he roared, " but put on your things."

" It is usual, sir," replied Sparks, " for——"

" Don't ' sir ' me—drum-major's my title."

" For a soldier to know why he is confined."

" Corporal Welsh, dress yourself immediately, and take Muggleton and Sparks to the guard-room—the latter for making a most disrespectful remark."

" I'll go," said Poor Ray, mournfully. " You think Corporal Welsh will make a few words over it, and then you'll report him."

" Silence, or I'll knock you down."

" Knock me down if you dare!" returned Poor Ray.

" Ah, ah, ah! I know who taught you that sentence! Fall in here! fall in! To the guard-room! Quick, march!"

Away they went, the remainder of the boys sitting up in their beds.

Corporal Welsh followed behind.

Drum-major Slasher left the room in a deep study.

On arriving at his own quarters, he took down the defaulters' book, and, after mature consideration, he wrote—

" Drummer Ray Muggleton—for being drunk and making use of mutinous language to Drum-major Slasher.

" Thomas Sparks—for interfering with Drum-major Slasher's duty, and making use of a disrespectful remark."

" If that doesn't get them cells," he murmured, " I don't know what will; and I'll tell such a tale to-morrow, that if there is any doubt about the question, it won't remain long. Now, Rachel Williams, I'll see and take note how Ray Muggleton—a mere youth—affects you. Poor Ray, as some of them call him! Ha, ha, ha!"

CHAPTER XXII.

CELLS.

T was cold in the guard-room—that Poor Ray and Sparks soon found out as they lay side by side on the hard, wooden guard-bed in the black hole.

Prisoners alone know how long a night seems.

Early in the morning their breakfast was brought in by Woolling.

After cleaning their accoutrements, and washing themselves in a dirty bucket, the bugle sounded for orders.

They were marched to the orderly-room between two soldiers of the guard.

Drum-major Slasher, as usual, had given his version to the adjutant, and that gentleman had kindly passed it on to the superior officer by his side.

Yet it must be understood that if the adjutant had possessed the remotest inkling that he was being made a tool of by a drum-major, that individual would have been severely punished.

Being a thorough gentleman, he believed, without hesitation, that a man holding the rank of drum-major would never dare stoop to a lie, hence he supported him; and adjutants must give all possible aid to non-commissioned officers; if they did not, the discipline of the service would not be worth a straw.

The colonel calmly surveyed the two prisoners for a considerable time, even after the reports were read.

Slasher commenced and told a long story respecting Ray's faults.

"Do you hear?" said the colonel, in a severe voice. "What have you to say?"

"That it's all false, sir."

"Oh, yes, of course,' said the adjutant, who laughed, and the colonel followed suit.

"When will you have any sense? I have threatened to discharge you times innumerable; that has had no effect. Defaulters' drill you laugh at, so I must give you forty-eight hours' imprisonment; the first twelve to be passed in solitary confinement."

Poor Ray never spoke.

The adjutant was evidently predisposed in Poor Ray's favour, for he sat balancing a pen between his fingers, as if wavering in his own mind whether he should come to the rescue.

Drum-major Slasher was eyeing him like a hawk.

"Sir, I think," said the adjutant, slowly, "if you gave him another trial, it would have a good result."

The colonel shook his head.

"This youth, if you remember, sir, gallantly jumped in the river to save a person's life; he is not beyond redeeming."

"It was foolish for him to do so, as he was nearly drowned himself, but still I like the manly courage that prompted him to do it; but, Captain Jenner, remember this mutinous language to the drum-major has nothing to do with what he did outside the barrack-gate some time ago."

"True, sir, but I think we could give him another opportunity to regain his lost character."

The colonel drummed with his fingers on the table.

"I have made up my mind, Captain Jenner, what to do, and that is to imprison him for a short time. You hear, Muggleton, how the adjutant has been speaking for you?"

"Yes, sir."

"His words with me have great weight. My intention was to give you forty-eight hours' cell; the first twelve to be passed in solitary confinement; that I alter to this—twenty-four hours to be passed in solitary confinement. And you, Sparks, fourteen days' pack drill."

Sparks was released, and went to his room.

But Poor Ray was marched back between a file of the guard, a prisoner.

A heavy load lay at Poor Ray's heart.

Twenty-four hours' solitary confinement.

And it was solitary enough.

Time appeared to be flagging, the sun to stand still.

So prone is the human heart to waver, that the colonel wrote a note to the provost-sergeant, requesting that Drummer Ray Muggleton's hair should not be cut, but the order, like many others, came too late.

He put his hand to his head.

It felt like a field of stubble, and he must hide in barracks till it grew again.

The dark part of his life seemed wrapped in Drum-major Slasher, who, from the first moment he beheld him until now, had hated him.

CHAPTER XXIII.

THE CANTEEN—POOR RAY ORDERED TO BE DISCHARGED.

THE canteen is merely another term for a military beer-shop.

Singular it is, but most soldiers when they get into trouble fly to it.

Tom Sparks, Roberts, and Poor Ray, sat drinking at one of the heavy beer-stained tables, cut and notched with the figures of nearly every regiment in the service.

Roberts had a smooth tongue, could turn up the whites of his eyes, curse the drum-major, and act the part of a spy to perfection.

He expressed great regret at Poor Ray's cropped head, and begged him to come to the canteen and drown his sorrow in porter with the coin that Drum-major Slasher had provided him with.

Poor Ray, not being suspicious, complied.

Tom Sparks, who was cunning enough for a fox, was also invited.

But Roberts, who carried the air of a sneak, was too much for both.

He was now obeying instructions that his master had given him.

Poor Ray, we are sorry to say, was a little unsteady, Sparks a shade or so worse, Roberts worse than either—at least, he pretended to be.

"Now, Roberts," said Sparks, clenching his fists, "isn't it too bad? See what old Slasher got me and Poor Ray."

Roberts shook his head, as he replied—

"He ought to be boiled in oil. He is kind to me, but I don't like him."

"I shouldn't go in and out of his room the same as you do," observed Poor Ray, thoughtfully, but there was an air of sheepishness about him.

HIS EYES FLASHED WITH UNBOUNDED EXPRESSION AS RACHEL CAME UP.

"But don't you see, Ray, he's a queer un."

"Ah," growled Sparks, "he got me pack drill for nought. See what I'll do yet! There will be such a filabaloo in barracks. I'll get up some night, blow the alarm, and shout—fire, fire!"

Roberts burst out laughing and clapped his hands.

"What good will that do, Sparks?" asked Poor Ray.

"Wait and see."

"How that can spite Slasher, I can't make out."

"All in good time; the barracks shall be turned into a scene of the wildest commotion."

"Good gracious!" exclaimed Roberts.

"Bravo!" said Poor Ray.

Sparks remarked in a whisper—

"I shouldn't care to give Slasher another chance, it might end in the black hole."

"He's out, I tell you. I saw him go out myself," said Roberts; "sweet on Rachel, you know."

Poor Ray got up to go, but he slightly staggered as he took Sparks' arm, and walked across the parade, leaving Roberts, who slipped off quickly to his master's quarters.

"What news?" said Slasher, eagerly.

"Both drunk; you can go up into the room, speak about music for some time, change your conversation, do you see, and appear thunderstruck when you find the fellows drunk."

"Leave that to me, Roberts! here's a shilling for you. Mind, you'll be corporal yet."

"I hope so."

"Go away quietly."

"Trust me."

The young villain grinned.

Corporal Welsh was reading a book as Poor Ray entered.

He turned his eye from the page.

"You have been drinking, Ray," he said.

"A little, that's all."

"Don't tell lies, you are staggering now. What did I tell you this morning?—that you and I shall have to part company unless you amend."

In rather feeling accents Ray replied—

"Corporal Welsh, I am not drunk, and I will not drink any more; no, I won't, if you will forgive me."

There was no answer.

The imploring eyes of poor Ray were suffused with tears as he turned them upon Tom Welsh, who kept turning the leaves over.

He never raised his eyes to encounter the eager face bent down so inquiringly upon him.

The action, simple as it was, cut the youth to the heart.

Staggering with grief, he went to his cot and covered his head.

The boys stared at each other, well knowing the love Poor Ray had for Welsh, and he himself, knew it too; it was cruel.

This freak, if we may call it by such a term, had nothing whatever to do with Rachel.

At this moment Roberts walked in: he was soon followed by the drum-major.

"Corporal Welsh," said Slasher, at the same time taking a quick survey of Poor Ray and Sparks, "do you remember whether we played a waltz on Sunday night at tattoo? I say we did not, can you tell me?"

"We played no waltz, drum-major."

"Then I've won. There is a beautiful set of quadrilles published by Cramer; never heard such quadrilles. But what have we here? Who's that with his head covered up?"

"Poor Ray," said Woolling, as Welsh hesitated to reply.

"Call the fellow by his proper name. Yes, he's been drinking with Sparks in the canteen; one of the sergeants told me so just now; they shall both be put in the guard-room."

"Put in the guard-room!" said Sparks. "Why, do you mean to say I'm drunk?"

"Silence!"

"If I go to the guard-room then, drum-major——" exclaimed Sparks, assuming a threatening attitude, but he had the good sense to leave off at that and merely shake his head, leaving the impression on the drum-major's mind that he would do a dreadful deed.

Poor Ray heard every word.

He had a presentiment even then that there would be another night for him in the black hole—that den of horror—when he inwardly resolved that, come what might, it should never see his face again.

He uncovered his head.

"Do you see, Corporal Welsh, he is drunk—crying drunk—the tears are in his eyes. To-morrow I'll do my best to get rid of him."

Welsh made no reply, though Poor Ray threw an appealing glance towards him.

"Get ready. I must confine you," said Slasher, as if he were very sorry at being compelled to do such a disagreeable duty; "but I dare say it will be the last time that I shall be so troubled."

"Drum-major, please, I am not drunk," said Ray.

"None of that whining here," said Slasher.

A thousand conjectures flashed through the youth's mind.

If Welsh would only speak, all might be well, and, in his desperation, he was determined that he would make him.

"Corporal Welsh, before I go to the black hole, I wish to ask you a question—Am I drunk?"

After a long pause, these words were uttered—

"Such a question no one should put to another in the presence of his superior."

Slasher continued—

"What you, Corporal Welsh, might say to the contrary, would only be prejudicial to Drummer Muggleton."

Poor Ray spoke not another word.

He was marched off, and Roberts sat down quietly talking to Sparks, saying in substance how very much he regretted it.

Shall we follow poor Ray to the black hole?

No; rather let us draw the veil over that long miserable night.

When daylight struggled ineffectually to get through the bars of his prison house, Poor Ray's face was sorrowful and pale.

The orderly room again!

It was terrible work this time.

The Rubicon was passed.

"Your conduct is disgraceful," said the colonel. "Look at yourself now, as you stand before us, blackguard—ruffian—written in your countenance. The corps can no longer be disgraced by such as you. The drum-major has strongly recommended me to discharge you; his recommendation I heartily concur in. You were taken off the streets, a miserable wretch; to your old haunts you shall return."

"I implore and entreat you," faltered Poor Ray, "to hear what I have to say.'

"No, no," replied the colonel, quickly; "all that you might say would avail you nothing; my plan I will carry out, if only as a lesson to others. What do you think, Captain Jenner?"

There was a hesitation on the adjutant's part.

The colonel had spoken so emphatically throughout, that he feared to interfere or suggest any other remedy.

He merely replied—

"That, I suppose, would be the most judicious step."

"Just so, Captain Jenner."

The adjutant looked very hard at Drum-major Slasher; he began to smell a rat.

"Muggleton, your discharge will be made out, and by to-morrow evening you will be sent about your business."

Slasher was in ecstasies.

That evening Ray sat in The Grove, where he expected to meet Welsh, to whom he had sent a note.

Not a soul was to be seen; nothing but high trees.

The bugle call could be heard distinctly; but his bugling days were over.

He knew not the time; it was passing unheeded by him; but the band playing the retreat, reminded him that it was sunset.

Then, and only then, he despaired of ever seeing Welsh.

In bitterness of spirit, with no one near, he knelt down and prayed aloud.

It is extraordinary to relate that the colonel, who had never been in The Grove before, passed that evening; he was fond of solitude, but he had a more favourite stroll, lying in a direction opposite to The Grove.

Poor Ray heard him not as he approached, but continued to pour forth heart and soul in supplication.

The colonel was struck with amazement.

This, then, was the ruffian drummer boy, the black sheep that infected the corps.

This was the youth that he had called ruffian in the morning.

Then a thought flashed through his mind that perhaps the boy was right.

He might not have been drunk.

The drum-major had evidently a little animosity against him, and perhaps he had been punishing an innocent youth.

He would hear what the boy had to say.

"Muggleton," said he.

At the sound Poor Ray started to his feet.

"Muggleton," said the colonel, "you are a good young man. I am sorry that I spoke to you as I did yesterday.

"I have signed your discharge; it is in the orderly room. It shall be torn up.

"You go back to barracks. Stay, tell me truthfully why the drum-major speaks so bad of you?"

Poor Ray told all, even the terrible night in the Lea Woods.

As he finished the colonel exclaimed—

"The villain! But from this time forward I will be your friend. Tell no one of this interview."

"No, sir."

They parted.

The surprise of the drummers as Poor Ray entered the room was great, especially Roberts, who began to hiss him.

"What do you mean by that, bad luck to you?" shouted Tom Sparks.

"Pooh, whatever you like."

"Then take that."

At the same time a blow accompanied the words, sending Roberts reeling.

But the coward had not heart enough to return it.

"Explain," cried the boys, in bewilderment.

"I am not to be discharged," said Ray. "The colonel told me, Corporal Welsh, I am to stay here."

"Hurrah! hurrah!" shouted the drummers.

Welsh's tenderness returned.

"Forgive me, Poor Ray, for my harsh conduct," he said, and held out his hand.

The cheering was so great that it caught the ear of the drum-major, who at once hurried up.

"What's the matter?" he shouted.

Then he caught sight of Poor Ray.

"Begone!" he cried, "or I'll kick you downstairs."

Had the colonel been at hand to

hear such a remark, Slasher would have been tried by court-martial.

"He's not to be discharged now," said Welsh.

Slasher turned a deadly hue.

"Don't tell me that; begone."

"No!" exclaimed Poor Ray, rather threateningly, "dare you lay a finger on me and you will be sorry for it."

"The colonel be——"

Quietly the door opened, and the colonel entered.

Whether that gallant gentleman heard the words we cannot say, but we are inclined to say not.

"Drummer Muggleton," said the colonel, "will not be discharged. I have changed my mind; for the future I shall look after that youth myself."

"Very good, sir."

"I think he will be a steady young fellow yet."

"Not the slightest doubt, sir.

The colonel smiled faintly, and then said—

"I wish to speak a few words to you privately."

Slasher, with the colonel by his side, went out and left the drummers to themselves.

"Wouldn't you," said Sparks, addressing no one individually, "give the mines of Peru to know what the colonel is saying to him?"

"There is every likelihood of a change in the ministry," exclaimed Woolling.

"Hurrah for Corporal Welsh, our future drum-major," roared Sparks, waving his forage cap in the air.

The cheers were quickly taken up.

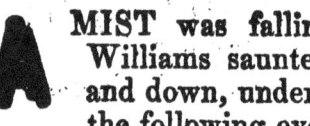

CHAPTER XXIV.

RACHEL.

A MIST was falling as Rachel Williams sauntered slowly up and down, under the verandah, the following evening.

She saw Welsh so often, had so many interesting walks with him, that by way of a change, with promptings of another kind at her heart, she felt very anxious to see Poor Ray.

Try how she would, somehow he was never to be seen like any of the other drummers.

She could find Welsh at any moment, and the drum-major, like her shadow, never left her, but the youth with the cropped head, that most persons would be ashamed to be seen speaking to, was difficult to catch a glimpse of, except on parade.

A friendly chat with him appeared out of the question.

She admitted, as she walked to and fro in expectation of seeing him, that he was rather too abrupt, too independent.

Yet feelings in her bosom plainly indicated that she looked up to him as the only youth she could ever love.

But to be treated indifferently, to send answers back that he was busy and could not be seen; suffering from indisposition; and such like replies, which she knew were only excuses, galled her so much, that several times she made up her mind to speak or think no more about him.

Drummer Woolling was standing at the end of the verandah, when she called to him and whispered—

"Tell Poor Ray that I am anxious to see him. Don't let any of the others hear you. Tell him not to keep me waiting, as I am in a great hurry."

"Right," said Woolling; "but don't I wish I was him?"

Poor Ray was very much engaged with a tale that he was exceedingly fond of.

Woolling whispered in his ear.

"Oh, what a nuisance! I must finish this chapter. Wouldn't leave off here for a shilling."

"But she's waiting, and in a great hurry. You're a lucky chap. The things she gives you, too."

"All right; tell her I'll be there directly."

The chapter was finished.

Rachel was thinking of all sorts of little charges to bring against him.

"Good evening, Ray," she said, sweetly, her eyes sparkling.

"Good evening," answered Ray, as he took her proffered hand.

He was thinking of the chapter he had just finished.

"Where do you get to?" she asked. "To look for you is like searching for a needle in a haystack. Come to-morrow as far as The Grove—a beautiful spot."

"Don't care about it, Rachel."

Her countenance fell.

"Where will you go to then? You are hard to please."

"But," he answered, "I don't understand you. First, I see you very thick with Slasher, then with Corporal Welsh. Now it appears you are tired of them, and send for me—it's foolishness, what I call flirting. You shouldn't do it. Not that I suppose for a moment, Corporal Welsh means love. Oh, no, he likes your company, that's all."

"He thinks a great deal of me, then."

"Who?"

"Welsh."

"Pooh! you only fancy so. Which would you like to marry of the two?"

"Neither."

"Somebody else in the regiment—a sergeant, I suppose?"

"No; some one in the band."

"Indeed! that's singular. Not Sparks?"

"No."

"Not Roberts?"

"No."

"The big drummer?"

"Can't you really guess?"

Her eyes twinkled with expression.

"Why, not me!"

"Yes, yourself."

"I shall never marry any one, Rachel. But fancy a fine young lady like you marrying a soldier. You ought to be on the look-out for higher game."

"I am content."

"There is Welsh," continued Ray.

"Ah! he——"

The individual alluded to came up at this moment.

"Good evening, Rachel, my darling."

She replied with the usual salutation, but her countenance expressed dissatisfaction, for she knew that Poor Ray would soon leave the field in favour of Welsh.

"Is that true, do you think, the rumour about being in readiness to proceed to Mafkat, in Arabia, to put down the Mahometan pirates?"

"It is; the route is in the orderly room, Ray."

"How dreadful!" said Rachel; "what fighting there will be!"

"So much the better," returned Poor Ray; "only we don't get medals for that work. Let me fight that I may either get a Victoria Cross or die in the attempt."

"When we reach that land of camels," observed Corporal Welsh, "the followers of the prophet may place a few at our disposal for a ride, eh, Rachel, to the eternal Mecca?"

She smiled faintly, invariably preferring Ray's commentaries on any subject to those of the clever Corporal Welsh.

Ray hurried away, and, as usual, the conversation instantly became dull.

Drum-major Slasher came up, giving a military salute, and with Rachel between them, these two non-commissioned officers walked up and down, each loving the idol by his side as the miser loves his gold.

CHAPTER XXV.

THE WRITER OF THE MYSTERIOUS LETTER HAS AN INTERVIEW WITH DRUM-MAJOR SLASHER.

A SLOUCHING figure of a man, well muffled up round the chin, wearing a long coarse frock-coat, and a deep, broad-brimmed hat, which had evidently been pulled over the eyes as far as prudence would admit, without creating suspicion, stood under the shade of the barrack wall, keeping a watchful eye upon every soldier who passed the barrack gate.

Ever and anon he put his right hand into the side pocket of his frock-coat, as if he feared he had lost some valuables.

More than two hours went by, but there he still stood.

"Curse him!" he muttered, "have I been wrongly informed?"

The man then relapsed into silence, biting his lips in rage and frowning under the broad-brimmed hat.

"At last!" he exclaimed, with a triumphant leer; "my spies were right, after all."

He hastily followed Drum-major Slasher, who came out of the barrack gate smoking a cigar.

He had made an appointment at a well-known music hall.

The stranger knew it.

After many streets and turnings had been traversed, the mysterious individual increased his pace, till he was close enough to put his hand upon the drum-major's shoulder, who started at the touch.

"Good evening," said the stranger, raising his hat politely.

"Good evening," said the drum-major, with a puzzled look.

"I perceive," whispered the stranger, taking his arm, "I am not known to you. Let us enter here."

The man pointed to a fashionable hotel.

With hesitation and fear, Slasher ascended a flight of stone steps, and entered a well-furnished apartment.

"Sit down," said the stranger, who quickly locked the door.

Slasher began to feel very uneasy, as the unknown proceeded to take off the woollen scarf, coarse overcoat, and a pair of false whiskers.

How different the change from a dirty, lazy-looking blackguard to a gentleman; but there was villany lurking in the restless eyes of the educated scoundrel

"To business," he said, taking a seat exactly opposite Slasher. "I am the writer of an anonymous letter you received concerning the lad Muggleton."

"Ah!" gasped Slasher, as he thought of the thousand pounds.

"Drink," said the stranger, pouring out a glass of wine, which he drained off himself, and then poured out another for Slasher, evidently to remove the slightest suspicion as to treachery from Drum-major Slasher's bosom.

He continued in a whisper—

"The boy must be got rid of, Slasher. A thousand pounds at his death—nay, more; two thousand. See, here are notes."

Slasher's eyes sparkled again.

"Here," again remarked the stranger, "are sovereigns, thirty—forty—fifty. For good money like this——"

"I could cut the throats of a hundred drummers," observed Slasher.

After a pause, he added—

"Who's Ray's mother?"

As he spoke he put his right hand towards the sovereigns which were lying on the table.

The stranger observed the motion, and said—

"Slasher, another time you shall know all. We sail for Arabia, you know, in a few days."

"We!" echoed Slasher.

"Yes, I go with you, unless the work is done before. Here are twenty sovereigns for you now."

"Oh, gracious!" exclaimed Slasher, out of breath, and rubbing his hands together. "I'll do it!"

"If you betray me," said the mysterious individual, "I'll blow your brains out!" and he produced a revolver. "You and I must not meet again; but if you have anything to communicate, write to William Flint, Esq., M.D. Time presses."

"He may fall overboard on the voyage," said Slasher. "Shall I get the money then?"

"Before we reach the shores of the Red Sea. You are a man, if I am not deceived, just cut out for the work."

"How did you find me out?" asked Slasher.

"Ah, ah, ah! How does the vulture scent its prey from afar? But reveal not a word, or you are lost!"

Quickly putting on his disguise, he accompanied Slasher a considerable distance, bidding him good-night in these words—

"Remember the boy Muggleton. Two thousand pounds—a rich man for life."

CHAPTER XXVI.

THE ROUTE FOR MAFKAT, IN ARABIA.

THERE was a terrible hubbub; a telegram had just been received ordering the regiment off forthwith to Mafkat, a town of considerable importance, with an excellent harbour, in Arabia, as the Eminel Mumenir, or Prince of the Faithful, had collected a number of enthusiastic followers, dressed in large, loose trousers, the head-dress consisting of several bonnets, some of linen, others being embroidered with gold, scarcely two soldiers being alike.

These fanatics foully assassinated

Europeans, day by day, on the outskirts of the town, in revenge of some supposed insult by English sailors, who, it was alleged, had cursed the pious worshippers of Mahomet, and who, being suddenly surrounded with natives, turned and made quick work of them.

To prevent further strife and bloodshed, and to protect trade, the English government had sent a small detachment of soldiers which His Royal Highness, Eminel Mumenir, cut off to a man.

The news was judiciously suppressed, for the English government determined to exterminate at once these raving followers of the Prophet, who, till Aden was taken by the English, believed not in powder or bullets, but trusted to the Koran, even when the English troops were pouring in shot and shell upon the devoted city, which brought them to their senses.

Another lesson was on the tapis for Eminel Mumenir and his followers, who, bivouacked on the mountains, little dreamt that the English government was now sending troops under the command of an able general.

It was night when the telegram arrived; every soldier and drummer was busily packing his knapsack and circling the baggage for rail.

The morning would see them clear of Manchester.

"We are in luck at last," said Corporal Welsh. "Good-bye to easy parades and every night in bed, and hurrah for midnight marches over mountains and burning sands; harassing the enemy in rear to-day, to-morrow in desperate combat with them."

"Hurrah!" cried the boys. "We'll show them what we red coats can do."

"Shouldn't we be supplied with revolvers?" observed Poor Ray.

Here he looked dismally at his little sword, or Roman dagger.

"True enough!" said Tom Sparks; "but never mind. I'll cut in with this."

"And won't I!" exclaimed Roberts

"We are off to the land of knives and daggers," cried Welsh.

"Hurrah!" cried the boys.

"The stirring times are at hand," he continued. "You will hear of hairbreadth escapes, brains blown out, poison, and all those delightful sensations that make us fighting-men ready to die. Isn't it better," he continued " to die in a field of battle, fighting for one's country, than to lie down and give up the ghost on a bed of down? Give me a soldier's death; no sinking away, no dying by degrees with their deadly nostrums."

"We shall see," said Sparks, "who are the plucky ones."

"I'll back," replied Roberts, "I shan't be a coward. Only give me a chance at the enemy."

"I'se hope they won't be murdering," replied Joll.

"Blowing up magazines; eyes, limbs, and legs, flying in all directions," whispered Sparks; "but who cares?"

*   *   *   *

At an early hour the regiment marched off to that old, stirring air, "The girl I left behind me."

A tedious ride by rail brought them to Portsmouth.

Her Majesty's ship "Crocodile" had been preparing some days to receive them.

A great number of the boys had never seen the sea.

As they marched on board and eyed the mighty ship with wonder, sea-sickness, and the many incidents the boys had heard relating to it, rose to their minds.

They walked about the ship and examined it minutely.

She was soon under sail.

The sea was rough, dashing and rushing so impetuously on, that Ray and others soon experienced sea-sickness.

Many of the boys, as the ship

pitched headlong into the sea and then rose again to ride on waves mountains high, thought how dreadful it must be for sailor boys aloft.

And many who till then had preferred sailoring to soldiering, changed their minds.

For days Poor Ray and others were lying in their hammocks, in all the agony of the direful nausea.

Roberts, who did not feel the effects, got a fat piece of pork, tied a piece of string to the end, and held it to Poor Ray's nose, saying sarcastically—

"You a soldier! Here, chaps, look at this miserable object."

"And bad luck to you," said Welsh, who happened to come up at the time, "ye spalpeen, I'd as soon you did it to me myself, as to this poor creature. Take this! and this!" which meant a couple of good ringing boxes on the ears.

"Are you any better, Poor Ray?" he inquired.

"I am dying, Tom; I shall never get over it."

"Get out of your hammock, man, and come on deck; it's beautiful."

"No, Tom, I can't; let me die."

"I'll get something to cure you—so I will."

Away went Corporal Welsh to the ship's corporal for a good piece of rope, concealing it from view.

He returned to Poor Ray, and assisted him out of his hammock.

Seizing him by the shirt collar, he applied the rope's end so vigorously about his person that Ray begged him to desist.

He, however, kept on.

"Are you better?" he asked.

"Yes, yes," he cried; "indeed I am."

"I'll come again in an hour's time, and give you some physic."

The dose was enough.

It soon cured him, for the next day, he, with Tom Sparks and his gang, played sad tricks upon the sailors, who vowed they were the biggest scamps in the service.

The captain of the ship being a gruff old gentleman, Tom Sparks went on deck of an evening to mock him, by feigning to call out to Ray.

One evening he secretly removed the captain's night glass from the bridge ladder, with the captain standing by, who never perceived him.

Sparks and his gang were delighted as they observed the captain searching for his glass.

"Ho, ho! there," said Sparks, gruffly; "captain, can you throw the main-deck overboard?"

"What's that?" said the captain, who did not exactly hear it.

"The colonel's compliments, captain, could you go to the cabin and take a stiff glass of grog?" observed Poor Ray.

"Tell him yes," he answered.

As he was descending, Tom Sparks put a drum in the way.

He fell over it and nearly broke his arm.

"Oh, sir," said Sparks, "what's the matter? Shall I help you to get up, sir?"

So great was the rage of the captain that he caught hold of the drum, and threw it into the sea.

Tom Sparks gave a roar like a wild beast, for it was his drum.

"You, sir!" he said, as if he had been addressing a shoeblack, "that was my drum; you shall pay for it."

The captain only remarked—

"You little imp," and knocked him down.

For this act the night glass was sent flying into the sea.

To record all the tricks and games played by the drummer boys, and sailors as well, would take columns.

It will suffice to say that during all their games the stranger mentioned in our last chapter, who was on intimate terms with the captain, hovered round Poor Ray, and several times addressed him.

Drum-major Slasher, too, was very kind to him, spoke well of him before the officers, till he got quite a favourite.

Several chances had occurred to Slasher to throw him overboard, but the sea, to his idea, was not rough enough; he might be picked up again.

The elements were against him.

Each night he prayed for a storm to come on.

His sanguine expectations were not realized, till one evening—it had been blowing hard all day—the sea, as the night came on, swept over the deck, driving many below.

But Poor Ray, with Corporal Welsh, sat talking of other times, till it was quite dark.

Slasher conjectured, as he saw Corporal Welsh retire below, that another such a chance might never occur again.

The two thousand pounds should be his.

Darker and darker it grew, till it was impossible to recognise the features or form of anyone on deck.

Slowly he approached the boy, who, out of foolhardiness, as if daring the waves to wash him overboard, was leaning over the bulwarks.

In an instant he put forth all his strength, seized the boy, and pushed him over.

A wild scream rang through the ship, and a voice cried out—

"Man overboard! 'bout ship!"

Instantly the engines were reversed, and the life-boat quickly manned, as young and old on board trembled to think a fellow creature was perhaps battling with the waves for life.

There was a noise of many voices on board, then all became still.

"Help! save me!" was the cry borne on the wind.

Voices of encouragement cried out to the lad; and a shiver ran through Corporal Welsh's form as he heard it whispered from mouth to mouth—

"It's Poor Ray!"

It seemed an eternity to many on board ere the life-boat returned.

Drum-major Slasher was below, white as a ghost, his knees shaking together.

Not so the stranger; he stood on deck.

There was a cry, and it passed like an electric shock through all.

"Ship ahoy!"

"Aye," answered the mate.

"He's found! found!"

Lights were hung out to enable the boat's crew to find the ship, and in a few moments they were alongside.

As they came on board, carrying the half-drowned lad between them, who was unconscious, loud cheers greeted them.

It was many days ere Poor Ray recovered.

Various conjectures were afloat, as who could be so diabolical as to throw an innocent lad overboard.

Ray gave the particulars.

A great many on board had doubts upon the matter; but Corporal Welsh felt as certain that it was Slasher as if he had seen him do it.

He cautioned Poor Ray never to go on deck again at night.

Poor Ray obeyed, and, in a few days more, the voyage was brought to an end, much to the delight of all.

THEY SET OUT WITH CHEERFUL SPIRITS, RACHEL RIDING BETWEEN CORPORAL WELSH AND POOR RAY.

CHAPTER XXVII.

MAFKAT, AND THE FOLLOWERS OF THE PROPHET.

THE regiment landed amid deep groans; as they marched through the narrow, dirty streets, the scum of the town greeted them with hisses.

Bedouins, in yellow turbans, threw up the dust in the air, chanting—

"Oh, ye red-coated cut-throats! Robbers—sons of dogs—Kaffirs—infidels—thieves!"

The priests, in like manner, in flowing gowns, stood at the corners of hovels, and in a raving manner quoted the Koran.

"Ye unclean, go from among us! Allah is great! Oh, ye Kaffirs, from the land of darkness, what says the Koran in the twenty-fourth chapter? 'They shall be rooted out, the sons of uncleanness, from off the face of the earth, and perish for ever.' The Prophet be praised. Allah is good!"

It was a scene of wild confusion—the unknown language, the Arabs running one to another with long knives, brandishing them about enthusiastically, the piercing eye and fiendish glance of unutterable hatred, as the cry of "Kaffir, infidel!" was taken up.

This ovation was far from being complimentary to the troops; it was to no purpose to utter "Salem alekum," or "Peace be with you," for the inhabitants followed the band, and in broken English poured forth imprecations upon them.

One pushed violently against Welsh, who certainly stood aghast at the unwashed fellow's audacity, but seeing he had the appearance of a madman, took it in good part.

The ruffian did it a second time, with a fearful expression.

The remark so stung Welsh that he took a pace back, and, with one blow, sent the fellow reeling among the rabble.

Frightful yells rent the air as the villain came up again brandishing a long knife, with which he made a thrust at Corporal Welsh's heart.

The butt end of a rifle dashed him to the ground.

In another minute the regiment was in a temporary barrack that had been rented by English agents, since the glory and pride of Aden had been laid low by the sons of Kaffirs—the refuse of the earth.

All was in disorder.

Orderlies, with despatches, were galloping everywhere, endeavouring to reduce the chaos to form.

The sentinels were quickly posted, with loaded rifles, and ordered to shoot any person who refused to answer after being challenged twice.

A cheerless room without fire to cook the rations was far from being pleasant, and the troops had to lie on the bare floor.

The following warning was read out at midnight to them—

"The troops in garrison will hold themselves in readiness to turn out at a moment's notice.

"Should a rocket be sent up from the general's quarters, the officer commanding will march at once, concentrate in the leading thoroughfare, and there await further orders."

"Queer times these," muttered Poor Ray, as he curled himself up in one corner of the room.

"You may depend on it," replied Corporal Welsh, "this is nothing yet to what we shall have to encounter."

"I wish I was back in old England," said Roberts.

" So does I," echoed Joll.

" It's fearful !" whined Roberts, who was shivering, and expecting to be blown up every minute, for a panic prevailed a few hours previous among them that the place was undermined.

But Sparks, who was a dare-devil, exclaimed—

" This is what I like. I hope I may get at the fellow with the long name, the Prince of Darkness. Kaffirs, indeed ! dogs, sons of herrings and sprats !—what beautiful names. Ugh ! it's cold. I should like a drop of whisky ; the dew off the mountain, as your countrymen call it, Welsh."

A great number of men patrolled the barracks, till an orderly dashed in on horseback with a despatch, ordering the colonel again to caution his men to be ready for any emergency, and at the same time that the guard should be vigilant and on the alert.

Tom Sparks had not forgotten the pack drill.

He had been waiting for an opportunity of avenging himself on Slasher, and it came.

A sharp gong in the town striking, denoted the hour of two.

Cautiously dressing himself, he crept down.

The town of Mafkat was asleep by this time ; not a soldier except those on watch could be seen.

Tom Sparks looked every way ; he pressed the mouthpiece to his lips, and, being an excellent bugler, the tones rang out, piercing the midnight sky.

It was the alarm.

It was dreadful, at least Slasher thought so.

Then he became bolder, and blew " the assembly."

In the twinkling of an eye there was an outcry—

" The Arabs are coming ! The Bedouins are upon us !"

In the drummers' room it was a curious scene.

Roberts covered his face and pre-tended to be asleep, but the hand of Welsh shook him roughly.

He then dropped on his knees to pray.

" Coward, come on !" cried Welsh.

" Turn out !" was the cry.

The colonel rushed from his quarters half dressed, and met the adjutant on the parade.

" What's the matter ?" he roared.

" I don't know, sir."

" Who gave orders for the bugle to sound ?"

" Fall in !" cried the soldiers themselves. " They are coming !"

To the surprise of all, even Sparks, up went a rocket.

The excitement being great, it was not particularly observed from what quarter it rose.

The men fell in silently.

Poor Ray, Sparks, and other buglers fell in behind their companies, but Drum-major Slasher was nowhere to be seen.

" With ball cartridge, load !" said the colonel, in an undertone.

The deadly weapons were ready in an instant.

The colonel then addressed a few suitable words to his men, and off they marched.

An Arab here and there was the only enemy they saw.

On reaching the main thoroughfare, no other troops were to be seen, as no warning or rocket from the general's quarters had been seen, for the regiments quartered in the town were so situated as to concentrate on a certain point, which gave them every advantage over their enemies.

The colonel could see he had been hoaxed ; strict inquiries were made to discover the offender, but without success.

Roberts guessed it was Sparks ; for once in his life he was afraid to tell.

Poor Ray threw his coat over him, and lay down again.

A voice whispered in his ear joyfully.

"I told you I'd make a hullabaloo; didn't I keep my word?" asked Tom Sparks.

"You did, indeed; but hush! Good-night! I'm so sleepy, Tom."

"Good-night, Poor Ray, and God bless you, as he will, for you'll see your mother yet."

Rather a singular benediction, but it was well meant.

CHAPTER XXVIII.

A DREADFUL NIGHT AMONG THE ARABS.

TO see in England a couple of soldiers riding on donkeys with a young lady between them, would create much laughter; but in Mafkat you could hire either a camel or a donkey for two rupees, from natives with famished looks and half naked, who mumbled over the Koran, while they teased European soldiers to mount "the ship of the desert."

The storm had partly blown over. Prince Eminel Mumenir had been warned by his prophets that the hour to rid the land of Kaffirs and infidels had not yet come; consequently, instead of fighting, he returned into the mountains.

Corporal Welsh, Poor Ray, and Tom Sparks, with Rachel Williams, hired donkeys for one rupee each, as they intended to visit a beautiful spot, known to English residents as Holly Horn, which for scenery has been compared with many places described in the Arabian Nights.

Rachel had by dint of persuasion induced Welsh to go for a ride to the spot famed in story, and bring the others with him.

A secret impulse reminded Welsh that there was still a slight hankering on Rachel's part to be in company with Poor Ray; he did not tease her with even a hint of such a thing, but endeavoured to remove the impression, by imagining it was merely a freak on her part, and that he never saw a brighter prospect of marrying than at present.

They set out with cheerful spirits, Rachel riding between Corporal Welsh and Poor Ray, all smiles and happiness, while Tom Sparks brought up the rear.

Holly Horn was ten miles distant, and as the afternoon was not too hot, they managed to get on well with umbrellas over them.

The spirits of the youths revelled in ecstasies.

Every mountain pass formed a subject for comment.

The pleasant remarks made by Tom Sparks created much mirth, as he whipped the donkey he rode on, and chattered in Irish to the roguish-looking vagabond who accompanied them as a guide.

This fellow was dressed in a brown Holland tunic, and had a bloodthirsty, villanous countenance.

"It's a mighty fine counthry, so it is, blessings on it," said Sparks to the Arab who rode by his side, scowling fearfully.

"To be sure it isn't the spot it used to be."

The Arab, in broken English, by way of saying something, asked what part of England he belonged to.

"Bad cess to ye for a spalpeen, haven't I the Dublin brogue, yez skaladop? It's a poor spec, donkey driving.

"Murdher and turf! ye son of an ass, it's a snail's pace yez are going at. May the prophet——"

"I'm a fool!" said the Arab.

"Perhaps more rogue than fool," remarked Welsh, who certainly did not like the appearance of the fellow, who was intent upon doing honour to no one but the prophet, for he attributed to that gracious personage deeds of such magnitude, that Welsh rebuked him.

"How exhilarating!" observed Rachel, showing her beautiful white teeth.

"Delightful," remarked Corporal Welsh, whose features were glowing with interest and love.

"Are you fond of the poets?" inquired Rachel, addressing no one individually.

"I like Gray best," said Ray.

"Wordsworth's style is sweet, pathetic, and simple," said Rachel, "I love him so much.

"As a vigorous poetess, Mrs. Hemans is much to my mind. If I wish to be melancholy, yet good, I take down her works."

Tom Sparks turned up his eyes.

"Talking about poets," he exclaimed, "is to me like talking Latin. I understand one about as well as the other."

It was after this manner the ten miles were travelled.

Holly Horn was, as auctioneers would say in England, pleasantly situated—a most fairy-like haunt.

Deeds of blood had been committed in the neighbourhood only a week before, but of that our pleasure party knew nothing.

The evening was passed in quiet rambling.

The time passed quickly, and to none more so than Welsh.

He had delightful opportunities of breathing forth passionate words, leaving Rachel to guess their import, for Poor Ray and Sparks had the hardihood to climb several high rocks, and jabber away to the cunning natives, who kept crying—

"Give me rupee!—rupee!"

After the excursion, the party entered a bungalow, and sat down in a semicircle, to partake of coffee, Corporal Welsh smoking, and eyeing suspiciously every Arab who came in on pretence of looking for some one of his friends.

It was getting dusk.

The Arab donkey-driver was nowhere to be seen.

From gaiety, a kind of gloom quickly hung over the party.

As night began to set in several rough, half-starved Arabs, with knives in their girdles, yelled fearfully at the door of the bungalow.

The face of one was bloodstained and brutal; Corporal Welsh had seen him before, but where it was simply foolishness to worry his mind in attempting to guess, so he gave it up.

"We had better see about returning," said Rachel, who felt symptoms of uneasiness.

The gloom from the surrounding trees gave a colour of dread to her mind.

"I second it," replied Sparks, whose wit had departed.

"And I," said Poor Ray, "should feel much better in the barracks at Mafkat than here in this region of desolation, beautifully situated; yes, for certain purposes. Hark, how the wind is getting up! I hope it won't be a stormy night. We must tramp back," said Poor Ray.

"I confess," whispered Rachel, "I dislike the locality."

"Great Heaven! what's that moving the blind ?" gasped Welsh. "There! see; a face is peeping in."

The blood of all present ran cold.

"See, the face has gone! How fiendish in expression. You saw it?"

"Yes," they whispered.

"Listen. What a noise."

"Well, you know," said Poor Ray, very pale, "don't let us be killed like sheep. I'll die hard myself, and defend my life in the bargain."

"But we have no weapons," said Sparks.

"Welsh has a sword," replied Poor Ray; "we have our belts; trust in God; we shall be spared.

"Poor Rachel! how deadly pale she is! We'll form round her, and die like Romans of old."

"I shall never forget those words, dear Ray," whispered Rachel.

"It's going to rain," said Welsh.

"Merciful Heaven !" exclaimed Rachel, half dead with fright.

A heavy roll of thunder followed.

"Come," cried Welsh, "let us be up and going. By the window we'll make our exit."

With difficulty the window was opened, and another moment saw all four safely outside.

It was dark, and heavy drops of rain were falling.

There were two roads, one leading to the right in an oblique direction, the other to the left.

The right was taken at a venture.

The four hurried on as fast as their legs could carry them, but being doubtful whether they were on the right road or not made it most distressing travelling.

A call or whirr, like that of a partridge, was heard.

They had unfortunately taken the wrong road.

It got narrower and narrower, and was strewn with the roots of old trees, as if some one had thrown them in the road purposely.

Welsh drew his sword, followed by Rachel.

Poor Ray and Sparks doubled up their belts, prepared for any emergency, as a more likely spot for an ambush could not be found.

As they walked on a light from a rude tent became visible.

It was quite near.

Corporal Welsh was suddenly seized.

In vain he tried to liberate himself.

He endeavoured to cry out, but with a like success.

A cloth was thrown over his head, and, directly after, he felt himself hoisted on the shoulders of four men, and carried along.

The vile oaths of the men, as they gave him to understand what manner of death he should die, chilled the very marrow in his bones.

He was, strange to say, let gently down, the cloth removed from his eyes, and he saw that he was in a kind of cave.

Several fiendish Arabs, in red turbans, and with rifles of English manufacture in their hands, chanted their war-cry.

Welsh breathed forth a prayer as they unbound him.

Rachel, Poor Ray, and Tom Sparks, were brought in, and placed by the side of Welsh for judgment.

The villain who had endeavoured to excite the rabble of Mafkat to slaughter the troops, stood before them in very coarse attire.

From what passed, it was evident he was the commander of these wretches.

The prisoners were so placed that they could not see each other, although not standing a yard apart.

"See," said the commander, "you had your day, now I have mine! Allah be praised !"

With that he struck Corporal Welsh on the cheek.

"I have not harmed you," replied

Welsh; "so that if you kill me, I shall be murdered."

"True, scum of the earth, and with thine own sword."

"But what excuse can you make for detaining these innocent youths, and the young lady?"

"Dog! how durst thou presume to question us? Prepare for thy fate."

"Oh, my God," cried Welsh, "let me not die like this!"

In an hysterical manner, Rachel cried—

"Spare him—spare all!"

"Impossible," said the commander.

"May I speak?" inquired Poor Ray.

"No!" was the fierce rejoinder.

The features of the ruffian, that bespoke murder and crimes of the deepest dye, forbade them to hope that any mercy would be shown.

Rachel's fortitude was leaving her.

Nature could stand the dread scene no longer.

Falling to the earth, she was left to take care of herself.

The three male prisoners were then placed in line.

Poor Ray was in the middle.

He caught Welsh's hand in his own, and retained it.

"Load your pieces," said the commander, addressing his men. "Six of you will be sufficient. Let the distance be eight yards. Ready!"

"Is there no hope?—no chance of mercy?" said Ray.

But Welsh and Tom Sparks, to the surprise of the commander, were silent.

"A thought strikes me," said the commander, putting his hand to his forehead.

"If you'll swear by the sacred Koran, and the prophet Mahomet, to release any of these men should they fall into your hands, you are free, ye Kaffirs of a land cursed by Allah."

"I swear!" cried Poor Ray, who, like a drowning man, was ready to clutch at a straw.

Ray was set free.

Tom Sparks was mute.

By the gestures of the men, who jabbered and hissed, mercy was not to be extended to him.

However, they gave way to the commander.

Sparks gave his word.

Welsh hung fast.

"Five minutes are given you, blind, ignorant Kaffir!" ejaculated the Arabs, who swarmed round him.

"If you give me five thousand, I would not," exclaimed Welsh, drawing himself up proudly. "Tom Welsh turn traitor—never!"

"Three minutes," said the commander, and his men's eyes glistened voraciously, like hungry dogs in anticipation of pulling his carcase to pieces.

Poor Ray fell down and begged for Welsh's life, but the Arabs kicked him away.

Welsh, with his true Irish heart, was perfectly resigned.

"Two," said the commander, firmly.

"One."

"Fifty seconds."

Poor Ray would again have thrown himself at the chieftain's feet, but was forcibly thrown back.

"Twenty seconds."

Rachel at that moment recovered.

In an instant Poor Ray made her acquainted how matters stood.

With a wild shriek which echoed through the dismal cave, she turned her eyes upon Welsh, who read, even in those terrible moments, that she would be his.

"I yield," he cried.

Even then Poor Ray thought he would have been torn to pieces.

The commander saved them.

Why he did so the history will tell.

They were allowed to depart, and some time afterwards found their way back to Mafkat.

No one ever dreamt as the party walked into barracks what agony of mind they had suffered, and the terrible moments of suspense that had not long elapsed.

But, by mutual consent, the subject was not broached till some time after, and then only in broken sentences.

CHAPTER XXIX.

A DEADLY SKIRMISH.

THE wind screeched with a mournful voice as it swept round a thousand men who were lying on the parade ground, with their rifles clutched and loaded.

Not a syllable was heard; each man was busy with his own thoughts.

The cutting blast spared them not.

"May the rocket ascend," was the fervent prayer, as the eyes of the troops rested on the general's quarters, where the English Union Jack was flying.

The silence, however, was broken by Tom Sparks, who for the life of him could not see the fun of lying on the ground like a deaf and dumb person.

"Devilish cold," he whispered, yawning, for he dared not speak aloud. "Why, in the name of Heaven, don't they let us loose on these fiends?"

"Curb your romantic ideas," replied Welsh. "You'll have enough of it yet on those bare, bleak mountains; the wind will cut you in two— phew! Will the rocket never go up?"

After a pause, he muttered—

"Is Poor Ray here?"

"Yes," he quickly replied.

"Keep by the side of me. Should we be engaged, don't rush headlong into action, but act with deliberation."

"This sword," whispered Poor Ray. "How can a fellow fight with it?"

"Faith! it's right what he says," growled Tom Sparks; "may the angels or Mahomet take me if I couldn't wipe the pates of their mightinesses at the Horse Guards with this dagger, bad cess to the robber who had the impudence to call it a sword. Oh! for a revolver to pick them off like blackberries from the bushes. Confound the wind, how it groans! Scorching you by day and nipping your ears like a pair of pinchers by night. I wish I was back again at the Duke of York, safe in bed."

"Silence there," cried one of the officers.

"Bedad to him, may he—ahem! but who's that? It's a challenge."

The sentinels, as they walked to and fro with rifles at full cock, challenged—

"Who goes there?"

"Staff officer!" was the reply, in a voice, scarcely audible.

"Stand, and give the countersign."

"Glasgow."

"Pass; all's well."

"Gentlemen," said the aide-de-camp, as a group of officers crawled round him, "in less than ten minutes you will be on the move. A large body of Bedouins are marching on Hesalbeto.

"The English gentry are to be murdered.

"Information to that effect has just been received from a spy.

"Colonel Daniels, the general requests me to inform you that you will march as silently as you can to the end of the town by way of Rajaform; there the troops will concentrate."

This stirring bit of information was eagerly commented on as the staff officer departed.

The usual challenge of all armies, "Who goes there?" met his ear.

"Did you hear that?" muttered, Welsh.

"I did," replied Poor Ray, who, like most men and boys on the eve of their first battle, experienced a peculiar sensation that does not fall to the lot of every mortal.

The wind lulled.

Then came a mighty, rushing sound, as a rocket shot right up into the sky, illuminating the upturned faces of the soldiers, as the innumerable sparks of glowing colours twisted and turned into a thousand shapes.

Then they expired, leaving the sky as black as pitch.

The troops rose instantly to their feet.

The words of command were given in a whisper, but the steady tramp, tramp, echoed loudly through the deserted streets.

Rajaform was a scene of commotion.

Aides-de-camps galloped furiously past.

There were dragoons with drawn swords, whose business was to cut off all stragglers.

The infantry had the work of first defeating and dispersing them.

All was ready.

The general, surrounded by his staff, gave in a firm voice the word of command.

"The brigade will deploy into line!"

On they went, with fixed bayonets, at a smart pace, leaving no bush or shrub which might form an ambush for the desperadoes under the command of Prince Eminel Mumenir.

The work of slaughtering Europeans was going on.

The night air resounded with shrieks which made the blood run cold in the veins.

No mercy was shown to the sons of dogs, the vile Kaffirs, who were, according to the Prophet's predictions, to be swept into the sea by the Arab soldiers.

Deafening shouts reached the ears of the brigade.

The sharp crack of the rifle, and the eager contest now at its height, for a moment attracted even the outlying picket of the Bedouins.

Ere they could give the alarm the red-coats of our own country were upon them with a yell.

A voice of thunder called out, and could be heard above the din—

"Followers of the Prophet, Allah has ordained the victory to be yours! Then on to the fight. Paradise is yours. These infidels are against our holy cause. Mahomet, with his arms widely extended, is longing to receive you. Your forefathers cry—On, on! Allah is with us! He hovers round you now!"

The carnage commenced.

Fierce yells and horrible oaths burst forth, as a murderous fire from the British mowed down the front ranks of the fanatics.

They grappled with the bayonets, crying—

"Allah is with us! Paradise is yawning to receive us."

Like tigers they frantically threw themselves on to the bayonets.

The dreadful work of shooting them down like dogs continued for some time.

The soldiers then grappled with the ragged and ill-armed Arabs.

It became impossible for shots to be interchanged.

Corporal Welsh, with Poor Ray by his side, slashed away right and left, and gave up the bugle for the rifle and bayonet.

Drum-major Slasher judiciously kept a good distance in the rear, watching for a favourable opportunity to shoot Poor Ray, who, however, kept too near the enemy.

The giddy Tom Sparks roared away till he made himself hoarse, as he fought with his sword amid dense smoke and bright flashes of light from the rifles.

But Roberts, like a faithful dog, kept pretty close to his master's heels.

Fighting madly on the extreme right, the troops of the prince actually gained ground.

It was only momentary.

The Arabs were losing ground.

A stunted wood was the key of the position; it was here the most deadly resistance was offered.

Arabs fell in heaps.

The Prince of the Faithful rallied them with encouraging cries, that could be heard above the din of battle.

"The spirit of Mahomet is hovering round you! Spare not the infidels! The Koran says, 'They shall be cut from off the face of the earth!'

"Your brothers are fighting with us now unseen. These miserable wretches of dogs are blacker than sons of Kishbeck, who, for their abomination, were turned into vile black hounds! These are their sons. Their carcases shall rot in the mountains of misery.

"Yea, Mahomet, the only true prophet of Allah, in his blessed book, the Koran, pours out his wrath upon them.

"The Holy City and poor of Mecca are praying for us! Then on to victory—paradise is your reward! On, for the distant regions of Mahomet! On, the brave descendants of Mahomet! Allah is with us! Let your shouts be—Paradise! paradise!"

With such like enthusiastic words he addressed his men.

The oration had a most wonderful effect.

With groans and shrieks of delight they threw themselves upon the bayonets.

The Prince of the Faithful evidently knew that if he lost the position he held in the wood, his troops would be flying across the mountains of Hayno.

He led them on with sword in hand, actually cutting down soldiers who had come up to bayonet him.

"Kill him," was the cry from the English.

"Dogs! imps of Satan! come on!" he replied.

"Can no one shoot him?" cried one of the officers.

"Spare him, men!" shouted the colonel.

This entreaty to be merciful was not listened to.

Revolvers were directed at him, bullets hissed harmlessly round his person.

None struck him, simply because the excitement was so great that to take deliberate aim was next to an impossibility.

He did not bear a charmed life, as his wild, raving followers imagined.

The troops being in such close quarters pressed hard upon him, as if they were determined he should not escape them.

Corporal Welsh engaged with him as he made a murderous cut at one of the officers.

"Die, murderer! the destroyer of many peaceful homes!" yelled Welsh, as he made a lunge at his heart, which was skilfully parried.

A loud, piercing scream followed, as Corporal Welsh tripped up, and fell before him.

Poor Ray saw it, but could render no assistance.

"Quarter!" cried Welsh.

"Vile Kaffir, die! Take the blade of this good sword down your throat like the son of——"

The prince started as if he had seen an apparition.

"The devil! it's you."

To the unutterable surprise of Welsh, the prince engaged with others.

He then retreated a step or two, and was hidden by his men, who still cried out—

"Paradise for ever! for ever!"

A panic ensued; they threw down their arms, and rushed frantically from the wood.

In vain their leader tried to rally them.

"Miserable cowards!" he cried. "You are shut out from Paradise for flying before these cursed dogs."

And fly they did, while the British troops hotly pursued them, firing into every valley and thicket that might afford the slightest shelter to the retreating army, which rushed pell mell like a disorderly mob, till further pursuit became useless.

Jaded and worn out, the troops were content to lie on the side of a bleak mountain.

The distant fires lent a strange aspect to the surrounding country.

Cavalry, at the charge, was sweeping down the road with terrific yells, sounding like distant thunder.

Their helmets, the gaudy dress, with long, glistening swords, made up a sight so passing strange that the troops admired the scene in silence.

CHAPTER XXX.

THE CAMP FIRE.

THERE is no scene so wild and enchanting as a camp by night.

The fires, the busy groups of red-coats, cooking their suppers, making grog, spinning yarns, with the outlying pickets in the distance on the *qui vive*, assist in a great measure to remove that monotony which so much besets a soldier's barrack life.

It was extraordinary to Poor Ray, who watched the animated scene—the fires lighted up the features of men who were familiar to him as his own face.

He loved the life, and cared not for the cold wind at his back.

There was the ration of rum in the tin canteen that soldiers carry on the top of their knapsacks, and he made himself quite comfortable, with Welsh and Sparks chatting good-humouredly together, as well as several sergeants who joined them.

"Welsh," said Poor Ray, after taking a good swig of grog, "it was nearly all up with you. I offered a prayer for the repose of your soul."

"By this time," remarked Sparks, grinning, "you would have been dead."

"I said my prayers that moment, I can assure you, Sparks. What a fellow for fighting! it's a pity he wasn't an Irish general. How he parried the cuts with his sword. I was nearly knowing the grand secret. Yet, do you know, the voice that uttered those frightful imprecations I feel certain I have heard somewhere before. I could swear it."

"What made him spare you," said Poor Ray, "is a mystery."

"I can't imagine," replied Welsh.

A LOUD, PIERCING SCREAM FOLLOWED, AS CORPORAL WELSH TRIPPED UP, AND FELL BEFORE HIM.

"Horrid work, burying the dead!" interposed Tom Sparks.

A silence of a minute ensued.

"Drink a toast," said Welsh. "Here's to the memory of those gallant fellows who fell—English, Irish,· and Scotch. Peace to their ashes, and repose for their souls."

The toast was drunk in silence.

After a pause, the subject of the brave prince was broached.

"He muttered some unintelligible remark to me," said Welsh, "as he hid himself. I fancy, Ray, some persons would call it a presentiment that we should see him again."

"Don't you think he is taken, then?"

"No."

"Not a bad drop of grog this," remarked one of the sergeants, who felt it quite an honour to be amongst the buglers.

"What do you say for a yarn—the night's long, eh?"

"Oh, hang yarns!" replied Sparks. "But, sergeant, as you appear to me to be very fond of telling tales, let me give you one, short and sweet. You never heard the sublime story, handed down to us from generation to generation—"The corkcutters?"

"Never."

"Get out your pocket-handkerchiefs. I'll make you cry, and show real grief."

Welsh and Poor Ray both grinned.

"Once on a time there were three brothers, and they were cork-cutters, and they all cut cork. These three brothers being cork-cutters, they cut cork. They were three brothers; mind you, don't forget that they cut cork. These cork-cutters, these three——"

"To perdition with your cork-cutters!" returned the sergeant, laughing. "It's the same over again."

"You are impatient. The pith was yet to come. Mankind is weak. I did not wish to give you too strong a dose at first. Suppose you tell one yourself, sergeant, and let it be sweet if not short."

"Master Sparks, I am sorry that I can't oblige you with lollipop stories, but the tale I propose telling is a true one. The old man, I mean my father, was a keeper; I, his son, like many respectable people's sons, was a scamp, got mixed up with poachers, soon knew a thing or two, that I shall tell you about."

"That's right, sergeant; a poaching expedition is very exciting."

"Silence," said Poor Ray, "for the sergeant's tale."

"Yes, silence!" echoed Welsh.

Sparks grinned.

At this moment the stranger, muffled up as on the night he took his stand at the barrack-gate, approached within a few yards, and then stood still.

"Who's he?" said Sparks.

"They say," replied Welsh, "he's a newspaper correspondent."

"Let us ask him to join us," said Poor Ray. "He looks very hard at me. I like his face. Don't laugh at what I am going to say; I fancy my mother has got features like his."

"Singular, very," murmured Welsh.

"What if he should be your mother's brother, eh?" said Sparks.

"I'll go," said Poor Ray, standing up, "and ask him to take a drop of grog."

"Ah! do," said Welsh; "a literary man will give us some queer anecdotes." As Poor Ray went towards the stranger, he turned round and walked away. This extraordinary conduct was commented upon.

"I'll find out," said Welsh, "whether he really is a correspondent or not."

Somehow Poor Ray saw that face days after; it haunted him.

Inwardly he resolved to address him the next time he had a chance, let that be when it would.

"The tale—the tale," cried Welsh.

The sergeant bowed.

CHAPTER XXXI.

STORY OF THE KEEPER'S SON.

"IT' was another such a night as this," said the sergeant—Sparks looked round and turned up the whites of his eyes, as much as to say he did not believe it—"that a party, consisting of your humble servant, Dick the Poacher, as he was called, and Joe, sat drinking in the back kitchen of the 'Traveller's Rest.'

"It was agreed upon that we should start at ten and pay a visit to my father's pheasants, the birds being plump and in very good condition.

"The pheasant plantation, as father called it, was within a stone's throw of the house—that house I had not entered for more than two years, through a quarrel with my step-mother.

"Dick got up as the clock struck ten, put a double-barrel gun into his velveteen pocket; I took some nets, a bag, and a stoutish piece of rope; and Joe slipped a single-barrel gun inside his coat, as his pockets were not large enough to hide it.

"We went quietly out the back way, lest some one might be inquisitive enough to follow, struck out across some fields, which brought us to the park wall.

"Here we found that we had left the dog behind; however, he soon came up.

"Scaling the wall with difficulty, we got into a lot of stinging nettles.

"The drop of spirits we had taken to give us courage was by this time dead within us.

"Dark firs and other sepulchral-looking trees surrounded us, very beautiful to look at in the day, but awful fellows at night, to make you fancy that some goblin or fiend is keeping you company, besides being good shelter for a keeper and his men to watch from.

"I knew every nook and corner; I could set a wire that no hare could escape from; like the Indians, I could trace the pole-cat, weasel, and badger to their different haunts; knew where to clap my hands on pheasants and partridges.

"I robbed the old man in one year of two hundred and forty-four eggs; but all went in drink.

"In consequence of my knowledge, to-night I led the way.

"We crawled on our knees to the old man's house to see if he had retired, but a light burning gave us a warning that he might even now be on the alert; not that I feared for a moment that he would know me in a wood. but we were frightened lest we should disturb the dogs round the house, more than twenty in number, besides two fierce bloodhounds that were kept for the express purpose of hunting poachers.

"If he should let them loose, it would be a case with us.

"We lay on the ground, waiting anxiously for the light to be put out."

The sergeant puffed his pipe for a minute, as though the recollection unnerved him, and then continued his tale—

"'Do you think,' said Dick, my companion, 'that he's in?'

"'I think so,' said I; 'but never mind; come on; we won't wait.'

"At that moment out went the light.

"'You stay here, mind,' said I, 'till I return; I won't be long.'

"I stealthily got over the wall like a cat, and went on tiptoe to my father's house.

"On the path I stepped on a rotten stick, which cracked, and one of the dogs gave tongue.

"'Down,' said I, in an under breath, and the dog was silent.

"I took a piece of rope from my pocket, and tied the handle of the door in such a manner that it was impossible, I thought, for any one inside to get out.

"After listening for a time, I heard the old man saying his prayers, previous to going to bed.

"That was a load off my mind.

"I joined my companions, who had loaded their guns.

"My duty was to hold the bags and put the pheasants in as fast as I could pick them up.

"It was a fir plantation.

"To walk in it was like walking on a carpet.

"We stood under the trees.

"There, overhead, were the fat, plump, dark objects that fetched such a good price in the market.

"Dick fired first. Bang!

"What a horrible noise it made.

"The echo was taken up, and carried, it seemed, miles—down fluttered the pheasant.

"Bang, again and again, till the fluttering in the bag reminded me that it was nearly full.

"My hands were hot with their blood.

"The dog growled.

"'Hush!' said Dick, as we fell on our faces.

"He caught the dog round its nose, to prevent its giving tongue, lest it might lead the watchers to our whereabouts.

"'What do you think it was?' inquired Dick, with a fierce, determined expression, as he gazed into my face.

"'Are you ready for a run?' asked Joe.

"I was thunderstruck.

"I had caught sight of a pair of shining eyes fastened upon us from a dark fir tree under which we stood.

"I griped Dick by the hand; he understood all in a moment.

"As quick as lightning we were rushing through the wood.

"Joe, not to impede his flight, threw down his gun, which I picked up.

"'Separate!' cried Dick.

"But I followed close behind him, as he carried the pheasants.

"There were heard voices shouting, 'Surrender! Here we are!'

"On we dashed, heeding not the briars and brambles that tore our faces till the blood trickled down.

"On we went, I say, as we did when in full pursuit of the Arabs—no pauses, no stopping to breathe awhile, but on and on, we knew not whither.

"I was getting exhausted.

"I felt sure that I must drop down.

"'Come on,' cried Dick, 'keep up with me.'

"'Great Heavens! Dick, stop a moment,' said I. 'Where are we?'

"But he kept on like a steam engine; and, to my horror, I heard a voice speaking to a dog.

"'After them. Good dog.'

"Dick stopped, as he muttered

"'It's the bloodhounds. We shall be torn to pieces.'

"Up they came, but they appeared to know me, and forward they rushed till they came up with our dog.

"A fierce growl, and the bloodhounds soon dispatched him.

"The bag was thrown aside, and in the confusion I lost Dick.

"Another hound that had been behind the others kept following me.

"Thought I, if I am caught, it will be a case with me, and the old man will be deprived of his situation.

"I knelt down on one knee as a man rushed by me.

"'Good dog,' he cried, 'after them.'

"The bloodhound gave a growl. He followed in my track.

"'Good dog,' said I, seizing the gun by the barrel.

"I watched an opportunity, and with the butt end I beat out the brains of the fierce hound.

"The man and I were soon close together. I could hear him panting for breath. He gave words of encouragement to others.

"'Come on with you; he is here,' said the man, dashing through the bushes, when, to add to my alarm, I heard that some one was in front of me.

"'But why play the fool longer?' said I, talking to myself.

"The gun was loaded and capped.

"I saw that I could not escape.

"I took aim and fired rather low. A cry of anguish told me that I had not missed the mark.

"But where was I? The wood swam round me. I rushed away, yet came back to the same place.

"Was the man dead?

"How my heart beat, as I heard a groan.

"That was a heavenly moment, for I had been thinking of Jack Ketch and the hooting rabble feasting their eyes upon my carcase, swinging to and fro in the air.

"I stooped down.

"A thousand lights played before my eyes. My heart was bursting with horror; it baffles language to tell. Had the earth opened its mouth and swallowed me, that moment would have been blessed, for no other harrowing feeling I had ever before felt equalled that which now filled my soul.

"I caught hold of the bushes for support.

"I was on the verge of fainting.

"The blood of the wounded man was dyeing the grass and leaves.

"The shots had struck him in the thigh.

"I tore off my shirt and endeavoured to staunch the wound.

"Through the darkness of the night I caught sight of his face.

"It was my father.

"'Father!' I cried, in a delirious voice, kneeling before him, 'it's your poor son! Speak, father, dear!'

"'Water,' he murmured.

"'I know not where to get any!' I cried, in despair.

"'To the right, there,' he faintly murmured.

"Sure enough there was a tiny stream.

"I drank of the water, and brought the old man as much as I could in my hat.

"It revived him, but he knew me not.

"'Father,' said I, again.

"He opened his eyes.

"That look of recognition I saw when I was fighting the other night; he gave me his hand in token of forgiveness, as I covered his face with my hot, scalding tears.

"I leave you to imagine how I took him home; but in twenty-four hours I was a soldier, and miles away from the place."

The sergeant covered his eyes with both hands, as if to shut out from his sight the recollection of that night, and then drew a deep sigh.

"Is he alive now?" inquired Poor Ray, who was deeply interested in the story.

"He is. I had a letter from him the other day."

"You have not seen him since then, sergeant?"

"No, I have not."

"What do you think of it, Sparks?" said Welsh.

"Not much. I like tales in the eating line. It's getting colder. May I never sleep on a mountain again! I am the first of the family to do so, and I shall be the last. Now for a snooze, to dream about bloodhounds."

Sparks curled himself up in his blanket.

The others took the hint.

The outlying pickets kept watch as the lurid glare from the camp-fires played fantastical tricks with the features of the sleepers, who were thinking what a luxury it would be to have a straw bed to lie upon.

Upwards of a week elapsed ere the troops returned to their respective quarters.

CHAPTER XXXII.

THE CONSPIRATORS—A QUEER VISITOR.

NOT many hundred yards from Mafkat barracks was a lonely field; heaps of rubbish, stones, and offal of the streets were deposited in this field of scum and dirt.

In the middle was a house half built, with the beams and rafters lying in all directions, as if the lazy Arabs had given up the work for ever.

An old, red-turbaned Arab appeared to be the solitary workman.

The English residents who lived out that way sometimes said—

"What a time that house is building, to be sure;" but no one ever thought of going among dead cats and dogs to see it.

The passers-by turned up their noses as they hurried on to get out of the vicinity, leaving the old man to read his Koran, and prostrate himself on the ground at morn, noon, and night.

Strange goings on might be seen here at night.

Down under the earth a great many feet, the followers of the Prophet were at work with shovels and pick-axes.

It was a mine running in a straight line to Mafkat barracks.

The Arabs had got so far as to be actually under the first sentry-box inside the barracks.

Even engineers, with all their instruments of skill, might have been taught a lesson by these rough excavators, who worked laboriously from morning till night, merely subsisting on a little boiled rice.

The tunnel or mine might be compared to a narrow courtway, with this difference; it was propped up in a master-like manner, that afterwards astounded the soldiers.

Here under ground for weeks Prince Eminel Mumenir plied the pick most vigorously, and the sounds were sometimes faintly heard in the barracks.

The rubbish was easily deposited with the heaps of mud from the streets.

Whilst cavalry were scouring the country, searching every bazaar and corner, right under their very eyes, so to speak, the Arabs were at their diabolical work with the fiendish determination of blowing up the barracks.

To blow up those brave troops who had beaten them.

The prophets of the Koran gave promises of bliss at each sound of the pick.

The duties for the soldiers became more harassing day after day.

The general had issued an order that all able bandsmen and drummers should carry arms at night, and do duty as sentinels.

Under this category fell Poor Ray,

Corporal Welsh, and Sparks, with many others who have nothing whatever to do with this history.

Corporal Welsh paced to and fro, with his arms sloped, his rifle being at the full cock.

The hour was drawing near twelve —midnight.

Welsh stopped suddenly.

He heard a faint noise as of some one hammering right under the sentry-box!

Could it be fancy?

But he expected the field officer every minute.

The sentinel at the barrack gate cried lustily—

"Guard, turn out; the field officer's coming!"

Sure enough it was the field officer, but without his orderly.

"Who goes there?" shouted Welsh, bringing his rifle down to the port, as the officer came dashing towards him.

"Field officer."

"Stand, and give the countersign.

"Dublin!"

"Pass."

The sentry presented arms as the officer approached.

"You have seen no suspicious persons hanging about outside, I presume?" said the officer, casting a searching glance at the sentinel.

"No, sir, no one."

"Any disturbance of the most trivial kind you must report."

"Yes, sir."

"Wasn't there a rumour a week back that the Bedouins were going to blow up the barracks?"

"Yes, sir."

"What do you think of it?"

"All bosh!"

"Yes, I daresay it is. How did the rumour get afloat?"

"Some of the men said they heard knocking, as if underground, at night."

"Indeed!"

"Yes, sir."

"Have you ever heard such noises?"

"Yes, only just now I heard knocking under this box. Hark! there it i again, sir."

The officer put his ear to the ground.

"Yes; it is knocking."

"I report the circumstances, then, to you, sir."

"Oh, what would you think if the knocking proceeded from pious Arabs working their way to undermine the barracks?"

"What! such a thing is incredulous."

"How many rounds of ammunition do you carry?"

"Sixty."

"Humph! the crisis is at hand," murmured the officer, as if speaking to himself. "Another three hours, and all will be well. I spared your life, young man."

"Spared my life, sir? Impossible!"

"Listen! I am Prince Eminel Mumenir, whose life is now in your hands. I spared you when your life was in my power. Have you forgotten the cave?"

"Merciful Heaven! and here!" exclaimed Welsh.

"Here, and why not?"

"But as a spy, in the dress of a field officer. I expect the genuine officer every minute. What a hazardous attempt; you carry your life in your hands."

"Fear not; I have my emissaries —spies, if you will. The officer in question will not be here this twenty minutes."

"But your business?" inquired Welsh.

"To ascertain whether the pickaxes could be heard. They are now exactly here. Three hours more and the picks will not be heard."

"How did you know I was on sentry?"

"Knew nothing of that. This uniform would awe a thousand Kaffirs into submission. Fortune, and the Prophet Mahomet favour me.

"Tell me truly, who relieves you? Any of the young men who were with you that night in the cave?"

"They are in the guard-room now, and presented arms to you."

"Tell them not to report any noise to the officer of the guard. I give you my word as a prince that neither of you shall be injured. You promise?"

Welsh hesitated.

Conspiring with Arabs to blow up the barracks!—a crime for which, if brought in guilty, he would be hanged without mercy.

"I must make a report."

"Do so, and you are a dead man. It isn't for the fox in the poultry-yard to cry tally-ho; other hands, not mine, will assassinate you."

"Consider, sir, blowing up the barracks! it's fanatical! All of you will be exterminated yet."

"The Prince of the Faithful will give you notice. It is ordained by Allah, the Kaffir shall be blown beyond the mountains of Toroani. Quick! time is pressing. Meet me to-morrow at sunset—the Mahometan hour of prayer, near the mosque. Your word."

"Be it so, then, till to-morrow evening. What do you say?"

"To-morrow evening," he said, "you shall know. Farewell."

He then mounted his Arab steed, and with the utmost *sang froid* returned the salute at the barrack gate, as the guard presented arms.

The perspiration rolled off Welsh, as he soliloquised—

"I'm in for it at last. The storm is brewing; but to-morrow night the general shall know all.

"I wonder how he got the countersign; but his spies are all over the country.

"The powers above—listen to them working!

"The scoundrels, they shall be blown from our guns."

It need not be said that it required little persuasion from Welsh to gain from Poor Ray and Tom Sparks a promise of temporary silence.

They were as true as steel, but the repeated knocking—like men in their graves trying to come forth—alarmed them much, as they fully expected to be blown into the air every minute.

Over the guard-room fire their words were few.

However, the serious glances they gave each other as they entered the room, would have sent a detective frantic to discover the meaning of the telegraphic communication that passed between them.

Yet Welsh dreaded the hour named by the prince—seven o'clock.

CHAPTER XXXIII.

THE SPY.

A GLOOM hung over the dirty town of camel-drivers, Mafkat, as a funeral pall.

The heavy, angry clouds, dark as Erebus—for the rainy season was near—rolled in a threatening manner, as if they knew the terrible work that was going on below.

On the minds of the three drummers it made a deep impression.

It was an omen of bad luck.

The witty and humorous tongue of Sparks was silent.

A despondency took possession of them as they sat conversing together in the drummers' room.

The shades of evening were falling fast, and a thick sepulchral gloom hung about the air.

The three were alone to all appearances, yet under the very bench that they were seated on lay stretched Roberts.

He had noticed the whisperings, and had seen the signal conveyed to one another from the eye.

There was some extraordinary work in hand.

He communicated with his superior. By his advice he was ordered to remain concealed in the drummers' room, as Welsh in the afternoon gave the boys to understand that he wished to have the room to himself for an hour.

"The door, I believe, is locked," said Welsh.

"Yes," returned Sparks.

"Make sure," added Poor Ray, as he walked across the room and tried it.

"As safe as a rock," he remarked.

"To work then," said Welsh, speaking in a tone so low that it was hardly audible.

"What is your opinion on the subject? Don't hesitate either of you to tell me what you think is best."

They sat thinking for several minutes.

Sparks broke the silence.

"Betray another is a word I don't understand, but our lives are in jeopardy. I'll be hanged if I can look anybody straight in the face. If you give the Prince timely warning to leave the country, that, surely, is acting honourable. Drop him a line to that effect, saying that by such a day the general will be in the secret. As for the other wretches, we'll bayonet them like cats and dogs."

"But think, Sparks; we shall be assassinated."

"Do you really think so?" said Poor Ray.

"Aye, as sure as we are sitting here. If we take a stroll through the town, or enter any of their bazaars, we may have daggers planted in our hearts. I wish to Heaven we were out of this country; it was a cursed day we marched in; see what it has brought us to."

"You'll meet the Prince at seven, I suppose?" inquired Poor Ray.

"I gave him my word as an Irishman, and I'll keep it."

"But he, or some of his emissaries, may murder you."

"Hark! What's that?" exclaimed Sparks. "I thought I heard some one moving under the bench."

"Fancy, my dear fellow. You'll imagine now every night that your throat's being cut, or that you are blown up to the sky, minus your legs and arms. See what a guilty conscience is," said Welsh.

"I shall be thinking of nothing," muttered Sparks, "but undermining the barracks."

"I suppose," said Welsh, "that neither of you care about coming?"

"To speak the truth, I'd rather not," replied Sparks.

"I don't mind," said Poor Ray.

Welsh took no notice, but went on to say—

"Should I not return by tattoo you will give immediate information."

And here Welsh lowered his voice to a whisper.

Roberts, in his eagerness not to let a word escape him, lifted up his head; it came in contact with the bench.

The three jumped to their feet, turning ghastly pale.

They had been overheard, then, but by whom?

"Who's there?" cried Welsh, in desperation, as he ran to his sword. "By Heaven, if you don't speak, this sword shall pass through your heart!"

"It's only me!" whined Roberts, whose face bore a hue similar to that of pipe-clay.

Welsh seized him and dragged him out before them like a dog.

"You have heard all that passed," cried Welsh, seizing him by the throat.

"No, upon my soul, I did not. I fell off to sleep."

"Liar!" shouted Welsh. "Who sent you here to be a spy on us?"

"No one, corporal."

"Tell me all you heard, or by my father, lying in his grave, nothing shall prevent me from taking your miserable life. Down on your knees, serpent; and then take this Bible, and swear after me."

Roberts hesitated, but a slight tap with the sword which just bruised the skin, made him ready to swear, if it were required, that black was white.

"Repeat after me, 'I, Walter Roberts, do hereby solemnly swear on this sacred book that I hold in my hand, that I never will reveal by word, sign, or gesture, the words I have just heard.'"

Roberts repeated the words and kissed the book.

"That will do," said Welsh. "Violate your oath and you will die!"

"What, corporal, do you think I could do so after my oath on the Bible? Never!"

"Then you did hear a word or two?" exclaimed Poor Ray.

"I did, but don't understand it."

"Walter Roberts," said Welsh, solemnly, "look into my face. Try and read what is passing in my mind now. Can you guess?"

"Yes," and the artful villain commenced to sob.

"Go, I say, for I guess by your eye that you know all that the prince said to me. Remember Judas Iscariot! In your case it would be advisable to take your Bible and read that narrative."

Roberts slunk out of the room, and met the drum-major under the verandah in close conversation with Rach. Williams. Roberts turned awa' from his superior.

What he read in Welsh's eye had more influence over him than all the promises made by Slasher.

CHAPTER XXXIV.

SEVEN O'CLOCK.

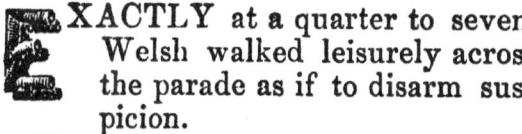

EXACTLY at a quarter to seven, Welsh walked leisurely across the parade as if to disarm suspicion.

He had no revolver to trust to should there be treachery, nothing but the Roman dagger by his side, in close quarters a very useful weapon.

His heart beat with misgivings.

A load was dragging him down as he thought of the prince he was about to meet.

Placards had been posted, offering large rewards for this man, dead or alive, yet in another minute he would be face to face with him.

True enough, near the mosque there stood a dirty, vagabond-looking fellow.

"One of his spies, perhaps," thought Welsh.

But his surprise was great when the man, who had a hump between his shoulders, addressed him in Arabic—

"*Salem alekum*—Peace be with you."

Welsh returned the compliment, throwing a furtive glance at the man.

"My orders are that you follow me."

"That I cannot do; my engagement was here at this spot, and no further."

"Whom do you fear, O Kaffir? You are safer in our hands than you are in barracks, ah, ah, ah! See, it's dark.

"Half a mile down yonder road will bring you to your destination."

"The prince bade me, O infidel, to respect you."

"Lead on; I follow."

They walked on in silence through lane ancle deep with mud.

Welsh had his hand grasped round e handle of his sword, as the locality was such that an honest man would not feel his throat safe in such quarters, as the trees which overhung the road offered a great temptation to desperadoes.

"A short journey, you see," said the Arab, as he walked into a small hut.

Whispering to a spy, they were shown into a back room dimly lighted.

Cups of coffee stood on the table.

"The prince," said Welsh, in tones that bespoke uneasiness.

"He'll be here, O friend; but first permit me to bolt the door. Ahem! my disguise, you see, is a good one; not even my intimate friends know me."

With an alacrity that surprised Welsh, old garments were thrown off, the hump removed from the shoulders, as likewise an artificial pair of huge whiskers, and a counterfeit scar, till the prince appeared in his splendid dress.

"*Mon Dieu!*" exclaimed Welsh, "I should not have thought it possible, though I have read such things in books."

"Drink," said the prince.

Welsh hesitated.

"Never fear; it is not drugged; no occasion for that, you see."

And he pulled out two of Colt's revolvers and laid them upon the table.

"Business is the order of the day. You are poor.

"The miserable pittance that the Kaffir government allows you barely keeps you a step above starvation. Don't interrupt me, please. I know, O friend, what you would say.

"Here is a jewel worth ten thousand pounds; take it, only keep the secret."

"Infatuated prince, know you not it is impossible to drive the Kaffir from off the earth?

"You have been a terror to all English residents.

"Your capture is sure!

"It is a temptation—a great one, that diamond lying there—but my allegiance to my sovereign is of far greater value than that dross which would only lead me to the gallows."

"Then you die, son of a dog! I ——"

"By the powers!" cried Welsh, his blood rising, "if you were Mahomet himself, I would not suffer you to address me as a son of a dog.

"Welsh is a name respected in Ireland.

"Prince, by to-morrow evening —stay, read this."

And he displayed one of the proclamations.

The prince for a moment forgot himself, and held out his hand.

Corporal Welsh seized the two revolvers, and, with a spring, made for the door.

The prince drew his scimitar and rushed madly upon him, quoting the Koran.

"YOU HAVE SEEN NO SUSPICIOUS PERSONS, I PRESUME?"

Corporal Welsh eluded him, and took aim with the revolver he held in his right hand.

It snapped, and it sounded to Welsh like his funeral knell; he pulled the trigger of the other revolver; it was not loaded.

He gave himself up for lost as he threw them at the prince, who, by stooping avoided them.

Drawing his sword, he dexterously parried the blows.

As he thought of Rachel Williams and Poor Ray, it gave energy to his arms.

The black, shining eyes of the prince, who still kept quoting the Koran, were like balls of fire.

Welsh, with deliberation, watched his opportunity.

The odds in favour of such a skilful swordsman as the prince were great, and he feared every moment that his spies would enter, as the swords coming in contact made a considerable noise.

Welsh, as quick as lightning, feigned to make a cut at the prince's head, intending to cleave his skull in two, but failed; however, he followed it up by a quick turn of the wrist, and the next moment the prince's hand fell useless by his side, leaving him at Welsh's mercy.

Welsh was about to thrust his sword into his adversary's heart, but, remembering how his life was spared on a former occasion, he desisted, ran to the door, and made off at his best speed.

CHAPTER XXXV.

DEATH OF TOM SPARKS.

WALTER ROBERTS' mind was uneasy.

The conversation he overheard in the drummers' room, left him in a state of uncertainty and perplexity.

He felt an intense longing to tell his master, but scarcely dared; not that he cared for the oath he had taken, but the fire of vengeance in Welsh's eye alone made him hesitate.

But he should never know.

He would beg the drum-major not to divulge a sentence, or hint to either of them about it.

What a noise the matter would make!

Welsh, Poor Ray, and Tom Sparks, ought to be placed in arrest.

How could they harm him?

He knocked gently at the drum-major's door; that worthy man never kept him waiting long, but let him in quickly.

Roberts was as white as a sheet.

He knew he was going to do a dangerous thing.

"What's the matter?" exclaimed the drum-major. "Is the drummers room on fire?"

"No," gasped Roberts. "Have you got a drop of spirits?"

"Yes; here's a glass of rum."

"Thank you. I have horrible news to tell; it will make you faint."

"Tell me quickly—do."

"Should you tell where you got your information from, I should be killed. You told me, you know, to lie under the bench. I said I heard nothing, but I did. Welsh has received a large sum of money from somebody not to split. The Arabs are going to blow up the barracks."

"The villain!"

"For the love of your soul, and mine too, say nothing!" exclaimed Roberts, falling on his knees, now feeling sorry he had done the deed. "If you tell, the adjutant shall know what you wanted me to do that night in the drummers' room."

Here was a blow—a most terrific one.

The colonel would believe it, after Muggleton's affair.

Prudence made him, on second thoughts, give up going to the adjutant, as he secretly intended to; but he set the rumour afloat.

It soon got wind.

No one knew the author.

A telegram was sent to the general.

The inquiry was conducted with the utmost despatch and secrecy.

The Arabs were taken at their diabolical work, by half-a-dozen officers.

Even the soldiers, some days after, only laughed to think how foolish they had been in believing such idle stories.

Four of the fanatics were captured.

In the evening Poor Ray, Corporal Welsh, and Tom Sparks, strolled through one of the bazaars; an Arab, in rich costume, with white turban and gold tassels behind, addressed them—

"Salam alekum!"

They replied in the same words; and the Arab called their attention to some fruit.

He begged them, in broken English, to walk in and take whatever they preferred.

Not for a moment did they dream of danger, till too late.

A party of Bedouins were concealed within, and, before they had scarcely entered, sprang upon the drummers like tigers.

They tied and gagged them.

Not a word was spoken, as they were put in sacks, and remained for hours in that torturing position—a time which seemed an eternity.

They were carried a considerable distance, and hoisted up on to camels; they could tell that by the jolting, painful ride.

What passed through the minds of the three young men, bound hand and foot, pen cannot tell.

Poor Ray thought of his unknown mother, and feared he was going to be slaughtered; and he began to imagine how dreadful the effects of strangulation must be.

Sparks shuddered as he brought back to mind the last interview with the dreaded warrior in the cave.

The camels stopped; they were taken from them, carried along, and the sacks removed from them.

Ere a minute elapsed, they gazed upon a scene of horror.

A grave had been dug, and the eyes of the three soldiers beheld it yawning to receive them.

On a raised seat sat the prince; on either side were Arabs swarming like bees.

The prince stood up, and gave directions in a language that the three prisoners did not understand.

Amid fierce yells, they were told their hour had come.

Some threw filth upon them with their fists, and spat in their faces.

A discussion ensued among the Arabs, whether the prisoners should be torn to pieces with hooks or thrown into boiling oil.

The prince overruled them, and sentenced them to die a merciful death by hanging.

"Executioners," said the prince in a deep voice, "do your duty!"

Tom Sparks was seized.

"Allow me," he said, "to shake hands with my dear companions before I die."

With the rope round his neck, the request was granted.

"Good-bye, dear Tom Welsh.

Should you ever see any of my relations, tell them I died as a soldier should die."

They embraced!

"Stand back, imps of darkness!" roared the prince.

The rope was tightened.

Several swarthy Arabs drew it over a projecting rock—care being taken not to cut the rope, by placing a piece of cloth under it.

Poor Ray and Welsh were tightly held, or they would have attempted to rescue their comrade.

They closed their eyes till the prince had exclaimed—

"Take him down!—bury him!—it's more than the dog deserves!"

There was a dull sound, as the body of the unfortunate Sparks was pitched without ceremony into the grave.

"Robbers! cut-throats!" cried Welsh, "I will combat with twenty of you, only give me a sword. But to die the felon's death is more than I can bear. Ray, come to my arms!"

The agony of that moment who can tell?

But relief was at hand, and that by the merest accident.

An English lady had seen the three soldiers enter the bazaar with a richly-dressed Arab, and, from what she heard, gave information to the military authorities, who quickly despatched a body of men, led by an old rogue of an Arab, who guided them to the cave.

The rope was round Welsh's neck, as the soldiers dashed in and bayoneted their foemen.

The prince cried, and called upon Mahomet to preserve them.

But his hour was come, and he was pierced by bullets.

The rest that follows is beyond the power of any pen to describe.

The change was great from despair to joy.

The minds of the two prisoners had been tortured so terribly that for several days they were on the sick list.

When they recovered, they found that the short war in Arabia was at an end.

The troops joyfully turned their eyes homewards, but, ere they reached England, the orders were countermanded, for another tyrant was either to be taken or laid low, and that was Emperor Theodore, the monarch of all nations, and the king of kings.

CHAPTER XXXVI.

DRUM-MAJOR SLASHER AND THE MYSTERIOUS STRANGER.

TWO thousand pounds!

It was a large sum!

The thought of it haunted Slasher day and night.

With that amount at his disposal he might retire from the service, take a public-house, and settle down comfortably.

The sooner the better, he thought, as he did not know how soon he himself might be killed.

He never enlisted for that, and, if he could help it, his name should never appear in the returns of dead or missing.

Oh, dear no!

He longed to have the two thousand in his possession.

With a sigh, Slasher clenched his fist, as he sat down to think the matter over for the sixtieth time that day.

He sat for a long time with his legs crossed, when a faint knock at the door startled him.

Thinking it might be only one of the drummers, and as he did not wish to be disturbed in his reverie, he determined not to answer, for he had previously locked the door.

Again it was repeated, and a low voice said—

"Slasher, let me in."

Drum-major Slasher started, and then opened the door.

The stranger smiled as he gave Slasher his hand.

There was something in his features which troubled the other much.

"Slasher," said the stranger, in a slow, decided manner, taking a stool, and sitting face to face with him, "I have been deceived. I release you from your engagement."

"Release me!" cried Slasher, as a vision of Rachel Williams rose up in his mind. "Why?"

"You are no good. I'll do the deed myself," was the reply.

For several moments Slasher made no reply.

He did not believe the stranger.

It was only a blind.

He had another better fitted for the task than himself.

"If I have been dilatory," replied Slasher, "it was for your sake, not mine. Be cautious, my dear sir, or else your eagerness will ruin us."

"I ought to have been in England ere this. I never imagined he would have got out of the English Channel."

"Pray, sir, consider; he fell overboard. He's like a cat—has nine lives; but he will not live through the night."

"Stop, stop, Slasher. He must not die to-night, nor, indeed, at any other time by your hand."

Slasher appeared chopfallen.

The public-house, Rachel, all his castles in the air were floored by a few words, and he himself would perhaps be left behind in Abyssinia for the jackals to tear to pieces.

He determined to try what influence a good bottle of wine might have on the stranger.

He instantly opened a bottle, poured out a glass for himself and another for his guest.

They both drank, and the conversation became more lively.

The bottle was soon empty.

As Slasher had several more, he brought out another, which made his visitor laugh and talk perhaps more than he intended.

"Slasher," he said, "I will no longer hide from you the truth about the boy's mother."

"Does she live then?" exclaimed Slasher.

"Yes, and is anxious to see him. She has expended large sums on advertisements and inquiries."

"Is she rich?"

"Fool! If she were poor, would I give you or anybody else a certain figure to put him away?"

"No, sir."

"Then why speak so foolishly? Mark what I say. His mother——"

"Yes, his mother——" replied Slasher, eager to hear all.

"Is a lady worth thousands, and you shall have the sum I promised provided the boy dies on or before the second night after we reach Zulla, where we shall be encamped. I go with you as a newspaper correspondent.

"Mark where the boy lies down at night, and—come nearer—here is a stiletto."

"To-night, if you like. Why wait till then?" replied Slasher.

His visitor rose to go, evidently to try what effect it might have upon Slasher, who immediately begged him to be seated.

"Am I to understand it is settled, Slasher?"

"Yes; but who is he, after all?"

"A son of my sister, who is consumptive. An old aunt left her all she had. The boy, if he turned up, would inherit all. Ah! Agnes, you shall never see him."

"Agnes Muggleton, I suppose," said Slasher.

"Agnes Muggleton! no, Agnes Fielding."

For several minutes they sat in silence, Slasher thinking that if he buried the stiletto in Ray's bosom and dragged him out from beneath the tent, everybody would say it was the natives.

The stranger inwardly complimented himself for his cleverness in bringing matters, one way or the other, to a very speedy issue.

Evidently he knew Slasher's burning love for money.

Talking about vast sums has upon most minds little effect.

It is the yellow, irresistible coin, glittering before the eye in heaps, that strikes such men as Slasher with a mighty yearning to get it.

The stranger could read this in his face.

He pulled out a roll of bank notes, dived his hand into his pocket and threw sovereigns on to the table.

Slasher tried to count them, having a secret idea that some of them would fall to his lot before long.

He felt the keen edge of his stiletto, and then took a quick glance at his friend, who had his eyes fastened upon him. The stranger whispered—

"Slasher, I have a revolver here."

"My dear fellow, I beg pardon, I meant, sir—no insinuations, I beg. I'm square and above board; but drink."

"Thank you, no; I must go."

"I have a question to ask," said Slasher, smiling as he perceived the unknown return the notes into his pocket-book, leaving, obviously for himself, ten sovereigns upon the table.

Slasher pointed to them.

"Take them," said the stranger.

"Thank you, sir."

And Slasher grabbed at them as if for his life.

"You'll give me the two thousand when——"

"As a gentleman of honour, I will."

"Because," said Slasher, "if you did not, I'd—I'd——"

"I know what you would do, Slasher; but you were going to ask me a question."

"Is the boy's father alive?"

"No; he was a drunken vagabond; he broke his neck while hunting, thank God! My sister—the only one I have, worshipped the fellow."

The stranger pulled out his watch as a hint that he must be going, examined his revolver, then turned his eyes upon Slasher, who said—

"Good night, sir."

"Good night, Slasher. Remember!"

The door was closed.

Slasher immediately locked it, and took out the ten sovereigns to gloat his eyes upon.

CHAPTER XXXVII.

CORPORAL WELSH MAKES KNOWN HIS INTENSE LOVE FOR RACHEL TO POOR RAY—ZULLA—A STRANGE SCENE.

CORPORAL WELSH had often asked himself whether it would be right on his part to acquaint his companion of the attachment he had formed for Rachel Williams.

It was plain that her thoughts were centred in Ray, who, as far as loving went, thought more of himself than Rachel.

The question had troubled Welsh for weeks, and he thought, " Why not make Ray a confidant—who never dreams that I am in such a terrible state of wretchedness—*he* might assist me, and, if only to make the road a little clearer for me, remind her that it was next to insanity to indulge in the belief that he could ever be hers."

This was selfish reasoning, however.

Ray, as usual, was reading as Donald Johnstone, the kettle-drummer, tapped him on the shoulder, and informed him that Welsh wished to speak to him.

Corporal Welsh hardly knew how to commence. It was a delicate subject. He coughed to clear his throat, stopped suddenly, looked every way to see that no one was within hearing, and then said, in a nervous tone, as he fixed his eyes upon the youth who loved him so well—

" Ray, tell me candidly, what are your intentions with regard to Rachel Williams ?"

" My intentions, Tom !" exclaimed Ray, " I don't know what you mean."

" I mean that in a year or so, if you should live to return to England, do you intend marrying Rachel ?"

Ray laughed.

" Marry her, indeed ! I should think not. What do you think, she had actually the impudence to say you thought a great deal of her. Didn't I tell her, though——"

" Ah, what ?" exclaimed Corporal Welsh, his face burning, and his countenance expressing deep concern as if his life's blood was leaving him.

" Why, that she had great assurance to think of such a thing."

Corporal Welsh's eye dropped.

" You shouldn't have said that," he whispered.

" Isn't it the truth, Tom Welsh ?"

" No, Ray, it is not ; I wish it were not so. Ray, I don't mind telling you, I love her better than ever I loved my own mother, and yet she treats me with indifference—I, who am so sensitive. Ah ! if you only knew all, Ray, you'd pity me. Some men can conquer their love if it be not returned, but I succumb. I have tried a score of times to tear out this violent passion from my bosom ; but, Ray—Ray——"

Language often fails to convey the emotions of the mind. Some writers truly speak of feelings unutterable. Ray was, to use a familiar phrase, thunderstruck ; indeed, he made no reply, but walked on by Corporal Welsh's side.

After a long silence, Ray said—

" Why did you not tell me of this before ? But don't be downcast ; she shall be yours."

Welsh shook his head, and replied, " She loves you too well."

" It's nonsensical to talk in such a strain," said Ray. " If she does love me, before this day week I'll make her hate me."

"Don't let any one know, Ray, that I have been speaking to you; and don't use deceit. It may be better not to speak to her at all."

"Ah, but I must. I'll give her a hint that you love her devotedly, and then you act like a man, as you are. Pop the question to her, and you'll be happy."

"There is Slasher, Ray; to give him his due, he loves her too, I would fain hope not so passionately as myself. By-the-bye, that gentleman he's so thick with has sailed for Abyssinia."

"I can't make him out, Welsh. He seems to be here and everywhere else. I think he's some foreign spy."

"Slasher was telling me he's a newspaper correspondent; there will be plenty of work for him shortly."

"Theodore will stand his ground. We may have sharp fighting with the king of kings, as he styles himself."

"He's got guns, I suppose, Welsh?"

"Yes; we shall march through narrow passes, between rocks so high that their tips seem lost in the sky, chasms yawning, where a slip of the foot will send us rolling ten thousand feet down between precipices."

"Won't it be fine, Tom?" said Ray, rubbing his hands in delight; "we shall have a medal, I suppose?"

Welsh shook his head, and relapsed into silence, whilst Poor Ray hastened away to prepare for embarkation.

Mafkat was left, comparatively speaking, most peaceably. The priests, as usual, quoted the Koran, and, in their own language, cursed the sons of dogs, as the merry sounds of the English fife and drum made pleasing contrast to the deafening gongs, and their miserable drums, beaten with the fingers by half-famished wretches.

The natives eyed the soldiers with glances of deadly hate, as they swarmed to the pier, calling in their own tongue on Allah and the Prophet to sink the vile Kaffirs.

"Good bye to yees," said Corporal Welsh, as he stood on the deck, bowing and kissing his hand to them in mockery. "Allah be praised that we are leaving you!"

"They have taught us a nice language," said Poor Ray, laughing; "but," he added, with a sigh, "poor Tom Sparks is left behind, with many other bright fellows."

"Who knows," said Corporal Welsh, "how many will be left in Abyssinia? A soldier is made for fighting, not moralizing."

One loud, continuous cheer rent the air, as the ship gracefully sailed out of harbour.

All Mafkat looked on in mutual wonder. The priests lifted up their hands, as if calling down the wrath of Heaven upon the heads of all on board.

The ship put on all steam, as the orders were to exercise the utmost despatch, and they flew as it were through the water.

On their voyage Poor Ray made known to Rachel the conversation which took place between him and Welsh, only keeping back that which Ray had promised not to reveal.

They were standing on deck at the time.

Rachel heard it, nor can we say she was surprised. Ray from the first was utterly indifferent as to whether she loved him or not.

It was foolish, she knew, to be infatuated with a boy, who only laughed if she spoke seriously to him.

In reply to Ray, she only made a simple remark, and then left him bitterly, we must say for the time, disappointed.

Poor Ray imagined he should be troubled with epistles from her, begging him to favour her with a line of explanation, but he received nothing of the kind, and therefore inwardly concluded that her love was not deeply rooted.

Once he saw Welsh and Rachel together; while in another part of the ship stood Drum-major Slasher, frowning horribly.

That evening Welsh came to him, pressed his hands, and whispered—

"Ray, to-morrow I shall know my doom, whether I am to be happy or wretched."

The next day Rachel accepted him out of revenge, as much as anything else.

The troops, after a most pleasant voyage, disembarked at Zulla, in Annesley Bay.

Boxes, hampers, saddles, artillery, etc., made the place look like a fair. Elephants and mules stood thick together. To enumerate what the expedition carried out would be almost impossible.

The same kind of mud hovels were to be seen as at Mafkat.

The heat was terrible, but they encamped in a most healthy district for the night.

Tents were pitched, the drummers having a tent of their own.

Drum-major Slasher pointed out what part of the tent each should lie in; he selected for Poor Ray a slight piece of ground where the wall of the tent did not exactly fall down to the ground, so that it was easy for any one passing to put his hand under.

A despatch came in late at night stating that till further orders the troops would not push on, but keep the ground of their present encampment.

Slasher heard it, and trembled.

As the drummers were undressing themselves for the night—which means merely taking off their tunics, and placing them on their knapsacks for a pillow—some one tugged at the tent, as if trying to pull it down.

Poor Ray had covered himself up with his blanket; he jumped up to see who it was put his head under what is termed, in military language, the wall of the tent, and saw two bright eyes shining upon him.

In a moment they were gone, but Ray knew they belonged to the stranger.

CHAPTER XXXVIII.

DRUM-MAJOR SLASHER COMMITS A CRIME.

THE next evening was dull, which was something unusual in these parts.

The jackals and other wild beasts left their lairs in search of prey, howling and making strange sounds, which alarmed some of the drummers, none more so than Roberts, who, because he slept next to the door of the tent, changed places with Ray.

It grew dark long before the drummers went to sleep, for under canvas it is, generally speaking, a rule among the men to spin yarns every night.

It came on to rain—not such rain as we experience in this country, but, literally speaking, waterfalls, which drenched every soldier in the camp.

It came through the tents like water through a sewer; and as the night was of a pitchy darkness, the troops grumbled till the storm ceased.

Drum-major Slasher had a very small tent to himself.

When the storm cleared away he got up, put on his great coat, and looked at his watch.

It was just two o'clock.

No one was stirring.

Cautiously he drew aside a portion of the canvas which guarded the doorway.

Not a soul was to be seen; the tents could scarcely be discerned, it was so very dark.

He drew the stiletto, and slipped it under the sleeve of his coat.

Then he stepped out from his tent and walked towards the drummers.

He had not far to go; the only obstacles being the many cords round the tents.

Before he got ten yards he fell over a tent-pin.

Cursing the military authorities, he got up, and again fell.

The fall bewildered him.

He knew not where the drummers' tent was, nor his own either.

He was lost for a time.

The wild cry of some native reached his ear.

Then the roar of the beasts that were prowling about, and the occasional challenge of the outlying picket of the British army, broke upon his ear.

The rain came on again, and it was so dark, that Slasher could not see a single tent, nor even the stiletto he clutched with a determined grasp.

He crouched on the ground, shivering and half repenting that he had ever promised to do the deed.

But it was too late now to retract.

He had given his word.

That he was soaking wet would tell no tale, as all the troops were so more or less.

Fainter and fainter the rain fell, till it finally ceased, and the heavens grew lighter by a shade.

The distant roar of thunder could be heard as Slasher crawled up to the drummers' tent, which he could now faintly discern.

He had marked the spot where Ray was sleeping; he applied his ear to the wall of the tent; the breathing was regular and heavy.

"Now," he muttered, "the darling Rachel shall weep! And the consumptive mother may die, and leave all the property to—to—ah, I am delaying while I'm talking. He still lives!"

A slight rustling, as of a man walking on tiptoe, made him pause and look up.

He saw no one—it was fancy; but to relieve his mind of any suspicion, he crawled round to the other side of the tent.

There was no one to be seen.

Gently removing the lower portion of the tent, his hand came in contact with a person's head, which must have been Poor Ray's, who muttered some unintelligible remark.

It was impossible to stab him to the heart unless he crawled into the tent; if he drove the stiletto through his brains, what would be the difference?

There would be no alarm in either case; but he had not forgotten the occasion in England when he dropped the phial.

He would be more careful this time.

The stiletto bore no mark; it had never been seen in his possession; he was sure of escape.

Then again he asked himself the question—

"Why delay?"

Softly he laid his hand upon the brow of the sleeper.

Drum-major Slasher felt sure a better opportunity would never occur again.

Grasping the stiletto with his right hand, he plunged it into the forehead of the drummer.

The hot blood rushed out as the victim moved convulsively, but still he kept his hold on the weapon.

All was still till Slasher thought he heard a terrible whisper in his ear— "Murderer!"

He turned but saw no one.

He then withdrew the weapon from the murdered drummer and wiped it in the sand, after attempting in vain to drag out the body; but it was impossible to do that without detection.

Again the sky became darkened; the thunder, which had been threatening, again rolled out in loud peals, and the lightning was so intense that at intervals the camp was as light as day. Slasher made a rush to his tent, but fell over the pegs.

The wind was rising, and it began to screech in his ears—at least he thought so—the word "Murderer!"

The lightning was succeeded by rain, and Slasher, to his horror, found that he was lost amid the countless tents of the expedition.

Covered with blood, and with the murderous weapon in his hand, he crawled into several tents, disturbing the occupants who speedily ejected him.

What was he to do if he went about in that horrid plight till morning, with Cain's brand upon him?

The army would know him to be the murderer!

He raved and tore his hair as he frantically rushed about among the tents.

The horrid whisper "Murderer, thou shalt die by the scaffold," sounded in his ear.

He turned his glaring eyes in an upward direction; the stranger was looking sternly on, but ere Slasher could speak he had vanished.

A shudder of horror ran through Corporal Welsh and Poor Ray, as they woke in the morning, and beheld the ghastly features of Roberts covered in blood, and the terrible wound in his forehead; for Roberts it was who had fallen under Slasher's stiletto.

Every one, young and old, in the tent was horrified.

"It was lucky, I think," said Poor Ray, "that I did change my billet last night, or I should have been the victim."

Welsh whispered in his ear—

"For your life say not a word to any one."

"No," answered Ray.

"Wait and see whether Providence ordains the villain to live," continued Corporal Welsh, who suspected Drum-major Slasher.

When the terrible deed became known, there was a loud outcry, "Who is the murderer?"

"The natives," was the answer of Drum-major Slasher, as, pale as death, he visited the scene; he could scarcely believe his own ears when he first heard of Roberts being murdered.

"Roberts! had he made a mistake?"

It was horribly true.

The two thousand pounds were not his, and the drummer who had served him in the capacity of a spy and servant, was slain by his master's hand.

He soon discovered that Poor Ray had changed sides with the murdered youth.

Though strict inquiries were being busily made, he saw no reason why he was not as safe as others, for no one, he fancied, suspected him, as the blood from his hands had been washed off.

The commander of the forces issued an order that for the future no native was to be allowed within the line of encampment after sunset.

This was evident proof to Slasher that His Excellency believed the murder to have been committed by one of their enemies.

Early in the day the drummers practised the "Dead March in Saul," and a grave was dug for Roberts by the pioneers.

As the firing party left the encampment, the regiments left their lines, and hastened towards the road that had only recently been made, to see the funeral pass.

"AN ARAB IN RICH COSTUME ADDRESSED THEM."

A rude coffin had been made, but there was no pall to cover it.

Drum-major Slasher held down his head, and pretended to be greatly grieved, and, as it was well known to the men of his regiment that Drummer Roberts was a favourite of his, the sham was readily believed.

The natives, with broad pieces of cloth round their waists, stood in mute admiration as the mournful sounds of the dead march were heard for the first time in Zulla.

A large gathering of officers and privates followed.

Three volleys were fired in the air as the body was lowered, and then all was over.

The army was soon ordered to be on the march.

The advance guard had left Zulla a day before to find their way, for Theodore was a strange man, who might attack them suddenly at the entrance to these passes, with only a few men, and such was the nature of the rocky country that in all pro-bability the English would have experienced great difficulties had they met with opposition at the commencement.

After several days' marching and road making, the advanced guard and the main body of the army were in high glee, for before them was the imperial city of Magdala, which ere long would be in their hands, and the British standard waving proudly above the battlements.

The next halting place was in the Tekonda Pass.

The country, so far, had been rocky and wild.

No language could fully describe the mighty grandeur of the Tekonda.

As Drum-major Slasher took note of it, the stranger gave him a meaning glance, and passed on.

Slasher understood it.

Poor Ray should be hurled from the lofty heights.

An opportunity was at hand.

CHAPTER XXXIX.

THE TEKONDA PASS,

THE sun sank in grandeur behind the mountains. The white circular tents of the British extended for miles. The camp was situated in a most picturesque spot: dark firs and other trees were scattered about as far as the eye could reach, among which the outlying pickets walked to and fro with white flags placed to mark how far they should go, and in what quarter they might expect to meet the enemy.

The sky in these parts of a fine evening is so intensely clear that it affects the eyes; and the troops, to guard against blindness during the siesta or afternoon sleep, invariably cover up their faces.

After the drummers had played retreat—for, go into what part of the world you will, that is indispensable—Corporal Welsh and Ray made up their minds to go alone. Drum-major Slasher felt disappointed at this.

They were soon in the Tekonda Pass.

The sound of the human voice echoed with such an unearthly tone that Ray did not so much admire the rocks.

It was dangerous, too, crawling up some parts like squirrels; now holding on by a ledge, with the unpleasant sensation that if it gave way, they would be dashed into the chasm beneath.

Poor Ray dare not look down; he half repented the foolhardy freak of following Corporal Welsh, who, like a monkey, was up a long way before him.

How they were to get down again was a question that seriously alarmed Ray, who had a presentiment that something terrible would happen.

There was, it is true, another and much more easy way of gaining the summit of the Tekonda, by a circuitous route, which Drum-major Slasher apparently knew, for he sat on the highest ledge in deep conversation with the so-called special correspondent.

They could see no one, though they heard Corporal Welsh encouraging Ray to come on, as they were very near the top.

"What is to be done?" asked Slasher.

"I will allure Muggleton to another part, and you, in the meantime, keep your corporal in conversation."

"We must change positions, then," replied Slasher. "Heavens, what a way down! One might die before he reaches the bottom. The projecting rocks are sharp as knives."

"Hush! Slasher, come farther back."

They went back several yards and sat down.

Corporal Welsh, puffing and blowing, reached the summit, vowing he would never attempt such a madman's trick again; his only fear was that Ray might lose courage and fall.

Welsh was astounded as he caught the figure of the stranger and his drum-major conversing together. It aroused his suspicion.

That man again!—whatever could be his object in playing the part he did?

At any rate, he would probe him, as the skilful doctor does the wounded soldier when searching for the bullet.

"Ah," exclaimed Drum-major Slasher, with feigned surprise, "who would have ever dreamt of seeing you here?"

Welsh made no reply.

The stranger stared very hard at him; Welsh stared also, and the stranger's eyes blinked before his.

"You don't say," said this gentleman, "that you had the courage to climb up the rocks?"

"Yes," answered Welsh, carelessly.

"What, by yourself?"

The stranger was amiably praying that the boy by this time might be smashed, and lying at the bottom.

"No," answered Welsh; "there's Ray close at hand."

"Ray?" repeated the drum-major. "Welsh, you ought to know better than to endanger the boy's life."

As he said these words, Poor Ray appeared on the top, panting with fatigue, his hands bleeding.

His heart gave a sudden leap when he observed the stranger.

Welsh had taken a seat beside them.

"You are plucky," said the stranger to Ray, who likewise sat down between them.

Poor Ray made no remark.

Welsh felt as if he could kick the man down the rocks. The villanous forehead, the restless eye, betrayed him a scoundrel; and it seemed as if he and Slasher were in league with each other.

Welsh spoke abruptly.

" What profession do you follow?" he asked.

The gentleman laughed as he replied—

" My dear sir, I have the pen of a ready writer. I am engaged for one of the London daily papers."

" That I question," said Welsh boldly.

" Sir !"

" I repeat that I question much whether what you say be true."

" Tut, tut," ejaculated Slasher. " Remember, you are speaking to a gentleman."

" Sir," said the stranger rising, " do you wish to insult me ? Have a care. I am prepared."

" I know you are," replied Welsh; " however, we wish you good evening."

" Not so; the boy shan't go with such a ruffian," said the stranger, as he put his hand on Ray's shoulder, as he was about to follow Corporal Welsh.

" Release me," cried Ray, as the drum-major too took hold of his arm.

" Villain !" cried Welsh. " Between you——"

" Silence ! " roared Slasher.

" It is a sinister motive. You want to injure the boy."

" Ah ! ah ! ah !" cried the stranger. " Injure him ! Why do you come out with him alone, eh ? "

" Ah ! why ? " echoed Slasher.

Corporal Welsh's blood boiled within him, as he replied—

" Why was Roberts murdered ? "

" Eh ! what ?" said the drum-major, releasing his hold of Poor Ray.

If Corporal Welsh had a doubt before, he was convinced now that Slasher was the murderer.

" Ah !" he continued, " you did not expect that."

Slasher looked towards the stranger. They understood each other.

Rushing in upon him, they seized Welsh, and dragged him towards the precipice.

Poor Ray gave a loud cry for help, but a blow from the drum-major laid him low; it stunned him.

It was a fight for life. Welsh struggled hard, but in spite of all his efforts, he was drawing gradually nearer the precipice.

Maddened at the frightful situation, he attempted to draw his sword. Slasher perceived his intention, took it from the scabbard, and threw it away from him.

Welsh was getting exhausted. He shouted to attract the attention of any individual who might by chance be coming that way.

He was near the edge, and Slasher laughed like a fiend. They tried to throw him headlong down, but he clung to the stranger tenaciously.

" Draw your sword," cried the correspondent, hoarsely. " Cut him across the hand ! Break his arm !"

" Wretch !" shouted Welsh.

Slasher struck him across the arm. The word, " Murderer !" was ringing in his ears.

In the excitement no one observed the approach of four officers, who had seen what was going on, and for the moment were horrified.

They shouted to attract the attention of the would-be assassins, but they heard not.

Corporal Welsh was hanging over, his right hand grasping the top. The stranger was about to kick his hand away, when he felt himself seized from behind with a vigorous grasp.

Corporal Welsh was eagerly seized by a pair of gentle hands.

When he saw that he was saved, he fainted.

Poor Ray recovered from the blow, and was astounded to see the drum-major bound with cords, and the stranger on his knees begging for mercy.

"Never, vile wretch!" cried one of the officers. "The horrible death you intended for another shall be your own fate."

The officers held a council of war, tried him, and pronounced him guilty, as a monster unfit to live.

On searching his pockets, they found papers which concerned Ray Muggleton, and a letter purporting to be written to Slasher, giving instructions as to what he should do on the evening in question.

The officers bound him, and laid him close to the edge, intending to throw him over.

A wild scream rent the air as the stranger rolled himself over and disappeared from their view. He fell from the highest peak of the Tekonda Rock.

Drum-major Slasher richly deserved similar fate, but the officers determined to take him as prisoner into camp.

When the drummers heard the startling news, it was plain enough to all that Roberts had been foully assassinated by his own drum-major.

It was the theme of conversation throughout the camp. Theodore for the time was forgotten. It was then discovered who Muggleton was and who his parents were. A telegram was sent to England, informing his mother that her boy was alive.

There was great rejoicing.

"You'll be leaving us shortly," said the big drummer to Poor Ray, "so as

not to have any more hairbreadth escapes."

"It was all but death with me," replied Poor Ray. "I've had some narrow escapes."

"I gave myself up for lost," said Corporal Welsh. "Instead of that, I shall be drum-major."

"Hurrah!" cried the boys. "Welsh, drum-major. Hurrah!"

"Yes," said Welsh; "and you may be certain I'll treat you all kindly. But our good friend here will be a grand gentleman; he'll soon forget poor Tom Welsh."

"Indeed I won't, Corporal Welsh; but I shall indeed be glad to meet my mother, whom I have no recollection of seeing."

"Ah! his mother," cried the drummers, enthusiastically. "We'll drink her health."

"You shall," exclaimed Poor Ray.

"What will Rachel say?" said another.

"Rachel!" said Welsh. "Men and boys, I feel as happy as Poor Ray here, in making known the fact that I am her betrothed."

"Hurrah!"

"We are all happy," said Poor Ray.

"There's Slasher. He's a prisoner. I would fain see him get off."

"He'll be hung in the presence of the troops," said Corporal Welsh; "and the villain deserves it. Before Ray had been in the regiment two days he tried to kill him."

"The monster!" they all exclaimed.

The conversation was suddenly checked by the sound of a bugle calling the orderly sergeants of every regiment in camp to take down the evening orders

Shortly after, the following was read out to the troops:—

"Camp, near Tekonda Pass.

"A drum-head court-martial will

assemble to-morrow at 9 A.M., to try the prisoner, No. 684, Drum-major Slasher, for disgraceful and fiendish conduct, in attempting to throw Corporal Welsh from a high precipice, known as the Tekonda Pass, which crime constitutes murder. The troops will be in heavy marching order. Newspaper correspondents are requested by the general of the forces to suppress this news. The following officers of the undermentioned regiments will compose it."

Here followed the names.

"It's all up with him," said Corporal Welsh. "His days are numbered."

"There will be a hanging finale," replied another.

"Who's to be executioner?" added a third.

No one answered.

The morning sun shone intensely on the burning sands. The buglers of the various regiments standing in line, blew the warning for parade.

Officers stood in groups discussing the probability of Slasher either escaping free, or paying the penalty with his life.

The assembly from every regiment in camp echoed over the vast forest of fir. The men fell in, their accoutrements shining in the sun, the white belts, the glazed knapsacks, and the glistening bayonets, forming one of those imposing sights which leave an impression upon the mind for weeks after.

After the officers had inspected their companies, the regiments were formed into one vast square, the officers and bands being in the middle.

Drum-major Slasher was marched from the guard-tent, between a strong escort with bayonets fixed; he wore an appearance of utter wretchedness; his face was pale, and his eyes fell as every soldier turned to gaze upon him.

He cast a quick, hurried glance at his own regiment, and heaved a sigh of despair.

The officers comprising the drum-head court-martial arranged themselves around.

After the preliminaries had been gone through, the following question was put by the president to the prisoner.

"Prisoner, No. 684, Drum-major Slasher, are you guilty or not of the grievous charge of intended murder which is brought against you?"

Drum-major Slasher, in a firm voice, pleaded not guilty.

Corporal Welsh was sworn, and stated what is already known to the reader.

Slasher declined to put any question to this witness.

Drummer Ray Muggleton, in like manner, gave his evidence in a most straightforward way.

Slasher cross-questioned him severely, but failed to shake in the slightest degree the testimony of this witness—indeed, from one or two observations made, he was injuring himself.

The officers came next, their evidence being most conclusive.

Slasher cross-questioned them but little.

The colonel of his regiment, when called upon to state what he knew of the prisoner's character, replied, that as a non-commissioned officer he was of little worth; and, had not this horrible charge been brought against him, it was the intention of the officers to degrade him to the ranks in consequence of what had transpired of recent date.

The prisoner, when called upon to plead, had little to say; he made a rambling defence, bitterly charging Corporal Welsh and others with conspiring against his own life.

The officers composing the court-martial leisurely examined the papers.

The bank notes found in the stranger's pocket were proved to be a clever forgery.

They consulted together for upwards of twenty minutes, and when called upon by the president, each handed in a slip of paper upon which was written—

" Guilty."

A dead silence reigned, as the president addressed the prisoner in these words—

"Prisoner, No. 684, Drum-major Slasher, having maturely weighed and considered the evidence, and, taking into account your worthless conduct as a non-commissioned officer, and the diabolical attempt to hurl a corporal of your own regiment from the Tekonda rocks, we have no other alternative than to find a verdict of guilty.

" The sentence of the court is, that you be hung, till you be dead, by the neck, to-morrow at sunrise, in the presence of the troops.   I will not harrow your feelings by making any comment upon your dastardly conduct; only I pray you to make your peace with God."

There was a slight cheer of approval, which was quickly silenced.

Slasher stood up as in a dream.   He heard his doom.   He essayed to address the president and the officers, but his tongue refused to move.   He staggered, as he was marched back to the guard-tent, with a ray of hope shining in his bosom.

There was every facility for making his escape: a tent was not like a prison wall.   This sanguine hope was cut off by the appearance of the provost-serjeant, who quickly put him in irons.   The guard was doubled, and the wretched man threw himself on the ground with a deep groan of despair.

CHAPTER XL.

SLASHER'S ESCAPE—THE CAMP ON FIRE.

AFTER a long, forced march, the expedition reached Fonetto, tired and jaded. The drummers found it hard to keep up, carrying their heavy drums.

During some part of the day, they marched through beds of perfumed flowers, then near the side of hot springs. Abyssinians, with shields at their backs, appeared on the line of march with fruit, but they were not allowed to buy. But on they kept, not daring to halt, as the advanced guard had reported that the enemy was not far distant.

Poor Ray felt ready to drop; his tongue was parched, and he begged to be allowed to fall out for a minute.

Welsh not only gave permission, but accompanied him.

Rushing into a low wood, they found a pool of thick, hot, muddy water, with some animal lying putrid in it.

They drank of it; it was horrible to the taste, and immediately brought on sickness. An Abyssinian boy, with fruit, popped up his head out of the high grass and offered them a melon, which they seized: it was delicious.

Poor Ray threw the boy a penny; he danced and cut so many capers that they both stood and laughed.

They quickly fell in, however, and continued to march on, greatly relieved, till they came up to a large strip of firs.

The bugle sounded the halt. The day's march was at an end. No one was allowed to drink water until after a long rest. The tents were put up, holes made in the ground for cooking, and in a short time the troops sat down to a good substantial meal.

A large marquee was erected—this was the canteen, to which all the soldiers flocked.

Corporal Welsh and Ray sat together enjoying the cool breeze.

"This is what I like," said Ray, "camping like gipsies. What do you say—shall we go for a stroll?"

"No one is allowed," replied Corporal Welsh, "more than one hundred yards from the camp. Suppose we were attacked by Theodore's army, we should be cut to pieces."

"I never thought of that," returned Poor Ray.

"Hark?" exclaimed Corporal Welsh; "what a fine chorus! it's the officers singing. Splendid! we'll take a leaf out of their books. Just go and tell the orderly bugler to blow the drummers' call—we'll sing for the men."

"Bravo! good!" cried Poor Ray.

Not finding the orderly bugler, he blew the call himself. The drummers rushed headlong to Welsh, who informed them that he would consider it a great favour if they would join with him in singing songs for the men, in front of the marquee.

Of course they would! What wouldn't they do for him?

So the drummers sat on the ground, some crossing their legs like tailors, others lying at full length on their sides, while Corporal Welsh sat in the middle as conductor.

They commenced duets, part songs following, and the regiments enjoyed themselves far better than they would have done in some of our 'dern music halls.

A vote of thanks was awarded to the drummers, and the company broke up as night, with its countless stars, ushered in the few hours which were left to Drum-major Slasher.

Rachel Williams, who was lovelier in Corporal Welsh's eyes than ever she appeared before, hung on his arm.

Poor Ray smiled as he asked her—

"What did you think of our singing?"

"Oh, indeed it was beautiful."

"We shall soon be losing him now, Rachel," observed Corporal Welsh.

"So I have heard," she replied, abruptly.

They wandered through the camp, and unintentionally marched close by the guard tent.

Involuntarily their eyes sought Slasher, whose face was covered up in his great coat.

"Poor wretch," said Rachel, "there he lies in a suspense which is worse than death itself."

"I hope myself," said Corporal Welsh, "they will transport him for a few years, instead of hanging him."

"To-morrow morning," said Ray, with a shudder, "he dies."

No other remark was made, and Poor Ray walked slowly to his tent.

Slasher's legs were much swollen, and he suffered greatly on the march, as he was surrounded by a guard, whereas the men marched in open order.

Twice he fainted with the heat, but his captors gave him restoratives and brought him round.

The anguish of his soul was bitter, lying there in that tent, listening to the songs which he would never hear again. The chorus and the hearty laughs mocked him. Groaning, he covered up his face. It was too late to think of repenting now. The chaplain came and begged him to employ his last moments in religious exercise.

Slasher shook his head and pointed to the irons, for they had not been taken off yet.

"See," he said, "the state of my legs."

"Unfortunate man," observed the chaplain, "I will go to the general and ask him as a favour for them to be taken off."

"Do so," said Slasher, "and I'll listen most attentively to you; but while these cursed irons are clinging to me, I cannot."

"Unhappy man," was the reply of the chaplain, as he left him and gained an interview with the general, who signed the necessary paper, and sent it by his aide-de-camp to the colonel.

The serjeant of the guard received the memorandum, which was as follows—

"The prisoner under sentence of death, Drum-major Slasher, is to have his irons taken off. Every precaution must be used to prevent the prisoner from making his escape. The serjeant of the guard and the men under him are held responsible. Two men will patrol round the guard tent during the night, and the bayonet sentry inside must not lose sight of the prisoner."

The sergeant of the guard read this to his men, who were alarmed at the risk they ran of meeting a similar fate.

The irons were knocked off, and the prisoner requested the chaplain to call him as early as six the next morning.

Slasher pretended to be asleep whilst the sergeant was reading the document. He was determined he would try to escape; it would be better, he thought, to be run through with a bayonet than suffer an ignominious death. He was a man again. Uncovering his head, he calmly spoke of his approaching end with indifference. The guard reproached him for it.

"I would not live now if I could; I deserve death—I am disgraced."

"Don't you attempt any of your tricks," said the sergeant, who knew him better than the men.

"What!" said Slasher with surprise.

"Don't try to escape; if you do, the guard will shoot you."

"Am I a coward, sergeant? Don't tell me that again, for I would sooner be shot by the guard than be hanged."

The sergeant had not thought of this; it was decidedly better to be shot than swung up by the neck. What was to hinder his prisoner from attempting it?

"Have you any cards?" asked Slasher. "We'll play a game or so; 'tis horrible to be lying here thinking. I'll play all night with anyone."

The sergeant complied. As the wretch was to die in the morning, what mattered it?

One of the guards got permission to fetch some beer. The prisoner drank some of it, began to talk loudly, and volunteered to sing a song.

This was more than the sergeant could permit.

Slasher occasionally kept his eye on a bayonet which, apparently, belonged to no one. The beer was soon disposed of; it made the guard feel sleepy, and they began to lie down one by one.

The march had worn them all out; and at length only one remained awake, playing cards with Slasher; he too threw them down, after a time, exclaiming—

"I shan't play any more; here's for a snooze."

There was only one to keep watch, and that was the bayonet sentry near him, who was dropping off to sleep.

The sergeant was sharp enough to feign a heavy slumber; he perceived that his men were asleep, and kept his half-closed eyes on the prisoner, who said sorrowingly—

"You are a lot to fall asleep! A guard too. Shall I make my escape to die another day? No."

Slasher lay down and covered up his head. The timely remark reassured the sergeant, and he dropped off into a deep slumber. Slasher, who had been watching like a ferret, sat up immediately, and grasped the bayonet he had before noticed.

The bayonet sentry was nodding. If the two men patrolling outside were alert, his escape was hopeless. He applied his ear to the ground and listened.

Not a sound could he hear. His heart beat violently as he lifted up the sides of the tent and crawled through close to the sentinel, who was dozing. Slasher made an awkward stumble, for his hand came in contact with the man's legs, who instantly seized him.

"Release me!" cried Slasher hoarsely, at the terrible idea of being captured outside his prison wall.

He clutched the sentinel by the throat. A quick blow followed; the bayonet he took with him was buried in the sentinel's heart.

Slasher knew not which quarter of the country to make for. He crawled through the camp, with the dying man's groans ringing in his ear. He than ran for his life through woods and up rocks, torn and bleeding, till the British camp was at a distance beneath. He then hid himself in a dense thicket.

A cry of "Fire" reached his ears, and he crawled out from his hiding-place to see what was the matter.

The whole country seemed in a blaze. Bugles sounded, and horses were seen running wildly over the plain. A portion of the British camp was enveloped in flames. By some unknown means it had caught fire and the conflagration spread rapidly, till the tents were struck.

The drummers had a very narrow escape of being burnt to death; and the doctor of the regiment ran distractedly about in search of his wife and daughter, for their tent had caught first. The lady, severely burnt, was rescued by a sergeant, who gallantly rushed in and dragged her out of the flames, while Ray, with several others, stood looking on.

"My daughter!" cried the lady, in heart-stricken accents.

"Her daughter is in danger!" said Poor Ray. "Dash in, some one."

No one heeded him, so he made a dart himself into the tent and rescued the young lady, who clung to him in a manner which much embarrassed him, and impeded his efforts to rescue her.

At length, however, he succeeded in fighting his way through the flames, and placed her in safety in her mother's arms.

Poor Ray's hands pained him very much for several hours, for the flames had touched them, and removed the skin; he was on the sick list in the morning.

The young lady, who was remarkable for her beauty, thanked him in the presence of her father, who presented him with a five-pound note, which Poor Ray spent among the drummers for them to drink his mother's health.

Then they heard the startling news of Slasher's escape, and that he had bayoneted the sentry.

Parties of men went in pursuit of the murderer. Day and night they hunted for him; Abyssinian natives were offered handsome rewards for his apprehension, but nothing was heard— at least for a time.

"CORPORAL WELSH WAS HANGING OVER, HIS RIGHT HAND GRASPING THE TOP."

CHAPTER XLI.

THE BATTLE—MAGDALA IN THE HANDS OF THE BRITISH.

THE day before Good Friday the outlying pickets perceived an unusual commotion among Theodore's troops, who were drawn up within an easy march of Magdala, the residence of the king of kings, situated on a rocky eminence which appeared impregnable. The sudden movement among the enemy was only a feint.

Magdala could only be approached by narrow roads from a distance. On Good Friday several batteries of guns of awkward structure were seen in position, and Theodore's soldiers on the watch.

Nature had made this spot almost inaccessible. With English troops to defend this fortress, it would have stood till doomsday.

Various tribes—the bitterest enemies Theodore had to contend against—brought valuable and reliable information to the English general, as often as ten times a day.

"I am getting tired of this work," said Poor Ray to Welsh, as they marched on at the head of their regiment. "I'd sooner fight."

"We shall soon be in sight of his palace; if he don't give us the slip, we'll show him what our Armstrong guns can do," replied Welsh.

"The officers say he exhibits uneasiness, and well he might."

An aide-de-camp came galloping back at that moment, exclaiming—

"Close up, men; we expect to be engaged. Pass the word to close up."

"I guessed as much," whispered Welsh. "See how we have been travelling all the week. Keep by me."

"I hope I shan't be sent to look after the wounded and assist the doctor," said Ray. "I'd sooner fight."

"I didn't enlist to be a doctor's cad either," remarked the big drummer.

Another aide-de-camp now dashed past and addressed the colonel—

"Your regiment, sir, will deploy into line and send out skirmishers."

"When?" asked the colonel.

"Immediately, sir. Theodore has made a stand. Magdala is in sight."

This news acted on the men's nerves like electricity. Fresh and as active as bees, they deployed into line, and the long wished-for fortress rose up in sight.

The troops cheered wildly. Between a run and a walk they hastened on, till orders came for them to halt, lie down, and load their rifles.

The artillery rushed past them.

The buglers and drummers were distributed along the line in rear of their companies. Some carried stretchers, in anticipation of a desperate struggle, and the doctors had their cases of instruments opened.

"Stand by me," whispered Welsh.

"All right," replied Poor Ray.

"There they are," said Welsh, pointing to a group of fellows in many colours, who were loading a cannon.

"Why don't they let us fire at them,

Welsh?" demanded Ray. "How nicely we could pick them off now."

"Hush! The general's close by; he knows better than you or I. Ah! there's our artillery loading; they'll get it directly."

"Lie down there, men," said the general; "your time for work will come soon."

Whiz went a shot from one of our Armstrongs, throwing up the dust around Theodore's artillerymen, who turned round and then commenced to yell.

They fired their guns, the shot going over the heads of the British, who could not resist laughing.

"Bang! bang!" our own artillery replied with rapidity and precision, knocking over Theodore's men like nine-pins.

Rockets and shells were sent flying in amongst them, spreading the greatest consternation, many running wildly about with their fingers in their ears.

"We are doing nothing," said Ray, clutching his sword tightly, and placing the sword knot carefully round his wrist, so that if the sword should slip from his grasp, it would be safe.

"Control your impatience. Ah! there's another aide-de-camp. Listen," said Welsh.

"Your men, sir, are to march in line about sixty yards, and fire; they will then make a charge, and take the guns."

The men rose to their feet, and Theodore's infantry, which till now had been concealed, opened fire upon them, yelling loudly.

The British troops marched on, the enemy's fire scarcely touching a man.

They dropped on one knee, and with a cool and deliberate aim, fired a volley like one man.

Death and destruction followed.

With a cheer they dashed on right up to the cannon's mouth, Theodore's troops making but a weak resistance.

One of their chiefs, who was at first taken for Theodore, rallied them.

For awhile they fought bravely.

Their useless weapons were no match for the deadly Sniders.

"Warriors of your king," cried the chief, "fight on, and the victory must be ours!"

And fight they did most desperately.

Poor Ray found himself engaged with one of Theodore's soldiers, who attacked the drummer singly.

The kettle-drummer received a blow from him, and fell.

Drummer Joll made such a sweeping cut, that he missed him, and was in return levelled by the Abyssinian's musket, who had expended, it may be presumed, his ammunition.

Ray parried most skilfully a blow aimed at him, and, though the chances were twenty to one in favour of the rude barbarian, seized the weapon by the barrel, and rushed in upon him, making short work of the fellow, for he drove the sword through his heart.

No one witnessed the scene.

Corporal Welsh was fighting like Irishmen will fight.

Amid dense smoke, Theodore's soldiers retired, leaving their guns for our soldiers to take care of.

This skirmish has been called a battle. It hardly deserved that title. It was no more than a skirmish in which discipline, and the brave conduct of the British, won them the highest praise and admiration.

Theodore had fortified himself within his palace, and the British troops were bivouacked for the night within range of his guns; but not a shot was exchanged.

"We'll be into his capital," said Corporal Welsh, drawing his blanket tightly round him, " before to-morrow's sun sets."

" We'll take him to London, and exhibit him," replied Poor Ray.

" Or Dublin," answered Welsh. " They may hang him if they like."

" The prisoners are released, you know, Welsh. A barbarian prince as he is, there's many a Christian general would have sacrificed his life."

" He has a purpose in that, Ray."

" He's game, I think. We shall have hard work to take the place if he fights. What rocks ! like those at the Tekonda Pass."

Corporal Welsh shuddered.

" Spin us a yarn," said one of the drummers to him.

" Sleep say I," replied Poor Ray. " We shall be in better trim for fighting."

Nestling up as close to each other as they could, they dropped off to sleep, though on the morrow Magdala was to be stormed.

The reveille, at a very early hour, floated in gentle strains over the camp.

The men soon threw off their slumbers, examined their rifles, partook of an early breakfast, and prepared themselves for the attack.

Letters innumerable had been written the evening before, and many that morning.

The British opened a terrible fire into Magdala. The Emperor Theodore replied to the salute with but little effect. Red-hot shot, shells, and rockets were poured in, till half Theodore's soldiers, panic-stricken, deserted him.

But he stood his ground with his favourite chiefs. The bombardment lasted for a considerable time. It was then found necessary to make a breach near the gateway ; this ended in a momentary failure.

The sappers and miners, through some unknown cause, were without the necessary powder.

The troops became impatient ; with a frantic rush they dashed up to the gateway, amid the bullets of the enemy, who opened fire upon them.

In vain the soldiers applied their muskets to the ironwork ; it resisted all their efforts ; ultimately they succeeded in forcing their way.

The gateway yielded.

Corporal Welsh* and Ray, at the head of a company of men, were the first to enter, Ray remarking at the time to an officer that the sword he held in his hand was almost useless.

King Theodore rallied his faithful followers, and with wild, excited cheers, they fought bravely for awhile.

" Down with them !" cried King Theodore, who fought most valiantly. " Followers of your king, the monarch of the wide world, you cannot be conquered ; I, the emperor of all the kingdoms under the sun, am with you !"

" Long live our king !" cried his soldiers, rushing upon the British bayonets.

" Confound him," said Corporal Welsh, " while he lives they'll fight. I'll put an end to his monarchy."

" No, no," cried several officers ; " he must be taken alive."

" Look !" said Poor Ray, with excitement ; " he's pointing a revolver to his head."

It was too true ; the emperor of the world had shot himself rather than be captured by the English.

His soldiers fled, and Magdala was in the hands of the British, who immediately hoisted up the union jack, amid such cheers as Magdala and its natives had never heard before.

---

* This is a positive fact : it was a drummer who first entered Magdala. It is mentioned in the " London Gazette."

Theodore was lying on his back, dead!

"Poor king," said Corporal Welsh, leaning over him, "I admire your gallantry; but there you lie, no more the terror of surrounding tribes."

The officers and men made way as his son came running up, panting for breath, his large eyes filled with tears as the poor little fellow took hold of his father's hand, and entreated him to speak.

"Don't you see," said Poor Ray to him, sorrowfully, "he's dead."

"Dead!" repeated the boy, in very good English.

Sorrowful were the exclamations of the boy as he knelt down by his side and covered the dead face, which bore traces of agony, with kisses.

The sight was exceedingly affecting.

The boy was led away, crying bitterly, and taken to the general, who patted him on the head and spoke kindly.

The bodies of the slain were buried decently, and every living creature was removed from the doomed pile of Magdala.

It was set on fire at night, and burnt till the palace of the late Theodore was no more than a desolate rock.

The troops stood to their arms, as dense clouds of smoke gave way to blazing lights, while huge stones were thrown up into the air.

The sappers and miners had been at work.

A mighty shock was heard, which shook the surrounding country for miles. Magdala was blown into the air! Next day not a vestige of it remained.

CHAPTER XLII.

EXECUTION OF DRUM-MAJOR SLASHER.

IT is surprising to witness in some men what a strange effect an alteration of the mind has on the lineaments of the face, particularly such a one as Slasher, who had committed the most fearful of all crimes—murder.

No one would have ever dreamed that in such a short time as a month Slasher would be no more like his former self than chalk is like cheese. He was thin, and doubled-up in appearance; his face was long, his hands bony. He subsisted on wild berries, not daring to show his face to the light of heaven.

Shunning the haunts of savage tribes, he prepared a juice from the bark of a tree and stained his skin a dark brown colour.

He knew a large reward was offered for his apprehension, for one evening he crawled near enough to a troop of cavalry, who were on the look-out for him, and heard them saying what a fine thing it would be if they only came across him.

That was enough for Slasher.

The expedition would soon accomplish its mission, and return homeward.

Whom, then, had he to fear? No one. But whilst they were hanging, as it were, on the skirts of his coat, he was in dread of his life, sleeping in no place twice—a hole in a rock to-night, to-morrow in a tree. And all this misery for two thousand pounds, which he had not received!

Life was becoming burdensome to him.

He feared to be alone, with no friend to talk to, his only companions being the wild beasts.

He grew bolder, and made excursions in daylight.

Ultimately he determined to start for Zulla, and there take ship for England and work his passage over.

A gipsy life in England would be preferable to life in the bush.

One great obstacle troubled him much. Was he in the right direction for Zulla?

There were no finger-posts in this country—no roads. He was lost.

At night he fed on leaves and the roots of trees, till, in a few days, he was like a skeleton.

At length he was pounced upon by some of the natives, who bound him hand and foot.

"What does this mean?" said Slasher to the chief of the party. "I'm an Englishman—a soldier."

"Your head is worth ever so many pounds. The soldiers of England have been looking for you," replied the chief, in a great many more words than we have recorded here.

"Wretches! let me go."

"No," was the reply. "Take care, or you shall be roasted alive."

Slasher submitted himself to his fate.

The natives, en route for Zulla,

brought word that Magdala was in flames, and that the English were on the march home again.

Slasher was delivered up by the natives to the military authorities.

"They have caught Slasher," went from mouth to mouth.

"He'll not escape this time," said Ray, throwing himself down on the ground, the others following his example, that day's march being brought to an end.

"No," said Corporal Welsh; "late as it is, if they hang him to-night, don't be surprised."

He had no sooner said these words than the assembly sounded for the soldiers to fall in.

"It's a hanging parade," cried the men. "They have got the villain."

Without any fuss or ceremony the men fell in, with unwashed faces, their tunics covered with dust.

The bugle had sounded just as numbers were going to sit down to a good meal, and the men did not exactly understand what hurry the authorities need to be in to take the life of a miserable wretch.

"It will take my appetite away," said Poor Ray, shivering.

"Who's to hang him?" said another, as the unfortunate wretch passed by them with a strong escort.

He was handcuffed. His hair was long and matted together. His clothes were in tatters. The boots he wore were cracked and all to pieces. His face was deeply stained. Numbers of his own regiment knew him not.

He was a deplorable object, and great as the villain's crimes had been, the most hardened soldier felt a slight touch of pity for the wretch as he stood near the fatal beam.

A rude scaffold had been erected; it consisted of two long poles driven into the ground within three yards of each other; a third pole had been placed on the top and secured with strong nails to make all secure. The two uprights were supported by stakes being driven in till the scaffold was as strong and secure as a rock.

The rope appeared to be a common drum-cord. A small basket for the criminal to stand on had been placed under the drop by the executioner, who stood by masked.

The proceedings of the first court-martial were read, and after the usual preliminaries had been gone through of taking evidence and other military details, the prisoner was called upon by the president of the court-martial as to whether he had any remarks to make why sentence of death should not be executed upon him.

Slasher trembled violently, but made no reply.

A large piece of black cloth was then thrown over the scaffold.

"Prisoner," said the president, "you are about to die; if you have any confession to make, it shall be taken down in writing."

The prisoner made no reply.

"It's my duty then," continued the president, "to command you to remove your stock from your neck. Executioner, come forth."

The masked soldier came forward, and placed his hand upon Slasher's shoulder.

"Suffer me, I pray you, to say a word," faltered the prisoner.

"Say on," said the president.

"Gentlemen of the court, and dear comrades, I am about to die. I confess I murdered Drummer Roberts and the sentinel, to make good my escape. I justly deserve the ignominious death which awaits me. I ask pardon from Corporal Welsh and Drummer Ray Muggleton for my conduct towards them, and hope they will forgive me."

Here the prisoner turned round to the two persons above named. Corporal Welsh bowed, and Poor Ray put his hand to his heart and waved it towards him.

"I ask one and all to forgive me in their hearts. Comrades of my own regiment, to you I say farewell. Executioner, I am ready."

A few minutes afterwards he was dead. He had paid the penalty of his crimes.

Poor Ray and Corporal Welsh fell out of the ranks, overcome by the sight, which created a deep sensation among the men.

CHAPTER XLIII.

HOMEWARD BOUND.

ANNESLEY BAY was crowded with ships decked out with flying colours of the gaudiest description. The wildest enthusiasm prevailed among the troops, who cheered lustily.

Thoughts of home and dear friends already stirred up the hearts of the soldiers, who longed to be going.

Ray sat quietly on deck, unobserved. To no man of the party was home more dear. Hockerton—homely, sweet, little town—and the manner in which he fled from it, cold, hungry, and cast upon the wide world, came back to his memory.

He pictured his mother a lady, such as he had read of, and then remembered that her own brother had been thrown from the Tekonda Rocks. Sorrowful news! He would have to relate how the well-dressed villain and Slasher planned and schemed to take his life from the very moment they left Manchester till they were caught in the Tekonda Rocks.

Everybody he saw on deck was laughing and shouting; but there he sat melancholy and alone.

Corporal Welsh, who, with Rachel leaning on his arm, had sought him everywhere, now stood before him.

"Ah!" said Welsh, laughing, "he'll soon be giving up soldiering; he'll have no one to bother him about flats, and sharps, but be riding in his carriage; but you won't mind writing to a fellow sometimes, will you?"

"No, I should say not," replied Poor Ray; "and I'll often come and see you both."

"Oh, thank you," answered Rachel, with a blush on her cheek.

"Let me know the day on which you intend to get married," continued Ray.

"That you may depend upon," said Corporal Welsh, who, with Rachel, then withdrew to another part of the ship.

Poor Ray followed them with his eyes, as did most of the men on deck.

Ray often looked with admiration

upon the doctor's daughter whom he gallantly saved from the flames; but of what use was his admiration? They would soon be separated for ever.

They had been sailing several days; no doctor's daughter appeared, like the other ladies, on deck of an evening. Ray was curious to know what had become of her—whether she was indisposed, or suffering from sea-sickness. The doctor's servant might inform him, but he was saved the trouble of asking any question, for the young lady, in deep conversation with an officer, rose up suddenly before him.

That was enough; Poor Ray turned away, and assisted the other drummers in making lines for fishing. A shark had been following the ship since they left Annesley Bay. A bait was set for it. The monster declined it, after swimming near it for hours.

Poor Ray sat watching the bait and the fish, and asking himself whether he could ever muster up enough courage to jump overboard, to save another from its terrible row of teeth, when one of the drummers foolishly got up into the rigging unperceived, to throw his line further into the sea, and fell in.

Poor Ray heard the plunge, and then the cry "A man overboard! The shark! the shark!"

One of the officers and Poor Ray jumped over together.

The consternation on board was terrific. The screams of the ladies, and hoarse shouts of men, were awful.

A couple of the officers fired their rifles at the frightful-looking creature, wounding it, upon which it became more furious.

A boat was let down, but the monster made a rush at it, upset it, and then turned to the three human beings, whose features were agonizing to behold.

The drummer clung to the officer so closely that it was impossible to make him release his hold.

Ray endeavoured to seize a rope, but in vain, as the sea was running high.

There were several Zulla Kaffirs and negroes on board, noted swimmers, who would, even at this period, have jumped overboard, but the passengers kept them back.

"Two hundred pounds," said the colonel, in the greatest excitement, "to the man who saves either of them."

One of the Zulla Kaffirs armed himself with a strong-pointed knife, and in an instant plunged towards the shark.

The fish was in the act of turning on his side to attack one of the three, when his attention was directed to the Kaffir, who instantly dived below, then rose, inflicting a severe wound on the shark.

Again and again the Kaffir appeared on the surface to take breath, only to dive down again and engage with the terrible fish.

In the meantime the three struggling in the water were rescued amid shouts of joy.

But after a time the brave, unfortunate Kaffir was seen to become fatigued, and the shark opened its huge mouth and speedily destroyed him.

It was to no purpose that his comrades followed, for the shark instantly disappeared, dyeing the water with its blood.

An oppressive feeling, caused by the event, weighed down every one on board during the remainder of the voyage.

Portsmouth again! Loud cheering; ringing of bells; flags; the streets crowded with people; mothers dashing into the ranks to salute their darling boys!

The troops took off their shakos, and poised them in the air on their bayonets; bands played, bugles sounded, aide-de-camps and generals rode at the head of the various regiments.

Poor Ray found a telegram awaiting him. He tore it open and read—

"To Drummer Muggleton, or Fielding, from Agnes Fielding.

"4, Park Place, Hockerton.

"I am dying to see you. Come at once if you can. I am very poorly.

"Your affectionate Mother."

Poor Ray drew a very long breath: he had no time for reflection, except to think that his mother must be very ill not to come and see him.

The great camp at Aldershot was their destination.

After a few hours by rail, they marched into the north camp.

The bugle sounded for orders.

The following orders were read:—

"Brigade Office, North Camp, Aldershot.—The general commanding the Aldershot division feels proud and happy in having such a fine body of men under his command. To the heroes of Abyssinia leave will be granted, to officers and men, commencing forthwith."

"REGIMENTAL ORDER.

"The colonel of the —— regiment has approved and appointed No. 842, Corporal Thomas Welsh, to be drum-major; this appointment dating from the day the late Drum-major Slasher was placed under arrest."

"Hurrah!" roared the boys.

"Three cheers for Drum-major Welsh!" cried Poor Ray.

"Hurrah—hurrah—hurrah!"

"Boys," said Drum-major Welsh, with emotion, "I thank you from my heart for the kind and hearty manner in which my promotion has been received by you all, and I shall do my best to prove worthy of it. But Ray will be leaving us to-morrow. I therefore propose that we give him a farewell entertainment."

"Hurrah!"

We have not space here to recount the night's proceedings. Everybody was happy.

Poor Ray was ready, yet loth to leave the familiar faces of his comrades. He felt sorry, very sorry to depart.

Rachel Williams came with tears in her eyes to bid him good-bye.

The boys thronged round him, pressing his hand.

"Don't forget the old regiment," said Welsh, as he shook him warmly by the hand.

"I won't; indeed, I will not, comrades; I can't thank you as I would like to do. I am indeed sorry to leave you. Farewell."

He passed out from the hut with a portmanteau in his hand. The drummers followed to the door, and on the parade, cheering him.

Ray turned round, took off his cap and exclaimed again and again, "Farewell! farewell!"

CHAPTER XLIV.

HOCKERTON.

AS Poor Ray reached the platform of the Hockerton station, a carriage drew up at the door.

The coachman put his hand to his hat and said, "Mr. Fielding, this is the carriage for you, sir."

Ray shook his head.

The coachman smiled, and said, "It's all right, sir," and the footman opened the door.

"Oh, no," said Poor Ray. "It would not look well in this uniform to be riding in a carriage."

"Shall I take the portmanteau, sir?" asked the coachman.

"If you like," replied Ray.

How peculiar it sounded to Ray to be called "Sir."

The coachman took the portmanteau, gave his horses a slight twitch with the whip, and drove away, Poor Ray following, to Number 4, Park Place.

It was a noble mansion, with a couple of stately trees near the portico. Ray took stock of it at once, and gave one loud single knock at the door. A servant admitted him.

A lady, with a pale face, was standing in the hall, near the carpeted stairs. The peculiar brilliancy of her eyes struck Ray at the first glance. The black hair streamed in rolling masses back from her forehead.

Ray hastened forward; he felt certain that it was his mother.

"My darling boy!" exclaimed the lady, extending her arms towards him, "come to your poor mother's breast."

"Mother, mother!" said Ray, as he kissed her again and again.

For a time neither spoke.

Tears trickled down the mother's face, as she pressed her wandering boy closely to her breast.

It was as the brother told Slasher near the Tekonda Rocks—she was dying of consumption.

The mother knew it. It was breaking her heart. With her arms round her boy's neck, she led him to the dining-room, where a sumptuous repast was prepared.

Ray, after partaking very sparingly, for he found it impossible to eat, sat near his mother with his arm round her neck.

He admired the transparent cheek, the high, intellectual forehead, and those eyes, which grew brighter and brighter, and the thin, white, delicate hand he held within his own.

Yet in that stately apartment he dreaded something, he knew not what.

"Mother," said Ray, "you said you were ill—what ails you?"

"Never mind now, my son, my darling—I'll tell you another time. I'm happy now. God alone knows when I was before! But tell me, my poor boy, how has it been with you all these years?"

"I have had some hardships and

"MAKING SHORT WORK OF THE FELLOW, RAY DROVE HIS SWORD THROUGH HIS HEART."

narrow escapes, mother. Your own brother tried, with the aid of another, to take my life."

"Where?" she exclaimed, with agitation.

"In Abyssinia. He lies at the bottom of the Tekonda Pass."

"My poor brother!" ejaculated his mother.

Ray told all he knew.

"It was to keep me from you that he might have your money," said Ray.

"By what name were you known among your comrades?"

Ray sighed as he thought of those unhappy days.

"Mother dear," he said, affectionately placing his arm round her neck, "tell me how it was I was left at Hockerton workhouse gates like a tramp's son; put there to take my chance or die. These thoughts have followed me through life, sticking in my throat in barracks, camp, and field; and I have said to myself in choking accents, 'It was my mother's hands that laid me there. God forgive her.'"

"Ray, my dear, lost boy," she replied, tenderly kissing his cheek, "it

"SHE LEFT YOU IN THAT STORM AT THE GATES OF THE WORKHOUSE."

"They called me Poor Ray—sometimes Muggleton."

"But the name of Muggleton, my son; it's horrid!"

"Yes; it might have been worse though, mother. Fatherby gave it me, the wretch! Does he still live?"

"Yes; he rendered me every assistance in his power to help me discover you."

was not your mother; it's painful to me to relate, but I must tell you.

"*It was my brother's wife,* a kind, generous-hearted creature. Her husband made her do it. One stormy night he hounded her out with imprecations, saying, 'Take the thing away—drown him, and the money will yet be ours.'

"She was here as a companion to comfort me. Your father had only recently died. Some six years ago, on her deathbed, she sent for me and confessed all.

"My brother never loved me as I loved him. It was my property he wished to get. All these years he has seen me suffering in agony, but never gave me a word of comfort. Ray, listen.

"In the adjoining chamber you slept soundly. Suddenly I missed you.

"Thinking she had taken you away to frighten me, I ran in the pouring rain to her house. She was there, dripping wet and out of breath. I did not notice then, but she had on a tattered dress.

"My brother was there. I begged and implored frantically, but not a word could I learn of your fate, though she told me on her deathbed that she had left you in that storm at the gates of the workhouse. I inquired there, but you had left. Ray, my darling, the remainder is known to yourself."

"Mother," faltered Ray, the tears trickling down his cheeks, as he hid his head on his bosom.

A veil of a transparent hue must be drawn over what follows. It is too sacred to be touched upon lightly, and it savours of sadness to write in this strain. Alas! as true biographers, there is no alternative.

They sat together the remainder of the evening conversing upon matters most important to both, and it would be difficult to say which felt the happiest.

Often afterwards they rode out in the carriage together; but the days were getting damp and chilly.

The news of the unfortunate brother's death produced a most disastrous effect upon the consumptive lady.

Would that we could follow the usual course and record how happy Ray and his mother lived ever after; but, alas! in real life it is not always so.

Agnes Fielding died within a month after Ray's return.

The excitement undoubtedly hastened her death.

The grief of the orphan was heart-rending—alone again in a large mansion, every piece of furniture draped in black; mournful was the scene.

He was rich; but what was money to him? Could he buy a mother's love with it?

Already he perceived land-sharks sailing round him.

The spell which bound him to Hockerton was broken. He could never live there—it was too quiet, after leading a soldier's life so long as he had.

He was persuaded by the rich and the great, who now courted his company, to settle down.

No, he was unhappy—he longed for excitement—better by far be a drummer again, than to pine away in a gloomy mansion. If his mother had lived, how different it would have been!

Drum-major Welsh would have been invited to spend a week or a month with them — with his wife Rachel—for they were married.

Ray sent many presents, and received in return a piece of wedding-cake.

The doctor's daughter, Welsh mentioned in one of his letters, was still with him.

So Ray exerted all the influence his money gave him, and after some time, procured a commission in a foot regiment that was stationed at Aldershot.

He then managed, by paying heavily, to effect an exchange into his old regiment.

Drum-major Welsh and he are often together.

The regulations say it must not be so; but considering their old friendship, it is not wonderful to hear that they sometimes, as the boys say, "chance it."

What is rather singular is, that those who marched side by side with him, and slept under the same roof, may be seen saluting him as he passes in the usual manner.

Ray never forgets, as some officers do, to return the compliment.

Of an evening he plays the flute, as it is an accomplishment he does not wish to forget.

The doctor's daughter, finding her deliverer was of a rich family, could do no more than accept the young officer as a partner for life.

She is to be married at Christmas, as the wife of Ensign Ray Fielding— no longer POOR RAY THE DRUMMER BOY!

THE END.

NOTICE.

Now Ready, Nos. 1 and 2 of that Splendid Story of Naval Warfare, entitled "Every Inch a British Sailor; or, the Cruise of Jack and Joe." A Splendid Coloured Picture Given Away. Order of all Booksellers Price 1d. Weekly.

EDWIN J. BRETT'S LIST OF PUBLICATIONS.

BOYS OF ENGLAND.—The oldest and best conducted book for Boys. Weekly, 1d.; Monthly Parts 6d.; Half-Yearly Volumes, 2s. 6d. and 4s.

BOYS OF ENGLAND RE-ISSUE.—Weekly, 1d.; Monthly Parts, 6d.; Half-Yearly Volumes 2s. 6d. and 4s.

YOUNG MEN OF GREAT BRITAIN.—An interesting Journal of Love. War, Romance and Adventure, for Men of all ages. Price 1d. Weekly; 6d. Monthly; Half-Yearly Volumes, 2s. 6d. and 4s.

SOMETHING TO READ.—The new double weekly Journal, containing stories of thrilling interest, together with a full-sized complete Novelette with each number. Price 1d.; Monthly Parts, 6d.; Half-Yearly Volumes, handsomely bound 4s. 6d.

BOYS OF THE BRITISH EMPIRE.—1d. Weekly; 6d. Monthly; Half-Yearly Volumes, 4s.

BOYS COMIC JOURNAL.—1d. Weekly; 6d. Monthly; Cloth Vols., 4s.

The Postage of any of the above Volumes, 6d.

INTERESTING AND COMPLETE STORIES EVERY WEEK. PRICE 1D.

BOYS OF ENGLAND NOVELETTE. | BOYS WEEKLY READER NOVELETTE.

COMPLETE VOLUMES NOW PUBLISHING AT 1s EACH. ILLUSTRATED. POST FREE, 1s. 2D.

KING OF THE SCHOOL.	DICK AND HIS FRIEND DUKE.
JACK-O'-THE CUDGEL.	NOBODY'S DOG.
HARKAWAY IN AMERICA.	OXFORD AND CAMBRIDGE EIGHTS.
RIVAL SCHOOLS.	UNLUCKY BOB.
FOLD FROLIC, HIS LIFE AND ADVENTURES.	EVERY INCH A SAILOR.
	FATHERLESS WILL.
NIGHT GUARD, OR THE SECRET OF THE FIVE MASKS.	CHEVY CHASE.
	STRONGBOW.
GILES EVERGREEN, OR FRESH FROM THE COUNTRY.	JACK RUSHTON.
	BY THE QUEEN'S COMMAND.
POOR RAY THE DRUMMER BOY.	CAPTAIN OF THE SCHOOL.
TOM DARING, OR FAR FROM HOME.	WHITE SQUAW.
WALTER THE ARCHER.	PAT O'CONNOR.
WILDFOOT, THE WANDEROR OF WICKLOW.	RIVAL CRUSOES.
	BICYCLE BOB.
JACK STEDFAST, OR WRECK AND RESCUE.	THREE BOY CRUSOES.

COMPLETE IN TWO VOLUMES, 1s. POSTAGE 2D. EACH VOLUME.

TRUE TO EACH OTHER.	ENGLISH JACK AMONG THE AFGHANS.
SCAPEGRACE OF THE SCHOOL.	PANTOMIME JOE.
SCAPEGRACE AT SEA.	WITHOUT REPROACH.
SCAPEGRACE IN LONDON.	

VOLUMES COMPLETE. PRICE 1s. 6D. EACH. ILLUSTRATED. POST FREE 1s. 6D.

JACK-O'-LANTERN. | RIGHTFUL HEIR. | WARD'S SECRET.

BOB BLUNT, THE TRAVELLER, Complete in Three Volumes. 1s. each.	BRETT'S BRLL ROOM GUIDE, 3d.
	ELINOR CLARE. Complete Volume, Cloth, 2s.
YOUNG APPRENTICE; OR, THE WATCHWORDS OF OLD LONDON. Coloured Illustrations. Complete in Three Volumes. 1s. each.	BRETT'S HOUSEKEEPER. Coloured Illustrations. Complete. cloth lettered, &c., 3s.
	BARONS OF OLD. Complete Stories in Two Volumes, Price 1s. each; post free, 1s. 2d.
MY SON; WHAT SHALL I DO WITH HIM? A Question for Parents and Guardians, 6d.; post free, 7d.	VALENTINE VOX. Illustrated Edition, Cloth, 3s. 6d.
BOY SOLDIER. Complete, price 2s.	STORIES FROM THE PLAYS OF SHAKESPEARE. 1d. each, or Volume complete, 1s.

HARKAWAY SERIES, PRICE 1s. EACH VOLUME, POSTAGE 2D. EXTRA.

Vol. 1.——JACK HARKAWAY'S SCHOOLDAYS. Complete in One Volume.	Vol. 10. —— JACK HARKAWAY'S ADVENTURES IN CHINA. Complete in One Volume.
Vols. 2 & 3.——JACK HARKAWAY AFTER SCHOOLDAYS. Complete in Two Volumes.	
Vols. 4 & 5. —— JACK HARKAWAY AT OXFORD. Complete in Two Volumes.	Vols. 11 & 12.——HARKAWAY IN GREECE. Two Volumes.
Vols. 6 & 7.——JACK HARKAWAY AMONG THE BRIGANDS. Complete in Two Volumes.	Vol. 13.——HARKAWAY IN AUSTRALIA. One Volume.
Vols. 8 & 9. —— JACK HARKAWAY'S ADVENTURES ROUND THE WORLD AMERICA AND CUBA. Two Volumes.	Vols. 14 & 15.——HARKAWAY AND HIS BOY TINKER. Two Volumes.

AMERICAN SERIES.

HARKAWAY AT SCHOOL IN AMERICA.

HARKAWAY AMONG THE PIRATES. | HARKAWAY AT THE ISLE OF PALMS.

[PRICE ONE SHILLING   COMPLETE]

JACK RUSHTON;

ALONE IN THE PIRATES' LAIR.

BEAUTIFULLY ILLUSTRATED.

ONE PENNY WEEKLY.   FOURPENCE MONTHLY.

PUBLISHING OFFICE, 173, FLEET STREET.